From The Women's Press Ltd
34 Great Sutton Street, London EC1V 0DX

Carole Spearin McCauley has written eleven books, including non-fiction on medical and computer topics, published in several countries. Her previous novels include *The Honesty Tree*, *Happenthing in Travelon* (The Women's Press, 1990) and computer-assisted fiction published in Germany. Her work has appeared in various periodicals, including *Omni*, *Mystery Time*, *Feminist Art Journal*, *Gaysweek* and the anthology *The New Fiction: Interviews with Innovative American Writers*. Six of her pieces have won prizes in international contests, including Writers of the Future (Los Angeles). She has worked as a writer at IBM-Warwick and as a reporter at the National Institute of Health in Maryland. She lives in Greenwich, Connecticut and is currently writing the further mystery adventures of Pauli Golden in a sequel to *Cold Steal*.

Excerpts from *Cold Steal* have appeared in *Women Live* (Dorset) and *Eidos* (Boston).

By the same author

NON-FICTION
Surviving Breast Cancer
AIDS: Prevention and Healing with Nutrition
When Your Child Is Afraid
Computers and Creativity
Pregnancy after 35

FICTION
Cold Steal
Happenthing in Travelon
The Honesty Tree
Six Portraits: Wild Birds on a Winter Mountain

CAROLE SPEARIN McCAULEY

Cold Steal

The Women's Press

Yet each man kills the thing he loves,
By each let this be heard,
Some do it with a bitter look,
Some with a flattering word,
The coward does it with a kiss,
The brave man with a sword!
Oscar Wilde, *The Ballad of Reading Gaol*

Out of suffering comes the cure. Better pain than paralysis.
Florence Nightingale

Science is a first-rate piece of furniture for a man's upper chamber if he has common sense on the ground floor.
Oliver Wendell Holmes

First published by The Women's Press 1991

A member of the Namara Group
34 Great Sutton Street, London EC1V 0DX

Copyright © 1991 by Carole Spearin McCauley

Cataloguing-in-Publication data is
available from the British Library

Typeset by AKM Associates (UK) Ltd, Southall, London
Printed and bound by BPCC Hazell Books
Aylesbury, Bucks, England
Member of the BPCC Ltd.

4 July – The Party

'All geniuses here' . . . Stevens and his whores. Research so like whoring. Hustle to get a buck.

Scared at first in the half light. Your hand shakes. Stage fright. Stevens' front, then back, lit like some idol. Who else would spend our victory party crucifying us?

Smooth steel growing hot in your hand, inside where he can't see. Second by second you caress it.

' . . . Can't get it up for work other people need. And mistakes. Shape up, or clear ou–'. . .

Tell it to the worms.

1

'Will you come to the party? It's not every night I get a million-dollar grant. You don't even have to write anything afterward.' Stevens' phone voice was urgent, unlike him.

Pauli's skin tingled, remembering his touch, firm but gentle, so oddly like Lizann's. 'No. I'd better not come. It's a great event, but your wife, she's running it, isn't she?' Pauli asked. 'How can you and I talk there?' Frustration and annoyance now burned through her. 'Stevens, how do you think that makes me feel?'

'We can kiss behind the pantry door. Between toasts.'

'Very funny.'

Stevens continued, 'Actually the evening won't be pure pleasure. I've got a problem here at the lab. A really bad one.'

'Oh?' At first Pauli had enjoyed hearing about all the dilemmas with staff, money and patients that he seemed not to tell his wife any more. Then she'd grown exasperated, because he seldom focused on her problems with equal fervour. As a gynaecologist, he'd heard it all before, lived professionally immune, apparently found none of it enthralling – except in bed, where, like other married people, he experienced what he never did with his wife.

Pauli began to weaken. 'All right. I'll come. Just say I'm researching another article, and we'll all feel good.'

'See you, Pauli. I love you. Wear your white dress. With all that auburn hair, you'll look gorgeous. I do like petite redheads.'

1

'You just want me to look like a nurse.'

'Don't be silly. I spent fifteen years with nurses, green and white. Believe me, the charm dies.'

'Like the patients.' A dirty jab that resembled a bent hypodermic needle, but how to end these conversations that trailed off into flirtatious chatter? Nor did she believe he loved her. 'Oh, I apologise . . . for that comment.' Pauli fumbled at words, sounding more sincere than she felt. 'It's marvellous about the grant, Steve. You deserve it. And I know you'll get a lot of work done with the money.'

'Thank you, dear. See you tonight. Come about eight.'

She put down the phone.

When she'd entered his lab months before, she must have overestimated the genial spirit of the place. Yet, except for Coral Deming, the mouse surgeon, Stevens managed intuitively to match the right people with the right jobs, leaving everyone feeling neither overqualified nor overwhelmed. Both the lobby guard and the charming secretary, Rainette, had joked with her while she waited to interview Dr Stevens St Steven and the other co-director, Dr Harry Stornell, on their battles in the War on Cancer.

The glaring whiteness of the lobby walls was relieved by a half-dozen ornamental stucco niches. In Spain each would have held a foot-high statue of Christ, a saint or the Blessed Virgin in various postures of torment. Here, in this black-glass polyhedron of a building, one niche held a photobox display of a nude athymic mouse, whiskers quivering, while the next one along held the updated model – the 'nude streaker.' This example, which lacked a spleen as well as a thymus gland, specialised in contracting leukaemia in infancy. Indeed, photos of medical and genetic wonders decorated the Medway Institute lobby, including these 3-D views of its claim to fame – or notoriety, depending on which skirmish in the War on Cancer you were fighting.

If ever there existed a rodent bred for extinction, that animal was the nude athymic mouse. Hairless, immunologically deficient, probably terrified, it had mutated until it possessed little natural resistance to either disease or tumour implantation. Dr St Steven's specialty, human breast tumours, benign and malignant, proliferated in it, and a single coal-tar injection could add stomach cancer to its breast cancer. Without a thymus gland to educate its white blood cells in defensive warfare, the mouse overdosed easily and fatally on reality.

What kind of people specialised in such grotesquery?

Leaving the lobby's vinyl loveseat, Pauli had next shuddered at a technicolour blow-up that showed a black-and-white 'mosaic mouse' – normal except for the fact that it happened to have four parents instead of two. Three-day-old mouse embryos, removed from the mother's uterus, were micro-injected sometimes with healthy tissue and genes from other mice, sometimes with mutagenic agents, sometimes with chemicals that killed normal cells, leaving those that produced a hereditary disease.

Somebody at the Institute had even turned breast-cancer cells into normal mice, using the embryo's drive to produce healthy tissue, to override malignancy. Each of the offspring, called 'chimeras', also had four parents instead of two.

The combined effect had made Pauli want not to reproduce at all, for the process seemed fraught with disaster. If I were a mouse, I'd call an intercourse strike, she thought. Except that these Brave New World surgeries rendered traditional intercourse passé, if not redundant altogether.

Now Pauli stared at the page in her office typewriter – an interview with a neurosurgeon about a complicated, controversial form of brain plumbing called 'scalp-to-artery bypass' that sent new blood into the heads of stroke patients through a constructed pipeline. All of a sudden she yearned for a combined head and heart transplant, the only possible solution to her own psychosomatic impasse.

She laughed at herself. Unfortunately, as yet there was no surgery for the soul. Coming next week, folks, in *Medical World News* . . .

The nature of her work as a general assignment reporter for a medical magazine guaranteed that she knew something about everything new and scientific (enough to fool the ignorant) but little in depth about any particular thing (not enough to fool the Ph.D.s – Piled High and Deeps – of whom

3

Stevens was surely one, besides being a medical doctor. Good for an hour or two on any topic, beyond that Pauli could tire and begin to ask ignorant, foolish or facetious questions.

Although long ago she'd convinced herself that romantic love was but a psychoglandular response to a passing stimulus (didn't that fit most relationships she knew?), her emotions balked sometimes. She'd asked Stevens not to call her at work. It blew her mind and destroyed what shreds of concentration she managed to suture together these days. Usually he phoned her apartment at night, when they could talk.

The page in her typewriter still stared at her, like something just rendered vegetable on the operating table. She tore out the words and replunged into the lurid red-blue illustrations of cardiac and circulatory structures in *Gray's Anatomy* on her desk.

What to do about Stevens?

Some days she loved him, some days she hated him for toying with her in his Cheshire cat smiling way, all days yearned to be in bed with him, if only to solace herself for Lizann's brutal departure. When Stevens wasn't brooding about work, his surgeon's fingers gave marvellous massages. He could charm even the shyest woman and delighted in oral sex.

Not that Pauli had ever been shy. Of the 'seven deadly sins' learned in childhood from the *Baltimore Catechism* and experimented with since then, lust ('concupiscence of the flesh') was her necessary favourite. Much more fun than typing medical quotations here in her cubicle. And much more problematic, because months ago she'd lost – the only phrase that fitted was 'clinical detachment'. And Stevens apparently never lost his at all. This invitation to his party was a freak occurrence.

But that was it! His way to deal with her – just enough warmth to keep her hanging on. No wonder his wife, Heather, was rioting in the bedroom. *If* she was ... Once, in a fit of curiosity, when Pauli had asked Stevens about Heather, he'd produced a wallet photo of a tall woman, ponytailed and blue-jeaned, one arm flung over a concrete vase on a porch. At least no babies played on the house steps.

'Our front walk,' Stevens had remarked, 'looks like an ad for a Victorian cement works. She likes antiques.'

So Pauli had expected this whirlwind with Stevens, beginning at the lab and her apartment and continuing into motel dates, to blow over as usual when her partner became unavailable, intending to remain so. Despite ten years together, Lizann had gone – but psychiatrists were wacky whenever they divided the biochemistry of human attractions into 'normal' and 'perverse', hetero- and homosexual. Like gravity here and gravity on Mars, it was all the same irresistible process when bodies approached at certain points in their movements.

Yet how to trust your own reactions when nobody else does? Male lovers before Lizann had accused her of infidelity with women; and women, with men. In fact, she could accuse Lizann right now! Whether Pauli acted upon attraction or not (usually not), she somehow couldn't win. It was hard when she seemed to be some sort of 'test for normal' for all her lovers: like litmus paper, would she turn blue or pink, boy or girl? And what happens when you're neither and both simultaneously, bearing desire for men and also for women inscribed on your flesh?

Everybody flirts for a while – flattering fun – then tells you to get your head shrunk or your vagina stitched to prevent spreading something they equate with VD or Aids.

All except Stevens – so far. To shock him out of office problems one day, Pauli had announced, 'You know, I'm bisexual.' Instead of moving to the other end of the bed, fumbling for Krafft-Ebing or appropriating her as fascinating pathology fallen to him alone, he blinked in surprise and then caught her hand.

Without hesitation he remarked, 'Everybody is androgynous. Only a few people have the guts to admit it.'

Since life had disciplined her for everything except understanding, she couldn't believe the gratitude in her heart – or the tears in her eyes. She reached toward his face, the soft voice, darkly waving hair, narrow shoulders, his disorienting combination of gentleness with strength that reminded her of . . . a woman.

'You've got love and faith, dear. What you need's hope,' Stevens continued, diagnosing her soul. Then, covering her bare back gently with the sheet, he began to talk about getting home for dinner from this motel room that she'd paid for . . .

In her office she thrust her hand on to the phone. Call him now and say you won't attend his July Fourth bash. With everybody gladhanding him, he won't miss you. But this decision conflicted with her need to be loyal to something in her life, to feel that something beyond her work mattered.

Pauli still gaped at this male version of herself – all her strengths and flaws, white-coated, writ larger, dollars plus lives flowing from Stevens' decisions about treatment, research, personnel. Why did all this become a man so well, like some opulent cloak he wore nobly, while she'd felt one inch high, floundering in the hem the year before Jacobs arrived to relieve her as interim editor at the magazine? Jacobs, a failed MD who believed all women were sneaky hysterics, didn't let either of those flaws handicap *him*.

Stevens never lost. That was the most infuriating thing about him. How did his crew of junior researchers and staff stand him?

On Pauli's second interview day at Medway, she'd backed into a green cubbyhole office in search of a telephone – and heard the furious female voice spouting into the receiver. 'No! Don't you understand your own bloody English, Edward? Tell him no! I'm already up to my eyelids in mouse surgery. Just because I won a needlepoint contest doesn't make me surgeon to the world. Morgan and Burl should know that. With Morgan's private mice, who knows what he's got there, anyway? I don't care *what* Dr St Steven ordered. All the changes he wants are chaos. Let me talk to Morgan.' After snarling, 'Tell him to call me', the woman flung down the phone. She then turned towards Pauli, the next intruder, with, 'What d'*you* want?'

'Just the public phone. Where is it?'

When the woman swivelled sideways towards a spare desk

stacked with cages, Pauli noted the most receding chin she'd ever seen on a normal human face. Masses of curly black hair, blonde frosted here and there, cascaded about it. Large tortoiseshell glasses with tiny owl decorations topped the rest. Above the severe white lab coat stuck the red nylon ruffle of what must be a blouse. About one wrist hung a gold charm bracelet from which more tiny animals rippled.

'The phone's hard to find. It's just a hole in the wall about three doors down.'

'Thanks. Sorry to interrupt your conversation.'

The woman waved a handful of silver and stone rings. 'Never mind. This place is a madhouse now. Everything rush-rush while we get squeezed from one tour and deadline to the next. If I didn't need the status, I'd scramble back to my university. Even the pay's lousy, because I don't have a Ph.D. yet.'

The black-and-white sign on her cubicle read 'Coral R. Deming, MA'.

Poor Coral. No wonder Stevens had shrugged a 'not necessary' when Pauli had enquired about other researchers she might interview among the four storeys of labs, offices, chemical, X-ray and cold rooms, the pathology and tissue-culture areas, and, of course, the quarantine animal wing. He'd liked the first article for her magazine on the Institute's overall work, and she hoped he'd like the pieces he'd just hired her to do on his researchers' individual projects.

And yet whatever she quoted from Harry, the co-director, or Morgan, the chief pathologist, had miffed him. 'This is a team effort, Pauli. Personalities who stand out make for jealousy.'

'But the news articles and press releases you want are made of that. Of quotes. These aren't dry journal articles.'

'I don't care. No individuals should stand out. I want readable prose on our new equipment and on the statistics and artwork I'll give you. For our quarterly reports, too, of course. You'll be paid well when you finish each item. Oh, you can meet some of my post-docs, like Arthur. Or maybe Burl and Merrill, our molecular bio prodigies, but their stuff is so technical, you'll get lost.'

'I doubt that.'

Although Stevens' honest earnestness did stand out and, with an effort, he could admit viewpoints not his own, whenever the situation arose, he acted surprised, betrayed, like some hurt little boy. As long as you agreed with him, you got along fine, all sunshiny systems go. The only pessimism or self-pity he tolerated was his own ('I'm the only obstetrician in town without kids. Jesus, it's obscene!'). But when you disagreed over anything, from a motel vs. apartment decision to Pauli's quandaries over her ailing mother and Sara, the magazine's vindictive secretary, he could somehow transmute the topic into a loyalty oath.

And then he turned snide so fast it made you want to kill him.

2

In his laboratory office Stevens stared at the joke poster that Rainette, his secretary, had made him: Male Chauvinist Mouse of the Year Award. A pink-eyed creature in a white coat, stethoscope and hypodermic syringe aloft, his whiskers twitching. Since the lab also researched cancer in rats, Stevens supposed he'd come off lucky in Rainette's animal art.

Now he thought it impetuous, but not foolish, to urge Pauli's attendance at the party. Both as a medical writer and as a woman, she was discreet, honest, loyal. He wished he could say the same for most of the Institute's non-animal population.

Months before, he remembered warming to Pauli's excited interest in his work. They talked easily as she was both a good listener and an accurate reporter for a difficult magazine on which the editor played hostile favourites, criticising somebody's every comma one week, ignoring the same employee for days following. Pauli remained the only woman there who was not a secretary. Others had quit dismayed, but Pauli was made of sterner stuff. Stevens liked that in a woman. He wished his wife, Heather, would display more of it, although neither she nor Pauli pulled masochistic tales of suffering, their own or others', upon him, as so many patients had done when he'd had a full private practice.

Like his father and the gynaecologists of his training years, he needed the barrier wall that he erected at crucial moments – deaths from haemorrhage, cancer, anaesthesia, the births of all the babies he'd pulled live and dead into the world, numberless recoveries from his various surgeries upon the reproductive organs of the human female. While he considered himself compassionate, even clever at handling women's responses, he hated to see his natural protectiveness misused to discuss nappy rash or sinus headache. He still wondered where compassion for human misery ended – and coddling people who should be solving their own problems began.

But running the Institute was proving no easier than private practice. Mice – creatures at the mercy of heredity and instinct – were basically predictable. You inject them with malignant cells or coal tars; they get cancer and die, all individuals of some strains dead in weeks. But managing *people* was neither neat nor convenient, however calm he appeared about it. For one thing, you couldn't stash them in cages or wards for the terminally uncooperative.

Unlocking his desk, he pulled out a manila folder of print-outs on the two latest and severest problems that weren't going away. Indeed, they threatened the whole Institute. He'd dealt with the dishonesty and weakness of others – junior and clerical employees whose personalities were mostly irrelevant to their functions. If they lied to hide ineptitude or laziness, no matter. They got fired eventually; there was nothing personal in it. But these new situations . . .

How hard he and Harry had worked to make each group of researchers feel at home with the Institute and in one another's houses, organising swim parties and barbecues when Heather would still cook.

He reread an airletter scrawled by one of last year's protégés whom he'd sponsored for a European research grant. Through Stevens' recommendation, Jim was settled in Lyons, analysing masses of data and lecturing as well. Stevens could be proud of Jim, if he could just decipher the handwriting: 'It was the first year at the Institute for both of us, and I never would have made it through, or here, without your – was it 'succor'? Must be 'support'. Jim didn't use fancy words.

With a pang, Stevens longed for Jim's sensible opinion on

this fresh crisis. Pauli could be controlled, but other reporters wouldn't be so agreeable.

As he gazed round this new white office, he recalled his former professional arena. Dr Stevens St Steven's previous office had walnut wood walls. Medium brown with a hint of red warmth, sober without coldness, it had genuine oil paintings on the walls, wooden end tables, tapestried chairs, the latest magazines with untattered covers. No muzak, no plastic.

It had combined professionalism with that touch of homeliness that announced, 'I have arrived and yet I still care for your pain, your fears, your comforts.' But that had proved to be the unsettling problem. After ten years' daily grind of frantic phone calls, hospital rounds, rushing to surgery, delivering babies at 2 a.m., prescribing Premarin to sobbing menopausal women, he didn't and couldn't, care any more.

Whenever he recalled his old office (where a younger man had now joined Simon and David, his former partners), he thought of Mrs Bartlett, and immediately winced – as he had the day she'd perched in his inner office. He'd examined her in one of the cubicles and now she was dressed again, looking, he supposed, as decent as she ever would or could – overweight, greying, distraught, pathetic, with furrowed forehead, sallow skin, her Peter Pan blouse collar twisted under a faded sweater that might have been yellow before it was washed against something green. With the fixed stare of a fish flung on to the beach, she reminded him of his mother's favourite sister, whom he'd always avoided as a whining bore. Like, too, his own sister, two years younger than himself, who had achieved decades of what she wanted by pouting, crying, staging either a headache or an upset stomach. She lived on tranquillisers and pep pills, as far as he knew.

Mrs Bartlett had consulted him for irregular bleeding several months before. He had regulated what remained of her menstrual cycle and assured her that she didn't have cancer, yet here she was again, complaining of abdominal pain. He knew what she wanted and needed – someone on whom to *depend*, someone to replace her husband, who had lost his job and ignored her, and the son who drank and drove too fast. But no good would ever come of such dependence, either for a doctor or for her. He must break it as fast as possible.

'There's nothing wrong with you, Mrs Bartlett. I've examined you again. You're in fine health. When you do begin menopause, just call and my secretary will make an appointment then. Don't forget your yearly Pap test. I've already showed you how to examine your breasts. Do it regularly.'

'But, Doctor?'

'Yes?' How long would he humour her, with ante-partum and post-surgical cases waiting in three other cubicles?

'I was wondering – Oh, never mind.' Clutching her purse, she rose from the hard-backed chair, her collar still awry.

He stared away from the angry tears flooding her eyes. 'Just phone my secretary,' he repeated, opening his office door, elbowing her out and shutting the door behind her.

He hated her pathos, her springing hope that somehow he could magically solve problems she'd failed to solve over forty-five years of living. Well, he wasn't supposed to be a shrink. What the hell did they expect of him?

Then he hated himself for hating her. What *could* he have said that wouldn't be a lie? She wouldn't follow the advice, anyway. Live and be healthy, Mrs Bartlett. Dump your relatives, your illnesses, your view of yourself and your life as fragile and doomed. Enjoy yourself, Mrs Bartlett. Even if you do get cancer, you'll at least have known *once* what it's like to be alive.

Oh, to hell with her and with the full 50 per cent (80 per cent, it seemed some days) of his patients just like her.

The next day he called Harry at the Institute and began the move to sell his share of the practice and return to full-time research. These crazy women were good business for psychiatrists, but not for him. He just wanted them to get their fish-eyes off him.

12

3

Heather picked up the phone in the kitchen and dialled Stevens' number. He hated her to call when she was upset, but she felt like annoying him.

'Steve, will you come home early? Please? I can't get Nancy to help with the sandwiches. She got a last-minute offer to go somewhere.' Nancy was the neighbourhood teenager who for $10 would either clean or cook before a party – if it didn't interfere with her love life.

'Heather, I told you not to leave it all till the last minute.'

Years ago, when they were first married, she would have cringed at his impatient criticism. Now she counterattacked. 'This is *your* bloody party! Now, will you come home and help me?' She wouldn't succumb to his usual trick of making a lot of shitwork sound like medicine's latest opportunity to improve your character.

'I can't come. I have something really urgent here to figure out.'

'You've always got something urgent, Steve. I thought –'

'Look, I'll try and get Rainette or somebody to come. I know it's a lot of work, but you're a capable woman.' In his high-handed way he was softening. For a few seconds she was glad he'd cut her off before she began what he called 'the whining bit' they both hated, but it was the only way to move him to do anything these days. Modestly worded appeals he ignored, just as he ignored their opposite extreme, hysteria. He and she had suffered too many false starts, backtracked and failed each other too often for either to believe in starting over, fulfilling illusions, old or new.

These evenings he ate quickly, went to his desk in the orange room to sort papers and reports, then fell asleep during the late-night movie, stumbling in to lie beside her in the double bed.

Before this lab job accelerated, at least they'd had Wednesday afternoons to act like a couple. She'd pick him at at the Institute. In good weather they picknicked in one of the city parks or at the beach; in winter they'd iceskate or see a movie. They'd end with dinner at a restaurant in the Spanish or Italian sections of the city, drive home and make love. Until a couple of months ago, when he began working Wednesday afternoons plus, of course, Saturdays and some Sunday afternoons. Now the only real difference in his schedule from when he'd had private patients was that, without hospital rounds, he slept an hour later each morning.

With all the free time he'd expected to have, they'd bought a three-storey Victorian house in an older suburb of the city and installed a few antiques, original New England pieces, before he lost interest in driving to country auctions.

On two different Wednesday afternoons Heather had phoned the Institute to see whether Rainette would give her a number to reach Stevens. When Rainette had none and Heather's calls to Stevens' former partners and one or two friends proved fruitless, she gave up in despair. Surely he couldn't imagine she wouldn't *notice*. But that was Stevens – methodical about his self-interest; blind, stupid and stubborn about anybody else's.

While she accused him mentally of not caring what she thought, she discovered she hadn't been listening to some new problems he was outlining on the phone – nattering on again about his endless office haggles.

'Stevens, if you don't get home, you can run this party yourself. I'm fed up with this whole situation. I'm moving out.' The calm fury in her voice surprised her. As many times as she'd imagined this scene, she had thought she would collapse in tears. *Say it. What have you got to lose?* 'Will you tell me where you go Wednesdays now? I know you're not working. If you got somebody else – have you? – well, she's welcome to you!'

Silence.

Just like Stevens. Tell him the sky is falling and he'd remark, 'Interesting. How many feet per second?' The bastard! As her fury ebbed, tears of frustration sprang to her eyes.

'Heather? All right. I'll *come* home. You're imagining things. I'll handle this other problem during the party somehow. Don't panic about the food. We'll get it done. Remember, I wanted to hire a maid.'

'I don't want *anybody* witnessing the mess we are right now.'

Stevens always hired or expected women to solve his life-support problems with food, clothing, cars, plumbing, household machinery. She cursed herself for being too clever by half at fixing things on three floors so he could act exhausted and get away with it. However, his mice apparently were proving just as difficult to control. Like the women, they seemed to demand more than minimal input. You could even give them cancer, but like everything else, they too required attention.

She rejoiced now that she and Steve had no children, despite months of painful tests and scheduled sex. One more failure attributed, of course, to Heather, so Stevens could pity himself as the only doctor in town without kids. Two male intern friends had already produced children with live-in women they hadn't even married – which drove Stevens towards deeper brooding when he delivered both babies to the excited young parents. Sometimes it was supposed to be Heather's 'stubbornness' that prevented conception of any-thing that didn't miscarry. Other times it was, 'You really look ugly. If you only fixed yourself up –', whenever she wore pyjamas instead of nightgowns. Stevens had actually set fire to one purple pair of pyjamas – a gift from her mother – hanging on the clothesline. She would laugh, except that lately he'd lost all interest and dropped asleep exhausted. Whatever sexual tenderness happened, she initiated.

Heather heard Stevens sigh into the telephone. Still no direct answer to her blithering about another woman. Which meant it must be true.

'I'll come in a few minutes. Don't worry. And don't leave. OK? I wanted you to depend on me. A child would have made –'

'I tried. Steve, you're not *here*. You're never here. What're we gonna do?'

'I don't know. But concentrate on the party, huh?'

As she hung up the white kitchen phone, she discovered she'd stabbed and restabbed a five-dollar salami. One end of it lay in gashed bits on the carving board. Not since her first year of medical school laying open the innards of charity cadavers had she been so nervous with a knife. And she'd originally aspired to become a surgeon, before dropping out of medical school and letting Stevens persevere for both of them. At least she'd been the only one of her sisters to finish college.

She and Steve might have made a team with her handling the office side, listening to women's complaints prior to his cutting them up. Drs Heather and Stevens St Steven – no uterus left untouched. You rape 'em; we scrape 'em.

Now she was getting silly. Again she stabbed the salami, this time right through to the carving board for no reason other than it made her feel good.

4

By 8.30 surprisingly and unfortunately, almost everybody had arrived. Either they considered it a joyous occasion or they all planned to leave early. The steam heat of a July Friday night had coagulated in all the rooms of the house. Heather switched on the only air conditioners they possessed, in the upstairs bedroom and in the maid's orange room off the downstairs hall. Stevens had intended this as 'the baby's playroom', but somehow it had instead collected both their sets of medical books, journals and slides, arranged in bookcases or piled against the tangerine walls and around the chocolate carpet until the room became 'the library'.

David and Simon, Stevens' former partners (David had given her the infertility tests), arrived first with their wives. All except Heather began a congratulations-on-the-grant and a furniture-stripping discussion in the living room with Stevens. From what Heather overheard ('. . . first you get down to the original grain, then you bear down hard and evenly . . .'), it sounded like second-stage labour stranded en route to the delivery room.

Heather answered the door buzzer again. This time Harry Stornell and his elegant wife, Lillis, stood on the wooden front porch. 'Hi. We gonna barbecue the fatted calf?' Harry joked.

'On a night like this?' answered Lillis. Heather was grateful, for it meant she didn't need to make conversation or do much beyond smiling the requisite amount.

'Can we help with things?' Lillis continued. As they stepped into the hall, Heather felt them both embrace her, not phony cocktail-party hugs but the real item, as if genuinely pleased to see her. Heather wondered whether Stevens' last office act of the day had been to inform Harry, 'Heather's cracking up. Be nice to her.' Heather hoped not, for Stevens would include some sneer or joke about 'a little identity problem she's having.'

Lillis wore a diaphanous pyjama outfit that looked cool, and Harry a navy shirt that looked hot. As she escorted them towards the kitchen to fix their drinks and load sandwiches on to their platters, she relaxed her back and legs for the first time in hours. The evening might be possible, after all. Confronting Stevens could come later.

By 4.30 that afternoon she'd hinged herself together enough to phone one of her old bosses from the days when she'd financed Stevens' medical education and put an end to her own. Her former boss, Dr Henderson, now ran the medical library on the other side of the city. To cover herself, she'd enquired whether he might know of a job for a friend of hers. In the autumn, he'd said, he would need an assistant librarian and would phone back on Monday with details.

With a job to go to, she'd *begin* to be financially, maybe emotionally, free of Stevens for ever.

By 9.30 all the junior and clerical staff, including Rainette and her husband, had arrived. Several senior staff were already wandering from room to room like unruly children waiting for dinnertime: Jim, the part-time veterinarian; Arthur, who did viral research; Morgan, the pathologist; Coral, the needlepointer; plus several post-doctoral fellows, such as Burl and Merrill, pursuing what Heather called their 'particular perversions' in genetics, tumour biology, embryo research. Because she and Stevens had entertained each of them as they signed with the Institute, they all hugged her. Arthur, who still had acne and loomed six feet six to Heather's six-one, leaned down to kiss her cheek, which thrilled her; many men had to look up.

Heather welcomed one new face – a tiny, copper-haired woman name Pauline – maybe Paulette? – in a white sundress. She had entered with Morgan, introduced herself rapidly, then glanced towards the living room, from which Stevens' hefty laugh rose above the crowd. She and Morgan then left Heather. Maybe one of Morgan's autopsy assistants from a previous incarnation? Shame to waste a gorgeous woman like that on corpses. Heather laughed. The woman in white must be a nurse from one of bachelor Morgan's hospital lives. Besides impeccable credentials, his golden boy exterior assured him jobs everywhere. From the easy way Pauline and Rainette chatted together, Heather realised the two women must know more about Stevens' life at Medway than she did any more. She envied a professional woman like Pauline. Could she ever get out of jeans and depression long enough to become one again?

Leaving Harry and Lillis in charge of food and drink, Heather escaped to the screened back porch and slumped on to a sofa in the final twilight. Maybe nobody would even notice her here. Of the whole house this was her favourite spot, from which she could watch bits of forty chattering people through lighted doorways or against the walls of five different rooms – the kitchen, hall, bath, living room, dining room – and even through the living-room bay window to the front-porch pillars. If only she could get such a complete view of her life.

She wiped perspiration from her forehead with a paper coaster. In the gathering black her lavender silk blouse and white jeans glued her to the vinyl sofa. She imagined removing all her clothes, running naked through the living room and hall, out the front door. But medical people had no interest in nudes.

How would she *stand* three more hours of high-tech chatter about hormones, cell receptors and mouse surgery from these people who considered her and Steve the perfect dual-career couple who had sanely avoided fights over kids by avoiding the kids? And her 'career', whatever it was, had veered and faltered several times from medical school through librarianship into real estate and the antiques business. Now Stevens scolded if she made any money at all;

an upper-income couple without dependants merely kept the income-tax bandits in champagne and caviare.

She watched Coral fulminating predictably about discrimination against women in science. Too true, but what good would it do her? Heather knew Stevens was considering firing Coral. Despite – or because of – her seniority at the Institute, she wasted too much of his time with her complaints and sabotage of his orders. Was she the 'something urgent' he'd mentioned during that lousy afternoon phone conversation? Just like Stevens to get rid of anybody who inconvenienced him.

'Even when we're not about to disappear down the matrimonial drain, nobody trusts us.' So that's what Coral thought of Heather – or any married woman. Well, mouse turds would freeze over before anybody married Coral.

Yet suddenly Coral stopped her diatribe, waved and smiled – towards whom? Ah, Morgan and Burl, passing through, drinks in hand. Poor Coral, if she fancied she stood a chance with a hunk like Morgan or a youngster like Burl. Next to her stood Arthur, listening to her with rapt attention. At least tonight she'd changed her tortoiseshell monstrosities for her partying, platinum/rhinestone glasses, now slipping down her nose. Heavy make-up covered her ever-enthusiastic crop of blemishes, Heather knew.

Heather, you're becoming a bitch. No, Dr St Steven, it's merely hardening of the categories . . . As Heather glanced up again, she saw Pauline watching her from the kitchen. The woman looked away instantly, as if embarrassed, as if guessing Heather was being insulted in her own home.

Heather's eyes stung. Must be pollution and cigarette smoke in the heavy air. Why didn't doctors worry more about lung cancer? She fought against rubbing her eyelids. The 'library', the only room invisible to her, was air-conditioned, although the machine was temperamental. Maybe she could continue collapsing there. Better still, go upstairs; let the repetitive noise of the bedroom's machine calm her.

Someone was extinguishing the lamps and front-porch

lights. Suddenly candles flared inside the glasses she'd set out. More people arrived with hoots and shouts.

'How ill this taper burns! Ha! who comes here?' flowed in pure ham tones from the living room. Must be Edward, the English lab assistant, who was addicted to amateur theatricals. Tonight he was in full flight:

> *I think it is the weakness of mine eyes*
> *That shapes this monstrous apparition.*
> *It comes upon me. Art thou any thing?*
> *Art thou some god, some angel, or some devil,*
> *That makest my blood cold, and my hair to stare?*
> *Speak to me what thou art.*

While he cackled convincingly and delivered the Ghost's answer, 'Thy evil spirit, Brutus', to his own rhetorical question, Heather crept through the dining room. Rounding the table by candlelight, she nearly fell over Coral, who was stacking two plates with food. Probably one for Edward – Coral was solicitous like that.

Heather reached the carpeted hall. Let Stevens direct the Julius Caesar show. She'd get him alone some time tonight.

Choosing a moment when the stairs looked vacant, she felt her way to the second-floor darkness. Ridiculous to sneak about her own home, but her brain and will rebelled at any conversation with the therapeutic and thespian horde downstairs. Steve must be in the library or outdoors. She couldn't distinguish him in any of the candlelit crews she'd slid past.

The second floor was even more airless, and ten degrees hotter, than the first, and she felt perspiration flowing again along her temples and between her breasts. But the bedroom proved blessedly cool. She closed the door behind her, dropped her clothes, put on her pyjamas and sank on to the quilted satin bedspread. Her former determination, born of the energy that rage provides, had dissipated. Now her head ached and she longed for someone to advise her on the mess her marriage had become. She and Stevens resembled the walls of the downstairs hall; she'd plastered and replastered, yet with summer's damp advent, the same crack appeared

21

anew under the turquoise paint. Any cosmetic job over a basic structural flaw was bound to fail.

Heather shuddered, wondering how she'd come to be so objective about her own misery. From her years of medical school, maybe; but more from Stevens, with his abstracted brooding towards solutions. If only she could fall asleep . . .

Heather rubbed her hands across her abdomen and winced. Damn red welt, six inches long, still hurt after three years whenever she perspired and wore fly-front clothing simultaneously.

Leaving Stevens would mean the welcome end of his love affair with her menstrual cycle, though they'd already despaired of scheduled sex to produce a child. 'Vatican roulette' had driven both of them nearly impotent. Even the ancient joke, 'You already had two trips to the maternity ward, what more do you want?' mocked her tonight. The first trip, which involved a D and C, had followed haemorrhage and a miscarriage. Infertility tests had followed that. Luckily Stevens and David believed in conservative use of the superovulating drugs or she'd still be hooked on Clomid. Then came several months of fearing she'd conceived anything from twins to sextuplets, who'd weigh a pound apiece and die prematurely.

The second surgery had followed a tubal pregnancy and more haemorrhaging. Tubal pregnancy meant the fertilised egg had got stuck en route to the uterus. Although Stevens mourned it as 'another lost child', it must have been defective. And who needed another damaged baby – arms, legs or brain missing? Water on the brain, like that mahogany drummer-boy statue with the big head Stevens kept polished on the mantel in the library. Grotesque.

She did possess a tragic talent for destroying the next generation. Of course, Stevens reworked it into *her* infertility problem. Funny thing: she liked kids. It was all the arguments that would result with perfectionist, absentee Stevens as their father that threatened her. Should have had kids years ago, before her and Stevens' battle positions got so entrenched. But few mothers had enough money, energy or ambition to leave, as she was planning to do. With every kid the stakes got higher, immobility greater.

Let him find another woman. May she have more joy of him than I've ever got... Who was he spending Wednesdays with? Not Harry's wife and not Rainette. They both loved their husbands, she knew. Ah, what could anybody know? Mostly that it hurt.

Only my gynaecologist knows for sure, and he couldn't care less.

Laughing and crying at this half-thought, Heather drifted in and out of consciousness. She felt light as a ping-pong ball, bouncing hospital ceiling to floor, lamp to window. Her mouth tasted like wadded cotton. When she shifted her legs, pain shot through her abdomen. Something unfamiliar there under the shorty gown: a heavy cotton-and-adhesive dressing plus the catheter's plastic tubing. The thought of herself draining into a bag made her giggle again. Another plastic tubing, an IV, hung into one wrist.

Someone entered the door to her room. Green surgical garb bore down on her. Minus her glasses, she recognised Stevens' voice before distinguishing his face. When he leaned to kiss her nose and stroke her head, she smelled rubbing alcohol and scrub soap.

'How you doing?'

'. . . don't know.' Through the post-anaesthesia haze, her words wandered, hid, reappeared, as if playing languid hide and seek with her brain cells. She feared Stevens' seeing her like this for the second time in three years. His standards for her conduct, speech and appearance remained so appallingly high. How many times had she tried – and failed – to show him that all his crazy codes for other people merely condemned *him* to a brooding life of unmet expectations?

'Good news.' He smiled. 'No tumour anyway. Ectopic pregnancy small enough, so we repaired the tube in time. You're in great shape, kid.'

Heather sighed. At her age she hadn't seriously expected cancer, despite Dave's hints, 'I've found a mass there. Maybe on the ovary. We should open you up.' When the haemorrhaging began, all he mentioned was fibroid tumours.

'Steve,' Heather pleaded. 'Can we stop . . . now? Use contraceptives? Five years. Doesn't work.' Her tongue slithered and tangled.

'What? Well, we'll talk about it later. You're as good as new. Dave guarantees it. I mean, Heather, of course you want children. Every normal human being does. You'll feel better tomorrow.'

'The . . . second time, Steve. Time,' Heather tried to protest.

'I'll be back this evening. Get some sleep. Let them know if you need an injection.' Briefly he touched her shoulder, then veered away.

As full consciousness returned in her, so did the pain – a constant sting and throb straight down her middle. They must have inflicted this vertical incision in order to lay open the total abdomen and remove whatever organs cancer might have begun to devour. Like a gutted fish, she felt sliced in half.

If he wanted a child after *this* – twice in three years – he could screw himself! After two tries, she was finished with it. See another gynaecologist in a few weeks, give a false name, get a discreet and renewable supply of the Pill – there should be some new brand of it that wouldn't give you cancer in exchange for peace of mind. That would fix Stevens' lust for fatherhood regardless of how she considered him or the marriage, regardless of the fact that he had no time and made none for either. He worked a ten-hour day, six days a week. Sundays he slept late, then napped or dictated letters after lunch.

No more need to cajole, flirt, bargain him out of exhausted moodiness. Oh, the joy and peace of giving up . . .

Heather woke with a start, her left leg tingling under her as if she'd been sleepwalking and fallen on it. Above the air-conditioner's drone she heard commotion, voices. People leaving already? Let Stevens deal with it. If she walked down now, she'd look rumpled, if not limping. How to get her leg functioning?

Again her mind wandered – half a continent away – to her last sleeping-leg problem. Her faculty adviser in second-year medical school droning at her above his glasses: 'What's this? Surgery's too hard a specialty for a woman. Your course work is good, but I've never seen a woman with enough stamina. And you know a surgeon lives by referrals. Other doctors entrust patients to him. I'm not sure they'd trust a woman. Of course, there are women like Dr Eiserson, but they're *exceptions*. Heather, you'd be better off in internal medicine or maybe paediatrics. Those are –'

'I don't agree with any of that, Dr Sims. I want to be a surgeon. That's what I'm in medical school for,' Heather answered, her voice unsteady. How could this man have been her faculty adviser for two whole years? And what illusions, founded in the exhaustion of her own seventy-hour weeks, had prevented her seeing it? If he thought such crap about medical women, why had he chosen her as his advisee? Maybe he hadn't; maybe she'd been assigned to him, like everything else in med school.

'Will you refer me to the surgery team, at least for the summer?'

'Heather, I can't do that. Dr Graceland over there simply won't take a woman. See the position I'm in?'

'He would if you'd convince him. You know my record's fine.'

'Are you telling me how to run my own department?' A sudden smile on his sagging face (it reminded her of a basset hound) revived her momentarily – until she realised his expression had softened to pity at her *naïveté*. To think she'd trusted this bastard for the last year and ten months. Fool!

She retreated. 'Please do what you can, Dr Sims. I'd like to call you on Friday and see what the answer is.'

'You already know the answer. I'll refer you for internal or for paediatrics but not for surgery. Be reasonable, Heather.'

'You're afraid of angering Graceland because he refers patients to you. You bastard!' she wanted to yell. Instead, she hoisted her books and staggered from the office, discovering her left leg, rigid with tension, had fallen asleep. She nearly crashed into his bookcase by the door.

When Sims, cornered on the phone, proved evasive, and

when her chairman repeated the wisdom of switching specialties, Heather dropped out of medical school. Sims signed her withdrawal form with proper gravity but without encouraging her to stay.

Again the blue funk over the surgery done upon her and the surgery she was never allowed to do. No wonder people dreaded middle age.

As the noises grew louder above the air conditioner's whirr, someone banged on the bedroom door. 'Heather? Heather!' From question into frantic command. Couldn't they leave her alone? The room was dark. If she just lay there . . . They probably needed something trivial, like fresh candles or more napkins.

Someone burst in. Yellow light stabbed Heather's eyes. From downstairs, a scream. 'Heather? Oh, thank God, we've looked all over for you.' It was Rainette, panting, her hand placed flat on her chest.

'What's going on?' Heather's voice sounded groggy. They'd think she'd been drinking.

'It's . . . terrible. I can't believe it. It's Stevens, he . . . Harry went to ask him something.'

Heather rolled over and sat up. Her leg still prickled. 'Sit down.'

Now Rainette was sobbing every other word.

5

Heather stumbled towards the stairs. Rainette lagged behind, Heather noticed, as if deferring to the mistress of the house over something . . . what? Well, she wouldn't be mistress much longer.

From below, Heather heard movement, then screams, but no laughter.

Lights blazed at her from the crystal chandelier. Why the screams? Screams-with-laughter belonged to the previous candlelit scene with medical men, like other men, drinking too much and feeling up convenient women. Even ugly ones raised a man's score.

The front door stood open, but the hall lay humid in the heat. From the landing Heather saw the first tense, whitened face. She had trouble identifying the open mouth and staring eyes as belonging to David. Unwinding the week's work with too much whisky and water until he gaped like a frog.

Next a blur of people gushed from the 'library' door at the right of the hall. They joined those just arriving from the living room, kitchen and porch. Babbling voices confused her. She heard only snatches: 'It's horrible . . . Who? He's lying across his desk . . . Get the police!'

Maybe a heart attack, or had somebody passed out in there? But most of them were doctors, so surely . . .?

'Here she comes,' called somebody.

David stepped towards the stairs and Heather. On his stiffened face his black moustache and crooked nose began to move. 'Heather! We couldn't find you. We thought you weren't well. Don't go in.' As if in comfort, he laid one tweedy arm about her shoulders. When his grip tightened, she realised he meant to restrain her away from the closed door of the orange room.

The smell of extinguished candles hung in the air. Six drowned faces, mouths agape, watched, making her feel like an actress who's missed one cue and is about to botch another.

'Don't be silly. This is my house.'

Hands still restrained her. She'd failed again at the role she never could pull off: the woman who decides instantly, without regrets, and has others – like Stevens, for instance – currying *her* favour.

Where *was* Stevens?

At first she'd dreaded meeting him against this backdrop of agitated frowns and stares. Hugging the turquoise wall, she now wanted him here to command this situation that people were restraining her from controlling. He must be in the library with whoever had fallen over.

She broke away from David, slid past others who were arguing, and shoved at the library door. If everyone was numb, she'd do something. She shut the door behind her. Compared to the long, airless hall, the orange room rendered a cool, shadowy welcome. But they should get the cracked window glass and rattling air conditioner fixed in here. Both let in mosquitoes.

At first the darkness confused her. Only one desk lamp burned, and Stevens' head and shoulders on the desktop blocked most of its light. He'd knocked it over. Now fear tore her. If he'd suffered a heart attack, why had nobody stretched him on the floor and massaged his chest until the ambulance arrived? Had anybody called one?

When she touched his shoulder, the blue plaid shirt was wet. When she tried to move her legs in the half-light, she found her bare feet mired in a wet spot, dark against the lighter brown of the cocoa shag carpet.

Her heart stopped beating, then shuddered until she feared it would leap from her chest. When she opened her mouth to scream, she found she wasn't even breathing.

28

Steve dead? How could Steve be dead?

Yet she felt his blood oozing between her toes. She watched irregular clots of it creeping and staining her insteps. Without touching him again, she managed two terrified steps backwards over the soaking rug and spattered folders to where the desk light wouldn't glare into her eyes.

Stevens' whole front, plus the once-beige desk blotter, lay in a blood wash as if someone had draped him with a scarlet Christmas sheet. Blood had pumped on to the desk, curtains and wall, then dripped between his legs to the floor.

If he killed himself, where was the weapon? Ridiculous even to think that Stevens would kill himself. 'Suicide's for cowards like *you*,' he'd yelled once during one of their fights.

Somebody had murdered Steve on the night that capped his whole life – getting that grant. Why hadn't she heard? Why hadn't any of that crowd heard?

She felt like throwing up. Staggering further backwards, she landed on the portable computer atop its white stand. Clutching it, she forced herself to peer again at him. His head lay skewed to one side. The red sheet's edge began at his throat with an open wound that a surgeon might make to begin a goitre operation. Somebody had neatly slit Stevens' throat. His wild, lifeless eyes stared at the lamp base.

Heather fixed on one protrusion from the red sheet. Stevens' belt and trousers were pulled open. The brass buckle she'd given him for his birthday ('It's real antique.' 'But, Heather, it's so gaudy.') winked from the mess. She stifled a scream. When she turned to run towards the babble of voices behind her, she wrenched to stop at the sculpture on the mantel. In the slanted light, it was the yard-high mahogany drummer boy from Haiti, found in a Connecticut antique shop, its salient feature the grotesquely enlarged head so intriguing to Stevens, despite her complaints.

Three smears of blood soiled the white mantel, and the statue itself now faced sideways, hiding the smirk on the boy's face that provided its eerie, retarded-foetus quality. Something fleshy – red and white – lay betwen the boy's hand and the waiting drum. One drop of blood, red on mahogany, had trickled down the tall statue.

All the autopsies she'd seen, the cadaver dissections she'd done, alone and partnered, flashed through her head. The tissue draped over the drum like some hooded worm had to be . . . Stevens' penis.

Heather retched convulsively, screamed and fell backwards into the door, which somebody was opening. Hands clasped her arms. Just before the tears began, Heather wanted to be sorry, but she couldn't.

6

Forcing herself to take the apartment stairs two at a time in the heat, Pauli caught the phone before it stopped ringing. Mrs Biasin, who owned the house where Pauli's mother rented? Another fall? Could be . . .

'Pauli, Pauli, are you there? He's dead! Nobody knows how but he's . . . dead. At the party. I thought you'd want to know. I'm across the street from their house.'

'Who are you talking about? Is it Mom?' First came fear, then Pauli slumped into her new summer habit – half-awareness to calls and people expected to convey unpleasantness. *If you can't digest it, screen it out.*

'It's Dr St Steven! Aren't you listening? Is your mother sick? I said *he*. The party tonight!' Rainette snapped at her.

It was nearly 1 a.m. Pauli was exhausted. Suddenly she yearned for the old days when women, including friends who were secretaries at cancer labs, were hesitant, almost apologetic, certainly never acquired sufficient self-confidence to snap at you. They would always allow for some incoherence arising from your pain or confusion, while you exhibited your portion of the female talent for anguish.

Although Rainette relished gossip, her voice was trembling. 'It's . . . terrible.' She must be joking! Stevens was alive just – Pauli checked her watch – eighty minutes ago. Pauli had said her goodbyes, driven back to her apartment, walked nearby to get some air.

'But, Rainette, I just drove *home* from the party.'

'Where have you been?'

'Out walking. I said goodbye to him. He was alive. Everybody was congratulating him about the grant, and you were complaining how hard he works you. You must be joking. How come *you* arrived so late?'

When Rainette spoke again, something had subdued her voice. Pauli heard background noises. 'Well, Tom and I did arrive late – on purpose. But I'm telling you, Stevens is *dead*. Something cut his throat while he was on the phone. There's blood all, just all over. The desk and rug. I saw it. And police around the house. They'll be calling you. Somebody told them you were the last to see him.'

'What?' Pauli shuddered. Something too much like a hot flush to be one washed through her body. Anticipating a thunderstorm, she'd closed all the windows. Now she dropped down, perspiring, on the floor, afraid to fall off any chair. Stevens dead! If not joking, then Rainette was lying. Why? *But I kissed him goodnight. He was warm. Say something, must say something.*

'Pauli? Are you OK?'

'It's horrible, Rainette. The police –' But Rainette couldn't know about Pauli's extra-Institute meeting with Stevens. Or could she? 'Look, I'll call you in the morning. . . I can't talk now. Good-night.'

Pauli replaced the receiver, got up, then slumped into one of the leather armchairs she'd bought at a used-office-furniture sale. As a child she'd dreamed of just such a white-walled, suede-furnitured, Japanese-lanterned apartment as the appropriate adjunct to the perfect professional life, unhampered by relatives, men, complications. Now, after ten years of first the apartment, then the uninvolving but increasingly demanding work, she felt drained. Without Lizann and now without Stevens, the whole thing mocked her by yellow lantern light.

1 a.m. What to do?

Maybe it wasn't true. Rainette might be wrong. Maybe they'd got him to a hospital.

Why would anybody hurt Stevens? *Because he, like you, isn't all there*? Because he'd spent so many years obedient to the whine of a beeper that even amid sex, he never left his coat more than a foot from the bed? But you don't kill somebody because he's not there. You just hate him.

She loved *and* hated him – a married man with no time for her or his wife. For three months she'd been, yes, lovesick over him, his power to thrill her whenever he looked at her or laid his hand between her legs. She loved and hated the yearning that destroyed concentration, her will to work, live her normal life.

Trying to open a casement window, Pauli found her knees shaking. How could Stevens be . . . gone? Nobody she knew got murdered. How had he died? Ask more. She'd asked less. What kind of reporter are you?

Maybe he killed himself? That must be it. In the middle of his own party? Stevens wasn't insane. Where was Heather tonight? After the first mini-introduction Pauli had asked twice but got no answers, even from Stevens. Heather on the twilit back porch had looked distant . . . scared? Much as Pauli envied whatever life Heather and Stevens managed to share, she hadn't wanted to confront her alone on that porch.

Is that what you tell the police? What the well-appointed medical writer reveals to the press:

'Kiss him? Yes, I did kiss him tonight – to congratulate him. But I didn't know I was the last to see him . . . alive.' *How about the murderer*? 'Yes, I was doing a series of articles on the Institute, the researchers' new work. And some statistics he gave me. Quarterly reports for the Medway board of directors.'

Steve, who murdered you?

Her fate: to get switched on by the man Stevens, and he suffers the bad luck and worse taste to get himself murdered. But murders happened in Manhattan, in Boston; they didn't happen here! From the living room to the bedroom she paced back and forth, wondering what she could throw that wouldn't wake the neighbours. She slammed two closet doors and an open drawer.

Her foolishness: should have known better. For years, until Stevens, she'd been the perfect woman to interview men day or evening in their labs or hotel rooms at a conference. She warmed to their ideas or minds, rarely to them. No involvement – that was the way everybody preferred it.

At first Stevens' face wouldn't return to her, was blotted out. Then she could picture how the velvety eyes, that glossy dark hair and smooth skin had distracted her from the first interview. Hearing his complaints about government red tape, public misunderstanding of cancer work, the high cost of ground coffee and white mice, she had concluded that any gynaecologist who can attract a clientele needs a female aspect, a sensitivity to women.

Next, instead of hormonal research, he'd stopped to tell her what he felt about his work. Delighted, she'd stopped taking shorthand and relaxed, prepared to enjoy a good story, bits of research gossip, whatever she needn't scrabble to record, condense and regurgitate in half a dozen deftly worded sentences. Preferably fewer; nobody tolerated verbosity. Unfortunately, people's souls proved less controllable; they could wax verbose until they sat stymied at the ineffable, inexplicable events in their own lives.

'I work six days a week,' he said. 'You know, I haven't taken a full weekend for six months. I thought when I quit practice, I'd get time off, but this new place . . . I'm due in Washington on Monday. I've got problems at home, budget allocation fights here. Cancer work is highly politicised, you know.'

She knew. Like other organisations needing funds, Medway lusted after the national publicity she could provide, although no one admitted such a lapse from scientific objectivity, of course. And when she'd asked Stevens' researchers 'What do your newest data show?', rarely did anyone answer, 'Nothing.' Even if it were nothing, they always made it something, though studded with hedges like 'preliminary', 'interim', or 'cannot be revealed at this time'.

She in beige panties and he in undershorts. 'Now what do you still want to teach me?' he'd asked as she climbed on top of him, kissing him impatiently to ward off the motel room's chill. 'You think I need a refresher? Maybe Anatomy 404?' Did gynaecologists know anything about women? She doubted it.

How to doubt the feel of his body warmed by afternoon sun on a blanket in the park, how his shirt creases were always misironed, how his eyes slitted whenever something, including her, opposed him. How nastily he'd rejected her apartment after the doorman had knocked with a package and glimpsed Stevens in a bathrobe on her sofa. He'd yelled at her for opening the door so wide. Although ten years' living and loving with Lizann had unaccustomed Pauli to most kinds of furtiveness, such furtiveness seemed to excite Stevens.

And now, according to Rainette's babbling, Stevens was gone. Pauli was the last to see him alive? Who had claimed that?

The police would appear soon.

Who could have killed Stevens? Who hated him enough? Heather? Coral? Maybe Edward in a fit of drunken drama? *Try to remember what you saw and heard at Medway.*

How much time before the police burst in? As soon as Pauli could move, she crossed the living room to her desk, tore from her cheque book and bank envelope the stubs and two cancelled cheques for April and May motel rooms. Usually they paid cash but when Stevens refused to use his cheques, Pauli had written hers. Foolish now, but the motel clerk, who seemed either bored or was paid enough to ask no questions, knew them anyway as 'Mr and Mrs Golden'. Besides, May was two months ago.

To avoid accommodating the police, she ripped cheques and stubs to bits and flushed them down the toilet.

Suppose the police ask your bank for the computer record of your account?

Why would they? Nobody at Medway knew you and Stevens were . . . Why wouldn't they?

Perspiring, she turned out the light and dropped on to some cushions, trying to coax sleep from the darkness. Must be 85° in the room, yet she was shivering with clothes on. And suddenly crying. Waves of tears surprised her, coursing across her face and into her ears and mouth. They would mark the butternut suede of her expensive sofa. To hell with it.

Stevens in and around her, like their first time on this sofa. Lizann also, after spaghetti dinners and wine ... Those times were finished.

Why did invasions of feeling always turn sexual in her? Why couldn't she substitute tennis or handball for it, like everybody else?

Rubbing her breasts, she tried to hold Stevens' face and navy-blue shirt in her mind. The images kept fading.

7

Heather awoke groggily. From the slit of sunlight entering the bedroom, it must be . . . afternoon. She should check on that job or someone else would get it. Dr Henderson might have a library opening earlier than expected because of vacations. No, it was Saturday . . . When she moved her head, the warm wet under her mouth meant she'd drooled on to the satin bedspread that covered her.

Stevens! *Steve, oh-h, Steve.* Was he still downstairs? Do the police remove a body? What would she tell them? *I skipped the party because I had a headache. No, I don't know who was there. Of course, we got along fine.*

Let somebody else worry about it. There would be an autopsy. Steve's parents or David or somebody would bury him. *You mean you don't know who attended a party at the height of your own husband's career?*

Why was she alone?

A needle. David had injected something. Well, at least she'd awakened again. *The sleeping and the dead are but as pictures.* How Stevens had hated college English lit ('Useless crap!'), and he considered Edward (who, doglike, had followed him to Medway) 'a first-class ass'. Well, he was beyond everything, including his own opinions, now. *Mrs St Steven, was your marriage a good one? Any troubles lately?*

Did the past how many years qualify as 'lately'?

Heather's silk shirt and jeans lay flung on a chair. She wondered who had undressed her down to underpants and bra. If it was David, well, he'd already cut more of her own insides than she'd ever see. Eerie how a surgeon experienced more of your inner reality than you did, except that nothing about it was personal. Indeed, Stevens told her that after the first few years, all he remembered was the grossly abnormal – women with grapefruit-sized tumours, one set of quadruplets, one teenager with no uterus at all.

Next to Heather in the double bed, the white phone shrilled. Three rings, four. Let somebody else worry about it. The police must be expecting her to answer so they could listen in. If only she had a lover desperate to hear her voice in her hour of need. How Hollywood ruins your mind.

When she lifted the receiver to her ear and mumbled, 'Hello', she heard a sexy female voice whisper rapidly, 'Hello, Mrs St Steven. We're having a summer special.' On what? Obscene phone calls? 'Do you want to protect your loved ones from hazard, disaster that could occur right in your home? Now, I'm representing the Quality Smoke Detector Company, and I'd like to make an appointment with you – no obligation, of course – to show you and your husband our line of smoke alarms for different places in your home. I know you have many fine antiques, and you do want to protect your family, don't you, Mrs St Steven?' Instil guilt and fear; then resolve them with money – the American way of business.

'I have no family,' Heather announced. What if the police were listening? 'You're interrupting . . .' What? Murder, incipient insanity, half a breakdown she'd have to finish on her own?

'I'm *very* sorry!' The sexy voice turned starchy nasty.

Heather slammed the phone on to the hook. When anybody said they were sorry like that, they weren't at all; it was just a phrase. Maybe that was some key to why Stevens died. Who else had received his stubborn hostility followed by occasional apologies that never sounded sincere? The police would be asking. Didn't they always think the surviving spouse did it?

Stevens' past year at the Institute flashed by her. Although she'd listened patiently to diatribes against staff stupidities, the janitor who got liquored up just before major holidays, the heating system that therefore cost a fortune, the plumbing that clogged, she realised she hadn't *heard* any of it, anything that related to who – except herself – hated Stevens.

Somebody else must have received his petulant aggression ('You're my wife; do what I want. What the hell's the matter with you?' – their standard midnight argument). But that somebody had possessed the courage to *act*, not drown, in her years of indecision, pain, passivity. Harry and Stevens had shouted over finances. Was that today? Maybe Coral couldn't stand Steve's scorn any more? Or Edward, whom Steve had insulted publicly over a dirty cage . . . was it yesterday? And Arthur wanted what? More lab space? Recognition? She couldn't remember.

Now all the years netted to one special night at the mahogany desk downstairs. Stevens, who was reading the usual storm of quarterly reports, reached out as she entered the room with cake and tea. He called her name, then buried his face between her breasts, no longer searching for passion (at least from her) but for . . . compassion, something she was supposed magically to furnish while never asking for any for herself.

'I'm tired, Heather.'

'Then love *me*. Forget about a child. Just be . . . the two of us.'

'I can't do that. We're still young enough.'

'Then why should I waste my life just so you can –'

The bedroom door was opening. Now David and this day were entering. Heather gasped at how much David resembled Stevens – same rosy skin, narrow shoulders, black hair, further emphasised by David's moustache. Men seem to need to clone themselves, physically first, then through their business partners. No wonder they think that women in business disturb that all-male cross-fertilisation by providing the real thing.

A man in a very unsummery grey suit followed David. He looked sallow and exhausted, as if he spent all his time hunched over a desk.

Tell them the marriage was marvellous . . . the happiest of

wives with your chic antique home in this upper-crust suburb. Who'll know the diference? Yes, you hoped to return to a job you'd held. No, there was no other woman in your husband's life.

Why would there be?

8

At 7.30 Pauli switched on the black portable radio and navigated from refrigerator to sink to stove, assembling an egg, toast, brewer's yeast, tomato juice. Once beyond the spate of auto and bank ads, the local Saturday morning news featured three burglaries, one fraud in social services, one suburban bank robbery, one suit over river pollution and one lost Collie.

No murder or suicide.

Had the news media not discovered Stevens yet? Were the police sitting on the information pending notification of next of kin or some such legalist manoeuvre?

Maybe Rainette's call had never happened? A nightmare like the ones Pauli got after drinking three Martinis. But she'd drunk only one Martini, talked with Morgan about the hospital's financial problems, watched Heather, gossiped with Rainette, joked with Edward about his candle-lit Shakespeare, congratulated and kissed Stevens –

At 7.35 the phone rang. Rainette again, apologising? Or maybe her mother wanting something? Maybe Pauli could spend a lazy Saturday just lounging around with books and radio in the hammock behind the house her mother rented. Mr Biasin had such a peaceful, verdant garden. Maybe –

'Hello, Miss Golden?' The man's voice sounded tired.

Pauli mumbled, 'Yes.'

'Detective Jordan of the Police Department. I believe you attended a party last night at Dr St Steven's house. We'd like to ask you a few questions. Just take a few minutes.'

41

'Is something wrong?' *Dumb, dumb.* Of course, you know what's wrong. 'All right. Where are you?'

'Don't trouble. We'll be there about 8.30. Thank you.' And he hung up before Pauli could explain her building had two Goldens, no relation, just chance. Either he seemed to know already or – let him get lost. How could she help catch Stevens' killers when she knew nothing about his life beyond the few hours – Fancy suburban houses crammed with antiques, paintings, silverware, stereos, videos and furs got burgled. Did Heather sport furs and diamonds? She didn't appear the goldfinger, social-climber type. Indeed, she'd disappeared completely despite Pauli's hunger to observe her, to gauge more what sort of woman Stevens had made his wife.

In a half-daze despite two infusions of fresh coffee (if it wouldn't destroy chromosomes, they should devise a way to give the stuff intravenously), Pauli wandered from room to room, opening windows to grab sweet morning air before humidity deadened it. She piled up dirty laundry, made the bed, set out a tray of clean coffee cups in the living room. Her brother, Frank, had sent her the pottery cups, 'hand-thrown', as he called it, from Colorado.

Could his mining outfit use a writer? Chuck it all, go West, young woman. Frank loved the mountains, and she loved Frank. Boulder, where she'd skied with him last winter, was a panorama of mountains meeting plain, populated by chattering, ski-suited youngsters who resembled multicoloured marshmallows as they overflowed the slopes, lounges and university cafeteria. How to feel old in thirty seconds.

Another wave of longing for Stevens clutched her, beginning at her chest, continuing along her spine, down her legs.

As she struggled with a bra whose hooks had bent, the doorbell rang. She threw on a sundress that sported its own bra. Had the police rushed to see her before questioning anybody else? Did that include Stevens' wife? How much did she know or care to tell?

When Pauli unlocked the door, an old man with a strained, high voice and a younger one, both in white sports shirts and blue ties, stood in the stuffy corridor. They resembled naval recruitment officers. The way the younger one replied, 'Thank you, Miss' to her offer of coffee reminded her of Edward at the lab. Same military school maybe. Escaping to the kitchen to fetch her coffee pot provided a chance to comb her hair and locate sandals in the closet. Serving coffee at 8 a.m. – some nerve being so early – recalled her mother's words, 'They're our guests, no matter how awful they are.' Gracious hostess. The act gained her time.

She shouldn't have left the pair. Back in the living room the younger one with a Hanging-Gardens-of-Babylon belly was wandering about, staring at her opened letters on the desk, a striped beach bag on the floor. Did he expect to find one of Stevens' socks behind the leather barrel chair? *Don't act guilty, Pauli.*

As she answered the first questions automatically, the younger one took down her replies in a small yellow notepad. She realised that, unlike her, he didn't know shorthand, meaning he must end all these sessions with an aching arm. She also realised that she hadn't grasped either of the men's names. The older one had a vertical furrow between his brows, thinning hair and a sallow face with a long, dented upper lip. The dent (or was it a harelip scar?) lingered when he pursed his lips; it seemed ready to swallow his nose. He spoke.

'As you probably know, Dr St Steven was killed last night at a party you attended –'

'It's horrible . . . whatever happened,' Pauli interrupted.

The detective nodded. 'I understand you're doing some special work for him.'

Pauli relaxed as she launched into her preparing-articles speech.

'So you saw Dr St Steven one day a week in connection with one article you wrote and five more you planned?'

'Yes. But he had so little time. It was more like a half-hour at the Institute, sometimes an hour, depending on what work questions we discussed.'

'Did you ever see him alone?'

43

Pauli shook her head. 'As Institute director, he had constant phone calls and people running in with problems. In fact, it was maddening to interview him. Sometimes I even phoned him instead of trying to see him because he was always late for appointments.'

The detective nodded. These facts must tally with what others had already told him.

'Uh,' Pauli began, trying to cut the suspense, 'I heard last night what happened. I'm shocked,' she blurted. The younger man looked up, observing her. The older one merely stared. 'I can't understand –' Pauli stopped, bewildered, perspiring. Shouldn't have mentioned it. If she didn't watch it, these deadpan types who counted on you to be nervous would discover more than they needed to know. She grabbed at her coffee mug.

'*How* did you hear what happened?' The detective steepled his fingers, still staring at her.

'Rainette called. I'd just left the party.' Pauli recounted what there was to tell – saying goodbye and recongratulating Stevens before 11.45, searching in vain to thank Heather, the hostess, driving home, walking.

'How did he die?'

'Knife,' the man announced.

Pauli winced and swallowed.

'Can you tell us what he was doing earlier that evening?'

'Well, first he was with us in the living room. Then he disappeared to the orange study room to read reports or something, I don't know. He was, well, a freelance employer, not my regular boss. I don't usually see these people again once the articles are finished . . . Why are you here so early?' Talking too much, Pauli.

The detective ignored her question. 'Somebody reported you and Dr St Steven were at the door of his library there.'

'Well, of course. He was alive.' Pauli sank back into her armchair. Maybe they didn't think she did it.

'We'll *assume* you left the party.' Confusing emphasis. What did they think? 'Did anything about Dr St Steven seem unusual before you left?'

Pauli hesitated. The younger detective lifted his felt-tip

pen. Did everybody *she* interviewed feel grilled like melted tuna on rye? But at least she managed it with a smile, enough charm to put them at ease. These guys hadn't even apologised for arriving at dawn. Oh sure, it was their job, not their fault, when people got killed.

'No. Well, yes, he always had problems. The staff changed every academic year. The salaries aren't anything like what private practice pays. The nude mice and special projects require germ-free areas that cost a lot in –'

The older detective, whom she'd nicknamed Tight Lip, interrupted. 'No. I mean in his personal or business relationships.'

'But he didn't discuss any, well, politics with me. I just asked him questions about the different work pro –'

'Did you ever see him outside work?'

Pauli answered too rapidly. 'Not really. We had lunch maybe three times near the Institute. Once in his office I guess we had sandwiches.' Their repeating the same question another way confused her. How much do they know? And how much is just fishing for what they don't know?

'And that's all?' The Lip pursed and pursued it further.

'Yes,' answered Pauli loudly.

'You live here alone? Did you come to the party alone?'

'Yes – and no,' Pauli answered.

'Yes and no.' The Lip smiled. 'A lot of yesses and noes in this case.'

'I drove my own car to the party,' Pauli explained, 'but I met Dr Morgan there. We walked in together . . . Yes, I live here alone. I had a roommate. She left for Europe last year. My mother's ill, so my brother will probably be staying here, and I haven't looked for anyone else.'

The young detective smiled.

'I'm sorry, but I have to leave soon to see about my mother,' Pauli announced. Do you order police officers out? Why not, when they'd ordered themselves in?

'She doesn't live in this building, then?'

'Oh, no. She's better off in an apartment across town. I'm gone all day. What would she do? I mean, the landlady at her place has been so helpful.'

'My mother's sick too,' said the younger one. Surprisingly, both men accepted Pauli's hint and now rose. The younger one added, 'You make good coffee. Fresh and strong.'

Pauli laughed. 'Like me, I hope!' Even the older one rearranged his scarred lip into a smile. Maybe they weren't such difficult types. It was just her nervous tension that either tied her tongue or allowed it to drivel on.

'Uh, Miss Golden, if you recall anything else that could pertain to Dr St Steven's death, here's our special number.' Pauli took the cheap, handwritten bit of cardboard. Well, the police didn't waste tax-payers' money on printing business cards.

As she showed them out, Pauli realised they hadn't once used the ugly word 'murder'.

Pauli sprawled, overheated, in the sun-dappled hammock. Her mother sat in a straightback, shaded deckchair. Briefly Mrs Golden interrupted her lengthening list of complaints against Mrs Biasin's 'nosiness' and other flaws to rewarn Pauli against skin cancer and 'I do hope you check your breasts regularly. Remember what happened to your poor Aunt Marian. I don't even want to name that terrible word, how she died.'

Avoiding Aunt Marian but agreeing to move from the sun in fifteen minutes, Pauli began to reason for the hundredth time over the Mrs Biasin situation. 'Mom, you're lucky she cares enough to look in, to walk up all those times a day. Most landladies wouldn't.'

'But she caught me . . . on the toilet.' Her mother hinged words slowly, painfully now.

'Well, close the door!' How did her mother always enmesh her in these wars over trivia? What Mom wanted – broken record from the past – was either another trapped listener who never disagreed or for Pauli or Frank to speak and act for her. Avoiding all confrontations and most actions made sure that Mom would never be blamed; somebody else had always done It, whatever, *to* her. She never did anything. Eternal innocence nurtured in the bosom of neurosis.

Despite summer heat, Mrs Golden was attired as usual in

cashmere twinset, coral necklace and 'sensible shoes', her hair freshly corkscrewed by the hairdresser who visited the apartment. If her hair, once auburn like Pauli's own, was constantly falling out, it was multiple sessions with chemicals and driers as much as poor circulation.

Over the winter Mrs Golden had suffered two strokes. She now walked right foot forward, fencing against the enemy within. The left side of her face and her left arm drooped. Since she rejected the idea of both physical therapy and a housekeeper, the time for tears and tantrums about a nursing home was approaching.

Pauli shut her eyes, felt the sunflecks touch her, melt the gnawing of what-to-do-now-about-which-problem. Call Frank and insist he visit nursing homes with her? Quit her job and flee to Colorado (the police would have fun with that)? Call Harry Stornell about the fate of the articles with Stevens dead? Call Morgan or Heather? Most of all, who had hated Stevens enough to murder him?

At least call Heather and say something respectful or comforting. *I was having an affair with your husband.* How to survive without Stevens. He could have divorced Heather. He and Pauli could have married. They might have had a child, as Lizann apparently intended to do in her belated dash towards 'normality'. Maybe, maybe. Pauli wiped her face, then unfolded herself from the sunny hammock.

Somehow she willed herself through the day of doing her mother's laundry, shopping and cleaning, and prepared enough chicken, fish and salads to last at least four days. The semi-mindless tasks – wheeling a grocery trolley, loading brown bags, stuffing sheets into a black hole and adding too much detergent – calmed her despite the heat that had passed 95 degrees by 1 p.m. By dint of driving, sweating, lifting, hauling and chopping, she forced thoughts of Stevens from her mind for minutes at a time.

She'd forgotten to ask the police so much, but what would they have told her? What kind of wound? Who discovered the body? Had anybody tried to get him to a hospital? Could a burglar have done it? Had anybody confessed? What kind of reporter are you, Pauli? His throat was slit. Yes, but if somebody does a sloppy job, people live through it, just like surviving a broken neck. Difficult but not impossible.

Pauli's mother, awed by what seemed such personal and lengthy attention, fussed for a while with a vegetable brush at the stove burners, then retired to bed while Pauli vacuumed the tea-stained carpet and considered ironing some of her mother's blouses. If sunstroke existed, how about ironing stroke? If the police were following her car, they wouldn't observe much today but Model Daughter. Surprisingly, despite the second-floor torpor of her mother's rooms, the comforting exhaustion of the labour gave Pauli the exhilaration of *doing* something, of fighting illness, horror, loneliness, everything gone awry the past year since Lizann left. Loving Stevens had rendered Lizann a memory, but now Stevens himself was –

'Ow!' Rising from untangling grey hairs off the vacuum brush, Pauli whacked her head into an open cabinet door. Blood sprang to the top of her scalp. Collapsing on a kitchen chair, she wet a clean towel at the sink and plastered it on to her hair. The hangover she was due for . . .

At 6.30, just before the newsagent's closed, she walked her headache down the stairs and six blocks along the still radiant pavement. The regular owner had hired a teenage paper seller, which avoided the need to stop and chat.

The local paper already screamed it across the front page: LOCAL DOCTOR SLAIN, complete with youthful photo of Stevens, a thinner, almost gaunt face Pauli hardly recognised. The black hair got lost in the poor reproduction.

> Dr Stevens St Steven, co-director of the Medway Institute for Cancer Research, was found dead at his Walker Terrace home early this morning. He was apparently killed by a knife wound during a party celebrating the Institute's third anniversary and the winning of a Federal cancer research grant. A police investigation is proceeding . . .
>
> Dr St Steven was well known in scientific circles for his papers and journal articles on hormonal aetiology of breast cancer and the correlation

between infertility or childlessness and increased
risk for the disease. The scientist is survived by his
wife, the former Heather Barto.

Plodding back, Pauli read while the print sweated on to her
hands. Like the police, the story avoided the word 'murder'.
And no mention of exact wound or weapon.

The Boston paper featured a six-paragraph piece carried
to the inside without a photo. They were probably saving
themselves for the Sunday edition.

An 'instant journalism' editorial stunned her. They
couldn't have written it on a Saturday morning just for
Stevens; it must have been canned in the morgue or
computer since somebody's else death, ready to go:

DEATH IN THE WAR ON CANCER

We mourn the passing of Dr Stevens St Steven, a
brilliant researcher and co-administrator of the
Medway Institute for Cancer Research. He brought
dedication to his work and dollars to his laboratory.
US medical science will be the poorer without him.

The 'War on Cancer', begun in hope in 1971,
now costs over 1½ billion dollars per year in
research and $104 billion more in treatment costs.
Yet in the opinion of many experts we are no closer
to 'an answer to cancer' now than we were then.
The disease strikes one in every four Americans,
and there have been more than a million new cases
this year alone. Dr St Steven died fighting this War
on Cancer.

The search for the 'magic silver bullet' against
the disease has become a politicised struggle of
citizens' groups, environmentalists, patients and
certain scientists who have drawn battlelines in
communities and courts against other equally
reputable scientists, corporation lawyers and
medical specialists. Subjects of legal suits range
from laetrile and vitamin use, through birth of dis-
eased children, to nuclear-power-plant regulation.
While experts snipe at each other's personalities

and positions, the public is the loser in these 'cancer and Aids epidemics', that have swept our contemporary environment.

So much of cancer work involves research for therapies and drugs for use *after* people become cancer patients. So little is spent on prevention or eradication of the disease. Very little of the 1 billion-plus dollars involves research into environmental cancer, although knowledge of carcinogenic substances and the laws to prevent their spread through industrial, air and water pollution already exist. By general estimate, 60 per cent to 90 per cent of all cancers (including breast cancer, Dr St Steven's specialty, thought by many to be nutritionally linked), is environmental.

Some of the projects directed by Dr St Steven involved basic biomedical research into cell structure, function and the ageing process. Other projects worked directly with immunotherapy, viruses and mouse tumours, both natural and induced.

May others carry on Dr St Steven's lifetime of effort.

To read the editorial, Pauli had slumped down under a tree. Grass and twigs prickled her legs. Her hands shook. This newspaperised Stevens no longer belonged to her at all, not flesh and blood, misironed shirts, fingers between her thighs, scrawled handwriting and abstracted brooding. This Stevens was already a public monument, five minutes' reading between dinner and TV. Probably swarms of sightseers and reporters who couldn't tell a cancer from a pimple were cruising past Stevens' house right now. Pathetic.

Mustn't phone Rainette and certainly not Heather. The morning's low-key police procedure must be a trap to get everybody to lead life-as-usual – except for details like bugged phones, watched cars and hidden cameras, until somebody deduced who did kill Stevens. The police would return. Sara, the magazine book-keeper and secretary, or a snoopy counterpart at the Institute or the motel (Pauli shuddered) would be sure to inform. Just her luck. How much would the police learn?

'Pauli,' her mother's voice wailed. 'You were gone . . . so long.' Mrs Golden's white sleeveless blouse had dropped off one shoulder. Pauli replaced it to hide the underwear straps.

'One of my friends got murdered. I feel lousy. Here, read about it,' Pauli muttered. 'I spent weeks interviewing him. Now the articles he wanted me to do are probably down the drain. I'll be lucky if I get paid.' She dropped the papers on to her mother's lap, pointing to the LOCAL DOCTOR SLAIN headline. Why protect her? Who protects me?

Mrs Golden's mouth crept into a vacant O. 'My glasses. Can't read.' Obediently Pauli untangled one pair of glasses from the cord of the other pair on the bedroom dresser.

'Terrible,' Mrs Golden commented after following lines of one paragraph with the forefinger of her good hand. 'My daughter mixed up with something like this? Such dangerous work . . . Cancer . . . don't want to say it.' Her voice, indignant at first, trailed away fearfully.

'But Frank blows himself up three times a week setting dynamite!' Pauli insisted.

Her mother looked hurt. 'Don't care. He's a man. Working's . . . no life . . . for a woman.' With great effort she enunciated the full last sentence.

Did strangling the half-dead with your bare hands count as murder? Matricide – what a fancy word for such a basic passion.

In thirty seconds Pauli slammed the apartment door and raced downstairs, nearly colliding with Mrs Biasin, laundry basket on hip at the back door. Mrs Biasin's mouth also made a vacant O.

51

9

It had rained all day, steamy mid-July off-ocean drizzle that mildews fabric and puckers paper. Awaiting Heather's visit, Pauli felt herself wilting. *Relax*. Sure.

In the bathtub Pauli had discovered another triad of lumps in her left breast. Two of the familiar, squishy cysts, which the surgeon aspirated yearly, but now something else pea-sized also moved fairly easily . . . although it felt harder. A solid lump? Damn rotten time for it with everything else. And not even forty yet. How old had Aunt Marian been when she – but hers ('carcinoma') kept recurring year after year.

Oh, can it. Or bottle it – Morgan's specialty. Anyway, knock it off. Wait till after your next period and, if it's (they're) still there, see Dr Williams.

At least four out of five lumps were innocent, anyway, until proven guilty. Like herself and Heather.

Assuming that the police would have bugged both her phone and Stevens' home phone, Pauli had handwritten a gold-daisied card to Heather, hoping to appear honestly sympathetic without looking morbidly curious. If she was compassionate enough to write, she hoped Heather would be curious enough to respond.

Dear Heather [don't write 'Mrs St Steven']
You and I met briefly the other night. [Don't mention 'party'] I've heard of your husband's death. The police have questioned me also. If

there's anything I can do to help in this crisis, please let me know. Dr St Steven was a fine man and professional person. [Don't mention 'the best of three male lovers I ever had'] Many will miss him.

I expect you're very busy, but if you'd like to come some evening for coffee or drinks, phone 626-4893.
Best wishes
Pauli

The terse 'Many will miss him' stung Pauli, made her feel hypocritical. When she couldn't devise anything else, however, she let it stand.

She'd sent the card on Wednesday following the party. She even rushed from the corner pillarbox, trying to make the office early, imagining Stevens would call as he usually did to confirm or change Wednesday afternoon plans, until she remembered. Stevens is dead. He'd be buried on Friday, from a funeral home she wouldn't see to a grave she didn't want to see. And Heather had phoned . . .

Still awaiting Heather, when the apartment doorbell chimed, Pauli glanced into the mirror at her drooping hair, tried to ignore her lumpy breast and to straighten her skirt. Dampness had crumpled across her thighs. Silly to invite Heather. If Heather hadn't killed Stevens – as far as anybody knew – then who did?

According to the newspaper, 'After greeting guests, Mrs St Steven retired to her bedroom on the upper floor, where she slept for some hours.' But right now everybody, including Heather, probably suspected Pauli, since the police gave no details beyond, 'After meeting briefly with Miss Pauline Golden, a medical writer, Dr St Steven was found dead at approximately 11.45 p.m. by Dr Harry Stornell, co-director of the Medway Institute. Investigation is proceeding.'

Again the chimes sounded. Having forced herself across the room, Pauli scarcely recognised the woman outside her door behind the dark glasses, honey-blond hair cascading from an intricate topknot, above an elegant ruby silk suit and black boots. If Pauli had expected the hippie with jeans, granny glasses and wind-tossed hair of Stevens' description, then Heather had dressed to impress Pauli with something. Stevens' misjudgment, the silliness of any middle-aged man who strayed from such sophistication? Heather's own togetherness triumphant over the past week's torture?

'Thanks for your note. I wasn't . . . sure about coming. But I hate the evenings. People driving by. I think they're staring at the house.' Heather's words rushed out.

'I understand.' Pauli smiled, grasped Heather's hand, removed the raincoat from her arm, sat her down on the sofa. Heather's right hand was moist and cold. As much as Pauli had daydreamed being Stevens' wife, it was no job for anybody now. How foolish her jealousy . . .

'The police . . . And he didn't leave a will. Everything's a mess,' Heather blurted.

Contradictory, aren't you, Pauli? Had planned to distance yourself from Heather as part of forgetting Stevens. Writing the note was to be a thank-you gesture for the party (if 'party' was how anybody described the scene of a murder), a way to assuage her own guilt by offering token friendship to a survivor. Her intellect again fantasising justifications that her body's intuition wouldn't tolerate for a minute: she hadn't fallen for Stevens, was only maintaining a pleasant work contact – until Stevens' death had revealed the whole shabby process.

Now Heather, real and upset, no longer that foreign category labelled 'Stevens' wife', sat before Pauli. If touched, would she shatter or cry? Suspicions surfaced, for which Pauli immediately berated herself: was all this devised, an act to make Heather appear the grieving wife because Heather suspected that Pauli was the woman? *Treat her kindly.*

'I'm sure you miss Stevens so much.'

'Yes, I – It's just been a horrible week, the funeral, the questioning.' Heather's face contorted. She rubbed one palm across her forehead.

Pauli sensed all her own skill at easing others during interviews draining from her. The only common topic of conversation was Stevens – guaranteed to knot muscles, tie tongues.

54

'David's been marvellous. He organised the funeral. Half the city came, just to stare maybe. I coped somehow. The police are still around with questions and things to sign. If they know who did it, they aren't telling me. It's horrible.'

Pauli struggled to avoid details of the funeral. 'Stevens told me you're a medical librarian?'

'Yes. That's one thing I've done. Probably the one I'll go back to.' When Heather fidgeted with the wine-coloured silk of her skirt, again Pauli felt trapped. Either let her talk, or wind this up fast. *Decide, Pauli.*

'You know Stevens was married before? I guess med school pressure nearly killed both of them. I mean, they never had any time together.' Heather stumbled, trying to rescind 'kill'.

Pauli's jaw hung open. Damn! Another woman Stevens had worked over, one more detail he hadn't mentioned. No need to ask whether there were children. No wonder he grew desperate the second time through as Heather aged towards thirty-five, forty? Heather's soft fall of blond hair wouldn't show grey, and her firm skin over wide cheekbones looked pink and vital. Only some tired creases around her eyes betrayed the past week's ravages.

'Were you and Stevens happy?' *Forget it.* Should have asked about the weather.

Heather's lips quivered. 'At first . . . I finished library school when everybody else was dropping out of everything. They thought I was nuts. Then I started dating Stevens again –'

'Again?' Pauli's sharpness shamed her. *All over, forget –*

'He and I had met in medical school before his first marriage.'

Pauli winced. Anatomy and physiology. Whizzed through it way back, but now what I know is latest technical stuff . . . Why discuss Heather's or Stevens' past? Maybe Heather would just accept a drink and leave.

To stall while devising something non-lethal to discuss, Pauli assembled a bowl of ice, gins and tonic, sesame and sunflower seeds. 'What d'you think I am? A bird?' Stevens had quipped when she'd dropped them into his mouth, sitting above him on the same sofa where Heather now trembled. *Forget it*.

Yet talking to a near stranger seemed to calm Heather (maybe psychiatrists were right), while it upset Pauli. Heather grasped her drink and picked up a magazine from the table. 'Listen to this joke.'

'I love jokes. Go ahead.'

'Closing averages on the human scene were mixed today. Brotherly love was down two points, while enlightened self-interest gained a half. Vanity showed no movement, and guarded optimism slipped a point in sluggish trading. Over all, the *status quo* remained unchanged.'

Pauli giggled. 'That's a joke? Sounds like where I work.'

'It *is* where you work. Don't you read your own magazine?'

'I get it mostly for my mother, although the print's too small for her now. Although I write it, I hardly have time to look at it.'

'What's it like, working there?'

'Good, except for Sara, the secretary-sort-of. We writers should be none of her business, except to pay us. But she's got her ledger pointed straight towards *my* job. Only there's no money to hire her at a reporter's salary. She's jealous, that's all. Takes on against my work by showing pieces to her 'brother-the-doctor', who says 'throwaway articles in a throwaway magazine'. Her other specialty is rewriting handouts from drug companies while I'm out of the office. Then when I get back, she waves her pages under my nose within everybody's hearing. And raves about the "important story" *she* covered while *I* was away. Ahh!'

'Hey, you're really steamed up. What're you doing about it?'

Sara's dumpy figure and slathery make-up swam in Pauli's head. She shrugged. 'What *to* do? I've discussed her attitude with Jacobs – he's our boss. He just says, ignore her, but it's hard when she eavesdrops on my every call.'

'But surely she can't doubt your competence?'

'That's what's so annoying – I mean her backbiting, not my competence. I've had pre-med courses galore, plus refreshers in new approaches to everything at both the hospital and the university. But she still acts like I'm a glorified typist.'

How to present more about the situation or Sara's viciousness without looking the fool for working there? *Shut up.*

Silence resumed while they both clutched at frosted glasses on the stained coffee table. Pauli had forgotten to wipe it. She tried to savour the tart taste of the limes she had sliced into the drinks.

'You don't *s-s-seem* like you killed Steve,' Heather stammered out of nowhere.

'Neither do you,' retorted Pauli. 'So that's what you came to find out? Thanks a lot.' How to get her out of here?

Now Heather froze, her leather boots rigid over her ankles as they slanted to one side. 'I'm sorry. I really don't want to talk about Steve. The police will – they're still questioning Edward because he had the last fight with Stevens at work that day. I mean, I came here to find out about you. You wrote the note. I was curious.'

'Why?'

'I know Steve had . . . someone. You saw him at work. Maybe you'd tell me. I wouldn't feel so . . . alone.'

Ah so, the deal. Hint you're the woman, in exchange she hints the marriage was no good, or maybe she'll switch again to grieving wife. And somebody will inform the police.

'I'm sure you loved Stevens. You're just upset now. It's all right.' Pauli smiled. She wanted to like Heather, but the woman changed emotional tack every other sentence.

'I did love Stevens! And he loved me in his own way. But he never had time, attention, for me.'

For me either, thought Pauli. God, we had the same problem. And now we're both floundering in the same wake of death. A frozen place somewhere inside Pauli melted. Suddenly she wanted to take Heather in her arms, caress the curled ends of the honey hair, the lean, long waist. Lizann surfaced; Pauli tried to blot her out. Not again, Heather's not . . . Why couldn't Pauli snub, cut tiresome people with impunity like everybody else? Whenever she tried it with her mother, guilt unnerved her for half a day until she wasted another Saturday scrubbing, hauling, fetching.

She rubbed Heather's arm through the silk sleeve. 'That feels good,' Heather responded. 'You must give good massages.'

Another wash of emotion engulfed Pauli. 'Look, I'm not ... the horrible person you imagined. I'm just ... lonely right now.' True as anything. Blow your image; look vulnerable.

Heather blinked. '*You*, lonely? But you've got everything – a great job, this apartment. Steve mentioned your articles, how talented you are to write about so many things. I can't imagine you lonely.'

'It happens,' Pauli commented.

'Look what I got – a dead husband, monstrous mortgage, sealed bank accounts, no job unless an old boss will hire somebody in ... a mess.' Heather showed pride, didn't want handouts.

A wild impulse surged in Pauli. 'Would you like to stay here for tonight? Are you alone in the house?'

Heather smiled for the first time. Tension lines left her face. 'That's really kind of you, but I'll go back now. Thanks. You're awfully kind. I won't forget it.'

Rising unsteadily, she pressed her left cheek to Pauli's at the door, grasped Pauli's hand and was gone. Her perfume, sweet and spicy, lingered around Pauli's face. Well, had she scored enough of a hit with Heather to prevent the police from hearing any tales about Other Woman Pauli, at least from Heather?

Slumped on her spine, legs sprawled, Pauli sat alone again. Just in time for a great abysmal movies-on-TV night, watching actresses assaulted and hysterical while she worried at her breast lump during commercials. She could sob along with the boob-tube women. Twentieth-century catharsis. Damn. She needed something after a half-hour with Heather. Call Frank in Colorado. If somebody murdered her suddenly, at least he'd miss her.

How about a vacation hidden among the cool mountains and trout streams of Estes Park? Lie in the sun on the toasted granite rock and melt it all away?

Steve, who killed you? Help me find out.

10

'Before I make my phone calls, I'll get you an article to look over,' Dr Arthur Huggard was saying as he loomed above Pauli. 'Then we can talk. I have just a few minutes,' he warned.

Pauli had wondered about Stevens' question marks in Huggard's one published paper on viruses that contained his hopes for his new anti-cancer serum. Although she'd planned the interview carefully, already he was retreating after only ten minutes. Busy, busy. Was that why he seemed so evasive?

Maybe the second article would be a relief, because he hadn't explained anything clearly yet. She still couldn't determine *which* potentially cancer-causing virus was his thing. Now he seemed wedded to several interlocking directorates of them. Everything sabotaged something else. Somehow a substance called 'interferon' got produced so that only half the viruses that plugged into cells ever checked out again. Something killed them. Yet she had a clearer explanation of interferon in its natural and synthetic versions sitting on her desk at home than he'd managed in ten minutes.

Dr Huggard leaned over a mess of papers tossed into the third drawer of his grey filing cabinet. Initially she'd liked Huggard's intensity over his particular, and perhaps breakthrough, brand of research, but now his uptightness was annoying her. His square jaw put her off as did the scruffy haircut and sideburns that thrust horizontally about his head. Had he combed it in a hurricane? His grease-spotted, baggy polyester suit drooped from shoulders and waist. The trouser cuffs dribbled along the tops of his blue suede shoes – mock Oxfords that Pauli hadn't seen since the 1950s. No doubt he considered them fashionable, perhaps even swinging. It neither bothered nor occurred to him that Elvis was dead and he was a few decades behind.

Neither Pauli's vivacity nor her earnest questioning had brought Huggard out yet. Now he handed her a dog-eared journal reprint. 'Page 25, it'll answer some of your questions.' Exiting, he turned and added, 'Miss Golden, I'd appreciate it if you didn't touch or read anything on my desk or the lab bench while I'm gone. It's all work in progress, and I don't care to have any of it quoted. With Dr St Steven's death, we're very upset here.'

Pauli looked up, too annoyed to answer, but he'd vanished. His desk was such a mess, who'd bother to disturb it, let alone snoop? Messy files – world's best security system. As for the lab bench next to the files, it was so overpiled with dirty glassware and beakers it resembled a dishwasher stacked by a drunkard. Did he also have a two-way mirror to check whether she was being a good girl? She was tempted to derange the dust around his silver mouse paperweight to let him know she cared.

The hell with him. His perfectionist, paranoid type could be miserable to work with, wanting to change every other word of what they quoted to you in the first place. The kind that never gets fired for incompetence – yet science and other enterprises advance despite, not because of, them. If they never existed, the world would be a happier place, and they're just intelligent enough to note that fact – and resent it.

Knock it off. Suppose the guy is a genius? Interferon research is certainly proliferating . . . Suppose also that he killed Stevens. With a shiver, Pauli scanned the journal interview with a pathologist.

Cancerous changes occur on a continuum. Examining a set of slides is not like looking at a traffic light that changes abruptly from green (completely benign) to red (obvious cancer). There is a confusing yellow transitional zone between green and red that shows progressive changes from early and minimal cancer to . . .

Murder, the worst of crimes, Pauli decided.

If two or three consulting pathologists disagree, you know you're in that yellow zone. That's why what appears to be breast cancer to one pathologist may not to another.

Picturing the lump in her own breast, Pauli shuddered, then dropped the Xeroxed pages on to her lap. Why had Huggard given her pathology stuff – Morgan's specialty – when he was a virologist? Strange, pedantic giant of a man. She imagined him making love to a fortunately faceless woman by explaining the workings of a penis before he fudged the final purpose of the total exercise.

She stared at the cartoon sign above his desk clutter:
THERE'S ONLY ONE THING WRONG WITH THE RAT RACE –
THE RATS ARE WINNING.
From it, a dayglo chartreuse rat frowned down, cross-eyed. Pauli laughed. However, Huggard's other sign, hand-lettered on to cardboard, lacked even irony to recommend it:
YOU CAN'T WIN
YOU CAN'T BREAK EVEN
YOU CAN'T EVEN GET OUT OF THE GAME.
She returned to reality when Huggard re-entered, his face clouded. Why had he left his own office to make phone calls? Pauli tried a few seconds' patient empathy. 'Is something wrong, Dr Huggard? You look upset.'
'Ah, politics!' He darted his hand out in a gesture meant to be a wave that wound up resembling a karate chop. Although it seemed to warn, stay out of this, his wrath continued to emit into the visible spectrum. 'Last year I announced a viral strain that actually causes four common cancers and is implicated in three others. This year I announced a purified protein serum that kills this virus. Actually *kills* mouse cancer cells in live mice and human

cancer cells in culture. I have discovered a cure for seven forms of cancer! Does anybody around this place give a goddamn?'

'I don't know, but *I'm* here because Dr Morgan –' Pauli began, realising that only Morgan had praised Arthur Huggard's work. Both Stevens and Harry Stornell had avoided Huggard's very name, let alone the purported genius of his work. No doubt the charm of his personality, but suppose that rattling the bars of his square little mind was the actual cure for cancer?

Pauli realised he was raving again. ' – don't work with people. I'm only a Ph.D., a doctor of philosophy, not an MD, a medical doctor, so I don't count. After I announced this work, I got phone calls from round the world. Letters and cables from Japan, Russia, everywhere. I mentioned leukaemia. I got a registered letter from a father begging me to cure his son's leukaemia. If you say you can't cure them, they think you're lying. Well, I could help him if I ever get the support I need right *here* to get human trials of my serum. But no! Not *one* person in this goddamn place so much as picked up a phone even to request one of my papers.'

'Surely Dr Stevens or Harry Stornell were impressed? They hired you.' Pauli tried to soothe – must be his bad day. But Huggard's face now turned Chinese orange. Pauli added hastily, 'I mean, the general support for immunotherapy work here must interest you. And if immunotherapy stimulates a patient's body to fight cancer, including cancer from a virus, what's the matter with that?'

'My dear woman.' The condescension in his voice barely avoided the words, 'You idiot'. 'If their bodies *could* fight cancer, they wouldn't get it in the first place, would they? Why treat only symptoms? If I were an immunotherapist, I'd beef up healthy people with vaccines, beginning, say, at age forty, so they don't get cancer the way we don't get smallpox or diphtheria any more.' When he stood, leaning forward, palms down on the desk, he resembled a preacher convicting the universe of sin and ignorance. His square jaw jutted as he towered above Pauli, appearing eight feet six instead of six six.

'But,' Pauli tried to interrupt, 'not everybody thinks cancer *is* a virus. Dr Stevens –'

'That ladies' man!' Arthur Huggard spat out the three words.

Pauli caught her breath, then hoped Huggard wouldn't notice her cheeks blushing. 'What . . . what do you mean?' she stammered.

'Steve was a gynaecologist. What the hell does a gynaecologist know about viruses?' Huggard's fly-away hair trembled.

Sperm are clever little invaders, too . . . 'You don't sound sorry he's dead.'

Steve? Subtract nothing from nothing, and what d'you get?

' – wouldn't even give me lab space. I got seven different projects going in these two little rooms. There's a vacant office next door. I've requisitioned five times to get it. I've got one – exactly one – part-time lab assistant/secretary/ bottlewasher. Edward may visit here once a week to clean a mousebox if I'm lucky. I do all my own surgery, wash my own scalpels, the lot. Whoever Coral embroiders for these days, it's not me! If they took me seriously, I could validate the worth of this whole institute. But they're all immuno-therapists. Well, immunotherapy's been around for ninety years. Who the hell's it cured? Using phoney vaccines to scar people half-dead already from chemotherapy and radiation. Next they'll be into diet therapy because immunotherapy's going down fast and they want a soft landing.'

'But false theories die eventually,' Pauli insisted. 'They just don't work.'

'Oh, so you think truth prevails in science?' Huggard sneered. 'Lousy theories not only *don't* get disproved; they get incarnated in places like this until they're not just vested interests but Revealed Truth. I've got *three* grants. That's about two more than anybody else. You think I can spend them? Not without bigger research facilities. Anywhere else I'd have a lab the size of a lecture hall and ten assistants.'

Get out or get some info from this guy. 'Uh, Dr Huggard,

I know your field is the molecular biology of virus reproduction.'

'Replication,' he countered instantly. 'One thing about you reporters. No matter how much time we spend with you, you write it wrong anyway.'

'Dr Huggard,' Pauli objected, 'you haven't spent *any* time telling me about your work. All I've heard is your fury over the politics of cancer!' Damn this man, blaming me for his own misery.

A glance at his desk showed the paper litter of a cup of cold coffee and a half-eaten jam doughnut. Caffeine and sugar junkie. His lousy mood was probably hypoglycaemia swollen into paranoia.

Pauli scrabbled for something to say that would ease into neutral territory for both of them. 'You know, Dr Stevens showed me one of your papers, and I've read it carefully. I believe your approach is very valid.' For the first time Huggard's mouth relaxed enough to produce something resembling a smile. The black bags under his eyes crinkled. He sat down now. Tirades over?

As Pauli flipped through her shorthand pad for the list of questions she'd planned to ask, her insides sank as she saw it and his paper sitting back on the desk in her living room. Besides, his hysteria had driven both the questions and his technical terminology from her mind. 'Uh, maybe today's not a good day. I do have some questions, but I'll phone you. How's that?'

'I'm busy. Are you sure you're not a spy for the police?'

As she rose, Pauli stared at him. Could this man really possess the cure for cancer in that head and these two little rooms? It defied probability, but so did half a hundred other things.

She took the long route out, avoiding Morgan's lab and Harry's office. Twenty minutes with Arthur Huggard made her even want to avoid Rainette, with whom she usually joked. Like acid, people like Arthur corroded wherever they touched.

Did the police know of Arthur Huggard's rage against his late and unlamented boss? Poor Stevens – with bitter maniacs like Arthur decapitating mice. Stevens had put no more question marks on Arthur's paper than anybody else's, but Arthur's reaction must have been more violent than easy-going Morgan, or Burl and Merrill, who were doing only one-year stints anyway.

But Arthur Huggard's whole career lay at an impasse. Did the police care about things like this?

17 July – The Lab

Bastard deserved it. Throat slitting was too good, quick, neat. Pushing me, pushing all of us. Nothing ever precise enough, ever pleased him. Male nag. We came here because of him. Ignored, sneered at us.

Ass-licking every politician that exposes himself here. Great White Father St Steven smiling up the Senator, calling us 'mental retards and women libbers'. Calling me 'used to be top-notch, works with serum now and then. Like the rest, demands space and salary but won't cooperate. All geniuses here.'

Then they laughed. Not even smart enough to shut his own door.

Big pricks die quick.

Tell it to the worms.

11

Half way along the grey tile floor of the Institute lobby Pauli smiled at the guard. And tried to smile at Dr Harry Stornell, but he was glaring over his half-glasses at an Adam's-appled young man. Harry shouted, 'The answer is no! No tours. I gave my statement to the police.'

Pauli eased by Dr Stornell's back. The young man must be a reporter. He appeared all of twenty-three, making Pauli feel ancient. Such people get hired, as she had been, because in an economy overstuffed with liberal arts graduates, minus dependants you can be had cut-rate at twenty-three.

It was 7 p.m. Setting sun rayed out of Morgan's lab along the white and fir-green corridor. The French windows were open. The janitor must be cleaning. Had Morgan's suite been a ballroom in some other existence, a vestige of a vanished mansion on this hilltop that now teemed with technology?

Hurrying made Pauli's bandaged breast ache. Unable to bear the suspense, she had sought one of the rare female surgeons at the Medical Centre. After painfully pressing and probing, the doctor had aspirated two cysts with a needle massive enough for veterinary practice and sent off the fluid to Pathology. The solid lump, however, had refused to aspirate, annoying Dr Williams and alarming Pauli. 'I see you're a repeat offender with these things, and family breast cancer besides.' (Mumbles from behind Pauli's medical record). 'Well, let's see you after your next period. You may need another biopsy.'

'But the fluid –' Pauli tried to ask while simultaneously scrambling off the examining table and pulling the paper gown about her.

'Report will be back in a few days. Don't worry about it,' Dr Williams declared over her shoulder as she left. The odour of sterile alcohol hung in the room.

Pauli shivered. Rubbing Dr Williams' flesh-toned plaster near the nipple of her left breast, Pauli recalled Stevens. Had he too exited rooms to avoid female questions? She was still waking at night, aching after him as if a limb, not just some breast fluid, had disappeared.

Since Harry was frantically busy, Morgan was hiring Pauli to continue whatever she'd begun for Stevens. All she had to do was collect folders Stevens had marked for her, plus papers on some of Morgan's projects.

Her first interview with him had included his microscopic slide show of horrors. Accustomed as she was to varieties of death, she was still shaken by these pathological pellets that, growing unseen in mouse and human, continued to steal life. A surgeon like Dr Williams might scalpel them out, and a pathologist like Morgan freeze, slice and mount them. Yet under the right conditions, cultured or transplanted from mouse to mouse, they never aged through a fixed lifespan of generations. Unlike ordinary cells, cancer cells became immortal.

And Morgan collected only the bizarrest – those with double nuclei, eighty chromosomes instead of forty-six, a technicolour freak show, 3-D under the electron microscope, until Pauli couldn't differentiate mouse from woman.

Unlike Stevens, who often fingersnapped or shouted at assistants, Morgan never lost control, striving to appear the charmer, cracking jokes and puns, whenever she saw him. Golden Galahad among the Petri dishes. Maybe he was singlehandedly revising the myth that pathologists are dour loners, fit only for the companionship of tumour and tissue slicer.

Not for the first time at the Institute, she yearned for a cheerier subject to research. How about measles? Or nymphomania? Now that would be fun to –

'Do you always smile at the wall?' Suddenly Pauli found Morgan, bow-tied and linen-suited, grinning behind her.

'No, I –' She stopped.

'C'mon in. I have to leave soon, but we can talk while I locate your stuff.'

Pauli eased into the leather armchair in front of the teak desk that decorated the inner office of his suite of lab rooms. How did Morgan qualify for such comfy furnishings while Stevens, the director, had rated only painted steel? Stevens didn't care, and Morgan must – while Arthur cared and got nowhere.

'What's Dr Stornell on the rampage about?' she asked.

'Reporters bugging him. Why can't they all copy the same statements we made to the police? Instead, each one of them bothers us, and they all ask the same questions. We tell them to clear off, especially the ones who can't even spell "carcinoma". Steve's death *is* a tragedy, but we all have to go on somehow . . . And don't quote me, huh?'

'Of course not,' Pauli agreed. 'Though, don't *you* wonder who killed Stevens? It has to be . . . somebody here.'

Morgan's eyebrows rose. He shrugged. 'If I knew, wouldn't I tell the police?'

'I heard the wound was very precise. The knife was very sharp, maybe even a razor-like instrument. Wouldn't it take a surgeon to inflict that?'

'Don't ask me. I'm not a surgeon.'

But pathology begins with dissection of mouse and human.

Morgan was asking, 'What's the matter today, Pauli? You're worried, abstracted.' He waved one hand before her face.

'Oh, close encounter of the wrong kind with my surgeon.'

'Infection? A growth of some kind?'

'Some breast cysts this morning. And for next month, one solid lump that wouldn't aspirate. The fluid's on its way to Pathology.'

'Aren't we all?' Morgan laughed. 'But seriously . . . let me know what happens?' He sat back, regarding her.

Sometimes I get the crazy idea I picked it up here among all your viruses and horror slides. Much as Pauli disliked her breast being the object of a joke, she could see why everybody liked Morgan, and why Harry sent him out, Exhibit A, to the microphone every time the Institute needed a spokesperson – Dr Morgan Dianis, quotable quotes on everything from cloning to environmental pollution.

'Pauli, here are papers four of us gave at a spring conference. And the print-outs for one. We can use a booklet summarising all four in fairly technical language. Now Pooler, he's the post-doc in genetics, he can't even write the technical stuff, and I'm coordinating so many projects I haven't the time. I've also got data that should become papers on several of my own projects. And –' Morgan paused dramatically, 'if you get bored, Harry's after me again about text and photos for a new display in the lobby. Disease of the month sort of thing, you know, make it sound formidable even if the funding got cut . . . Got all that?'

Pauli realised that instead of taking notes, she'd been watching Morgan perform. He was so *verbal* compared to Stevens. She nodded. 'Let me look over the new material.' Glancing at the nude mouse title and numerical tables in the first paper, Pauli forced her brain towards questions to elicit some general information. 'Do most of your projects involve nude mice?'

'Three do, three don't. The mice are expensive.'

'Can you tell me in one sentence why you use mice at all, instead of rats or monkeys? Or cells in dishes?'

'Do you know what a monkey costs?' He cocked an eyebrow at her. 'Cells in dishes can't walk, squeak or mate . . . Do you know what 100 mouse generations of brother–sister matings represent? And all that in a few years, because female mice come into heat the day after delivery, and pregnancy's only about three weeks. 100 mouse generations equal 3,500 years of human history. Remember how the ancient Egyptians married royal brother to royal sister to preserve the kind of human blood line they wanted? So mice are a kind of shorthand, a living time capsule, for human history back to 1500 BC. For tracing genetic patterns of disease and health . . . Short of experimenting on humans, of course,' he added.

As Pauli scribbled, she envied brains like Arthur's and Morgan's, furnished with specialised instant lore, to contrast with her endless generality. 'I also need something you said during the hospital people's tour, about how cancer may have only one cause.'

'That *isn't* what I said, but I'll forgive you.' He grinned. 'I said, the transition from normal tissue through interphase to malignancy may have one central *mechanism*. Since we've got rid of the major infectious diseases, it's fashionable now to say a disease like cancer is "multifactorial" – it may have something to do with environment or with diet or with ageing. Even the most direct correlation, that between cigarettes and lung cancer, doesn't show up for many years in most smokers. Anyway, if cancer does have multiple causes or is due to stuff beyond our control in the environment, that will be news,' he continued, 'because it's never happened before. In every other disease we know, many things may be going on and perhaps some predispose to getting the disease or aggravate it once contracted. But for each disease there's always been a chair of the committee, one central mechanism. And I don't expect cancer to be any different . . . Humans are not different from other animals, just harder to investigate.'

Pauli scrabbled for a sensible reply. 'People are more scared of cancer so they're paranoid about everything – water, food, vaccinations. There's a fixed anxiety now about health. When people didn't expect to be cured of disease, they didn't worry so much.'

'Right. Infectious disease are self-limiting. Within ten days you either live or die. People's expectations have been raised. Nobody expects sudden death any more – unless you get mugged on the street.'

Had Stevens expected death? Pauli felt suddenly absurd at Morgan's abstract discussion. 'Well, let me get busy. I'll see what questions I have.'

'You can use this office. I have some things to check with Edward before I leave. I'm glad you're still working on this, and I'll pay you for my own stuff, of course. Call me tomorrow if you want. You'll also see a note in there from a marketing rep at a computer company. She wants some stunning statements about what we use her machines for, small and large. Make up something and I'll sign it.'

'How about, "To err is human; to really foul things up requires a computer"?'

'Nah. Too close to the truth.' Morgan winked and was gone. What a relief Morgan was. Pauli could joke and talk business with him as if he were – her brother. No gut thrill, of course, none of that tantalising toying perfected by Stevens, though.

She settled into his leather and teak. As she reopened a battered manila folder, Morgan's transparent paperweight, or rather the words it magnified, inked on a square green card like a child's buspass, caught her eye:

> The disease of cancer will be banished from life by calm, unhurrying, persistent men and women, working with every shiver of feeling controlled and suppressed, in hospitals and laboratories, and the motive that will conquer cancer will not be pity nor horror; it will be curiosity to know how and why.
>
> H.G. Wells, *Meanwhile*, 1927

Pauli shuddered. The idea of anybody doing anything with zero emotion – 'scientific objectivity' – terrified her. Why wasn't curiosity an emotion?

On the bottom folder Stevens had written 'Pauline Golden – Promo'. Whatever cancer needed, it wasn't promo. It got too much of that already, self-serving and self-perpetuating everywhere. From the very back of the folder Pauli pulled out a handwritten sheet, expecting it to be the computer rep's note. With a shock Pauli discovered a whole page covered with Stevens' left-slanted writing.

Dearest,

It's very late, and I'm harassed with various staff and financial problems that just aren't working out right.

I know neither of us approves of my writing to you, but all phone calls still go through the central switchboard until we get the new system installed.

I want to answer some things you said. You believe we professional guys have scalpels for minds, frozen tissue specimens for hearts. And maybe ten-syllable words for emotions. That's why I need you; help me decipher my ten-syllable words!

I agree we exist in an unreal situation that freezes instants of time in both our memories – you stretched before your fireplace beating me at Scrabble, you naked as a medical mermaid in the motel bathtub grilling me on the latest in chemotherapy and transplant successes. Who else do we know who can be sexy and professional at the same time? I believe you are criticising me for something you feel guilty about in yourself. Am I right?

Pauli stopped, her eyes misting. With effort she continued.

You are my first special sensation since marriage. You are a rich fresh dimension in my life. Now don't raise your eyebrows in that ironic way you have. You're not filling a void in my life. I truly believe such a void does not exist. I also believe it would be self-defeating to heat up our relationship – but a loss to both of us to drop it.

You believe gynaecologists know nothing about women, see them only as numbers in a file, organs under surgical drapes. Yet you entered my world, have seen and felt me respond.

Pauli stumbled over some crossed-out words, then read on.

You are too defensive about whether your freelance articles get published. You fear getting dropped. Will you believe me when I say publication doesn't matter – you are helping several of us get our ideas down on paper. Leave it to Harry and me what to do with the work.

You believe 'deception takes too much energy'. You're used to relationships without strings with unattached soldiers of fortune, never with someone you meet for business. Suppose you were my patient. Would you also be embarrassed to see me at a party knowing I had delivered your baby, sutured your abdomen, palpated your breasts? If I'm not embarrassed, why should you be?

Stevens

The letter, undated and penned on a sheet of Stevens' old office stationery, stung Pauli. When she'd read it three times, she dropped her arms and head on to the open folder.

It must be for her, yet he'd never mailed it. So he had loved her, and she hadn't trusted him!

But his wife – did he *really* think the marriage that nearly drove Heather insane had no 'void'? Where had he suddenly buried all that bitterness over not fathering children? Maybe he and Pauli could have made a child. She loved babies, but they became – people.

Stevens' death – what a waste. She heard Morgan and Edward rattling trolleys outside the doorway. Had Morgan read the letter before giving her the folder? Had he shown it to the police? A juicy affair, but then, if you discovered pornography in your boss's desk, you'd take a good look – and leave it there. Besides, it was heterosexual. What could be more normal than that? Looking down, she discovered her damp fingers had smudged the ink on one corner of Stevens' letter.

Scientific objectivity. *You can do it; you've done it before*. Propping chin on one hand, she tried to concentrate on mosaic mice, microinjections and 'human breast carcinomas heterotransplanted into nude mice'. First the words blurred, then darted back and forth across the fixed image of Stevens' white face and black hair, motel bedspreads, the exquisite relaxation of love-making. . .

'Pauline, Morgan said you were here again. I want to talk to you about something.' Harry Stornell's voice boomed at her.

Pauli jumped. Look him in the eye. Harry dropped into Morgan's nail-studded leather chair and folded his arms across his paunch. Apart from his rouge-red cheeks, his skin looked dry and pasty under thinning hair. High blood pressure, Pauli guessed.

'I'll get to the point. I appreciate your trying to help us out during this, well, crisis period, but neither Stevens nor Morgan really consulted me about the writing you're doing.'

Politics, damn! 'The initial samples from your magazine were good, but what we need is solid research papers, not news handouts. Too many damn reporters around here.' He sighed. 'And Morgan should write his own papers by now. Anyway, what you've done seems too loose for scientific journals, but too complicated for brochure use.'

'But –'

'Let me finish.' His mouth tightened. 'I realise you're doing it as a sideline, and Stevens wanted one thing and maybe Morgan wants another. But your material isn't usable, and I don't want to put any more money into it.' He finished and stared at her over his gold-rimmed glasses.

Pauli's body began to burn. 'But I've got three articles started plus a summary of four conference papers Morgan wants. I don't understand –'

'I know, but that's your problem. Anybody, who'd quote *Edward* in what he writes. "Cute little buggers," ' Harry mocked.

'If it was inappropriate, you could have edited it out. After all' – she stared at him – 'you must have approved it? And that was deliberate humour for a public brochure, not a technical article. Most people have never seen a nude mouse.'

'So? They fall head over heels with them. Then they discover we give them cancer. Great idea. And quoting Edward! All you do with asinine work like that is make jealousy.'

Personalities who stand out make for jealousy. Stevens' words haunted her.

'Huggard told me you've been bothering him.'

'Bothering him?' Pauli exploded. 'He needs attention paid to his work.'

'So already you're an expert on what my staff needs?' Harry mocked. Finally the true reason. 'I don't want just anybody around here now. Submit a bill for what you've done. We'll call it quits. Morgan'll do his own work.'

'But I'm not . . . a spy! And Morgan's paying me himself for what he needs. What writing would *you* like then, considering Stevens is . . . dead?'

Harry's eyes widened. 'Get out of here, Pauline. Put the folders down. Stevens never knew what he was doing here, wasting money right and left from grants *I* got.' Bitterness tinged Harry's voice. 'What're you taking?'

Pauli clutched Stevens' letter, grabbed her briefcase and stumbled past Harry into the outer lab and the airless corridor. She expected him to chase her but he didn't. Morgan and Edward had vanished.

As she rounded the empty guard desk in the lobby, she was panting from trying to breathe, run and stifle tears at the same time. She nearly tumbled down the cement steps outside. In the asphalt-smelling parking lot her insides lurched. She couldn't locate her car keys – must be in her coat back *there* – until she dug them from her skirt pocket and realised she hadn't worn a coat.

Sitting with the door open to get the car interior off slow bake, she dropped her head against the steering wheel. Would he question Morgan about the handwritten sheet? How did these types with tantrums outwit her? She hadn't even offered a decent fight. If he feared reporters, she could have used that fear to keep her job.

But Stevens had died fast proving something.

What a fool not to have contracted for her articles. Without a contract she was nothing, an expendable X-chromosome they excised at will. What a fool to get so involved with Stevens to imagine he'd run the lab flawlessly. Well, Harry didn't think so, and must be glad Stevens was no longer there.

Pauli rubbed her breast, where perspiration was stinging the skin around the needle holes. If Medway hadn't bound her with a contract, that was their loss. She'd publish the pieces on her own – and work where she wanted.

But how to get Morgan's informal clearance?

12

In disbelief Pauli stared at one of Morgan's sentences: 'This mitogenic effect of HPL on xenografts of benign human breast epithelium proves further evidence that this placental peptide may be a factor in the aetiology of dysplastic breast lesions, lesions that are often seen in multiparous women.'

How did people (including doctors) write prose like that without throwing up – 'existential nausea followed by acute hyperemesis'? The idea made Pauli laugh.

Hesitating a moment, she changed 'prove' to 'provide' and handwrote an English translation above Morgan's medicalese: 'Based on work with mice, the hormone HPL (human placental lactogen) may be involved in formation of benign breast tumours, including certain tissue changes seen in women who are mothers of several children.'

'How you doing?'

Pauli jumped. From his lab room Morgan had sneaked up behind her again. She turned around in his desk chair.

'Your style leaves much to be desired,' she remarked, frowning.

'Yeah, ghastly, isn't it? Do you have a question?'

'I'll save them up. Well, I do have one. What do you make of all the question marks on your tumour transplantation paper? They're Dr Stevens', aren't they?'

Standing by her elbow, Morgan blinked, then stared down. 'Yes. That's his scrawls, all right. I don't make anything of them.' He pointed to a sign taped to his in-tray:

'*The* difference between science and the fuzzy subjects is that science requires reasoning, while those other subjects merely require scholarship.'

'Meaning?'

'Oh, Stevens oversaw all our papers – with a fine-tooth comb and calculator. A stickler for footnotes and logic besides. He knew he should have been doing finer things, so that's why he hired you.'

'Gee, thanks.' Pauli let her annoyance show. Morgan had let her in tonight through the Institute's sidedoor by disconnecting it with a barrel key and his regular key from the building's alarm system and the lobby guard's TV monitor. The old man, a different dwarf from daytime, dozed frequently. Why didn't Harry fire *him*?

She asked again, 'You sure Harry's left?' She watched Morgan's jaw clench with exasperation.

'Pauline, you're a worrywart. You wanted me to reason with Harry about keeping you on here. I told you I won't do that. I run my own operation, and not by begging him for favours. I know how to deal with Harry Stornell.'

What did that mean?

'Come on, I'll show you our latest results with the mosaic mice. They're not isolated like the nude mice. Anyway, take the stuff with you this time – regardless of what Harry thinks. I promise you per piece whatever Stevens offered.'

Pauli's heart raced. She still hadn't accustomed her innards to the casual mention of Stevens' name as if he still existed. For thirty seconds she rejoiced in Morgan's news, then she narrowed her eyes at him. 'Why're you doing this?'

'Well, you're not the first to note my style needs major surgery before it hits the intensive care unit.' He sighed. 'Anyway, soon I begin a year's work in France or Sweden, and I want this stuff ready for journal publication before I go.'

Pauli knew better than to question in whose name all these marvels would manifest. From now on, all her Institute work would appear either anonymously in 'News Notes' columns and pamphlets or under her new pen-name, Morgan Dianis, MD.

But besides being paid somehow from Morgan's own funds (better doublecheck that), wouldn't she outwit Harry, plus learn more about a top-notch set of projects, plus keep some of Stevens' hopes alive?

'You look so troubled,' Morgan commented.

'Can I rely on your discretion about this arrangement?'

He laughed, 'Of course. Actually, you know, you have no choice. Are you worried about my boss, or yours?'

Pauli squirmed. These charming bastards! How they turned the screws.

'That is,' he said, softening, 'I can see how much you want this work.'

Pauli tried to read his face. The handsome façade, the long-lashed eyes, seemed to hold nothing beyond his usual affability. She backed off. 'Let me take the folders. I'll let you know later what I can make of the stuff.'

'Well, I can get someone else. There was another reporter here yesterday. Not the one Harry kicked out, somebody else better equipped.'

Pauli ignored this. 'I'll let you know.'

Morgan's office had two doors. From the one that stood ajar on to the corridor, she heard sudden footsteps, then a light knock.

'Hey, I better get lost.'

Morgan laid a steadying hand upon her shoulder. 'Nonsense. I invited you.' When he opened the door wider, Arthur Huggard stood there.

'Morgan, do you – oh, sorry, didn't know you're busy.'

'Pauli insists she's just leaving. And I wanted to show her Coal-tar Mama out there in the animal wing too . . . Well, how's our Nobel Prize candidate? Arthur, how're your viruses growing?'

Instead of realising he was being patronised, Arthur unexpectedly smiled. Either he was currying Morgan's favour, or any notice from one of the Institute's MDs, no matter how insulting, was better than apathy. 'Hello, Miss Golden. Good to see you again.' Pauli repressed a smile at that one. 'I'll come back later after your tour.' With a swish of blue suede shoes he was gone.

With his index finger Morgan tapped his own head in the international gesture for 'crazy-crazy'. Pauli nodded. However, though strange, Arthur had at least been civil this time.

Pauli had never visited the Institute's animal quarantine wing at night. The black and white sign, 'MAMMALIAN GENETICS – Authorised Visitors Only Beyond This Point,' reminded her of the form she'd recompleted on each legal visit to the main lobby: 'I have not worked with experimental animals during the last ten days.' Heaven help sinners caught with hands in the viruses.

After Morgan's bright office the tan walls minus windows, the self-closing door that clunked behind them, the scrabble and odour of hundreds of creatures, caged, tiered and breathing in the shadows, made her flesh crawl. A manila name tag, tied to each transparent bread box, identified its occupants – mouse strain, date of painting or innoculation with carcinogens, vitamins, drugs, serum, depending on the experiment.

As Morgan turned to examine his animals, Pauli felt hundreds of red-bead eyes watch her. Translucent pink feet reached from the wood shavings up the box sides towards her. Whiskers twitched. A few mice – the dying – heaped themselves scruffily into corners, but most animals, being nocturnal, appeared ready for action under the sudden bath of fluorescent light. Pauli imagined releasing them. Would they rampage at the death sentences already injected into their living flesh? But such inbred animals, addicted to sterile cages, rodent chow, water, warmth, could never survive the hostile, germy world of housemice and tenement rats. On the way to death, they enjoyed a life of ease, if not pleasure.

'When do you do injections?'

'Well, not at this hour. Two mornings a week we slice fresh human breast tumours and transplant them under the animals' skin or into the brain. That involves the nude mice in the isolation area with the double doors we walked by. If we pretreat them with my antiserum, we get nearly 75 per cent positive takes, instead of the 20 per cent other people get. The animals get cancer and I expect to improve that to a

82

100 per cent as I develop a better serum. That's just one of my serums.'

'What's "better"?'

'More potent, purified. Any researcher needs something that produces only one testable effect, not a range of effects, so you don't know what caused what. But we learn to live with both failure and doubt.'

'You?' Pauli interrupted.

'Of course.' Morgan leaned back into a steel rack. 'The . . . pressure to produce results is tremendous. You work at something for ninety-nine days; it fails. On the hundredth it works. Then you spend the next 100 trying to prove what succeeded really didn't – that's it's just an artefact you won't be able to repeat. Then there's the steady doubt that many people consider detachment or coldness. It means while you give your guts to something, all the time you got a "maybe" in your head. Because somebody else comes along every day to brag about what they're doing or claim they're working miracles elsewhere, so you fear, Jeez, I'm in the wrong place. In science, nice guys finish second, and second's nowhere.'

In Pauli's head rose Arthur's wall: YOU CAN'T WIN, YOU CAN'T EVEN GET OUT OF THE GAME. Then there was Coral Deming's sign: I MUST BE A MUSHROOM – THEY KEEP ME IN THE DARK AND FEED ME SHIT.

'People talk about "serendipity" – finding whatever by accident,' Morgan continued. 'That's just stepping into a bucket of crap every working day and emerging smelling like a rose with another grant a year later. But I invited you here for our prize mosaics. And we've also got two new litters of nudes in the plastic bubble over there. They're not in the isolation room yet. So this little fellow here –' Morgan lifted down a plastic box on to a rolling lab trolley. 'Now this one, he actually had four parents, and two of them were pure cancer cells. Yet the mouse is normal – not a sign of a tumour. The processes of gestation in the uterus are so powerful they can revert even cancer cells back to normal.'

'You mean the embryo that became that mouse was built in a test tube from normal sex cells and cancer cells.'

'Well, when the egg and sperm have fused and produced

an embryo with just a few cells, under a microscope we inject tumour cells from two other animals. Then we implant the whole into a foster mother.'

'Like the test-tube human babies.'

Morgan nodded.

Pauli touched the transparent, sloping sides of the foot-long box and read the mouse's tag, 'Coal-tar Mama', from the black tufts streaking the otherwise virgin white of his coat. He resembled a miniature skunk with a bad dye job.

'Why do you call it "Mama" if he's male?'

'One of Edward's jokes. His sperm and egg came from normal non-cancerous white mice. Yet the black fur proves it's the cancer cells from tumours in black mice expressing themselves. Genes control coat colour even in cancer cells. In an age of publicity even cancer gets self-expression. That's supposed to be a joke, my dear.'

But Pauli was concentrating too hard to laugh.

'So part of his genes came from non-cancerous white mice, his black frosting from genes in cells of malignant tumours. Oh, Coal-tar Mama's the first of his mosaic race still alive here.'

'Why not rename him Adam?' The 3-inch mouse stretched a few normal-looking paws up the plastic sides towards Pauli. 'Can I touch him?'

Morgan's long fingers lifted the box lid, which contained an inverted water bottle and food pellets held by steel grating. Feeling the draft, Coal-tar Mama cowered in a corner.

Pauli pitied the tiny creature, first and last of his local race, bred of cancer cells from before the womb. 'He looks so . . . normal, but he's not much on courage, is he?'

'Well, he's two years old. That's geriatric-plus for a mouse. If he were human, he'd be senile.'

Pauli lowered her fingers and began stroking Coal-tar Mama's three soft inches. Both white and black furs surprisingly had the same seal-like texture. She'd expected the cancerous black to feel coarse, ugly. The mouse squealed twice and scrambled into its shavings, trying to escape. Gradually, however, Pauli felt its skin and muscles relax and its nose begin to poke, with cat-like curiosity, towards her fingers. A new talent – mouse massage.

'You're very good at that. Pretty soon he'll be asleep. Mustn't get too comfortable.' As if jealous, Morgan yanked the box and mouse away from Pauli's hand. Replacing the cover, he thrust it back on to the shelf. The mouse lay stunned; the water bottle gurgled. 'Why – ?' Pauli began, then stopped. Morgan had already crossed the room to check progress in the 4-foot-long plastic bubble, which stood at hip height. *God, people are weird here*. Coal-tar Mama, though an impressive freak-show exhibit, was obviously not Morgan's major or current interest.

'Come see my nudes.'

'What?'

'C'mon. Wake up, woman. The athymic nude mice. That's what you came to see.' Now Morgan was smiling as he shook hands with the vinyl sleeves knotted on the outside of the pressurised transparent bubble which sat inflated, breathing in and out on its trolley.

Pauli focused on the inhabitants of this Pressure City. Two plastic boxes, divided into covered nesting sections and open exercise areas, sat under the dome. Each held an oddly assorted family of normal-size, white-furred mother, minia- ture but normal white babies and – the jewels of Morgan's collection – two foetal-looking hairless fathers plus various nude babies. Already these fathers stood only slightly larger than their normal, white-furred babies, which would soon grow beyond them. 'We choose females who've produced at least eight pups per litter. When we mate them with the nude fathers you see, the nude gene is recessive, so we're supposed to get 25 per cent completely normals, 50 per cent normals with one nude gene, and 25 per cent pure nudes – unless the mother eats some of them or something else happens. We've even found a nude father with bitemarks on his back. She must have confused him with one of the kids as she dragged the lot back to the nesting box. As I told you, normal females come into heat the day after they give birth, so she can produce a litter every three weeks, but we retire breeding pairs at ten months, after maybe seven litters.'

Pauli stared at the scientifically deformed nude males and their tiny offspring, normal and mutated. 'How soon do you know the babies will be nudes?'

'When the hair fails to come in at five to six days. But there are other ways. Look at this fella's crinkled whiskers compared to this female's straight ones. And his hind legs are deformed. He drags one of them, see? That means he received one gene of the pair of genes that produces that limb problem. If he'd received both genes for it, he would have died before birth. This is a white nude mouse; we also raise black ones.'

Pauli stared at a second box open under the arching plastic bubble. What Morgan called 'whites', Pauli saw as pinky-grey wrinkled animals with red eyes, splayed five-foot toes, pointed elfin ears. The 'blacks' were merely a darker mole-grey with deep-brown eyes. They all resembled ancient foetuses. How did anything so deformed father a new litter every three weeks? Females must be desperate to make it with anything warm mounted on four legs, no matter how mutated . . . *They have no choice, silly, any more than humans lacking contraceptives.*

'These have no thymus gland,' Morgan was continuing, 'which means they get infections we don't even try to give them. Benign tumours grow well. And with my serum, transplanted malignant ones too.'

So far, nobody had duplicated either Morgan's special serum, or his results, but Pauli let it pass to avoid interrupting. Stevens had evaded her several requests to see this animal wing with, 'Maybe later, Pauli.' His interest was human medicine, not rodents. Edward had no authority to admit visitors even if she were still *persona grata* here. At least Morgan cared enough to make the effort.

'Somebody is developing an animal that lacks a spleen as well as a thymus gland.'

'The nude streaker?' Pauli laughed.

'Right. You read the lobby blurbs. Maybe you'll write some new ones for us . . . This is the surgical isolator.' Morgan was pointing to an inflated plastic cylinder; it hung like a half-amputated third limb next to the plastic sleeves with fingers that could reach and work inside the big bubble. 'For a Caesarean, we anaesthetise and open the female inside the large bubble. Then we lift her pregnant uterus into this separate tube off the bubble' – he tapped the amputated limb. 'Then we open the uterus, inspect the pups and deliver them to nurse from waiting foster mothers back inside the bubble.'

Pauli knew better than to ask whatever became of the original mother, now bereft of her uterus. She'd entered with so many questions, but a spasm of nausea seemed to have replaced them.

'Had enough?' Morgan enquired.

Pauli almost nodded, then caught herself. One eerie aspect of association with doctors is that they continue to evaluate physical symptoms, even at social occasions. Morgan had guessed her queasiness just as a skin doctor she met at a party had noticed brown blotches on her cheeks. When he remarked, 'I bet you've been pregnant recently', she caught her breath, raised her drink in salute – and edged away. Her one and only early pregnancy had ended in miscarriage two weeks before. She'd avoided surgery by mopping up the accident in the dorm bathroom herself and praying it had all ejected. The college clinic both refused to issue contraceptives and had never heard the word 'abortion' so it was catch as catch could. She caught.

The father was a guy named Ron, already arranging his plane ticket for a linguistics year in France. Not wanting a child either then, she didn't trouble him. Soon after, she joyfully met Lizann during a women's dance at the college's embattled 'gay and bi–' group . . .

Morgan was already across the room. He must have opened another box, for he was yanking a normal-looking white mouse by the tail, hoisting it into the air. Its pink feet flailed against nothingness. Deftly Morgan flipped it backwards into his other hand, exposing the mouse's belly while his index finger and thumb immobilised its head and teeth. He'd donned latex gloves.

'What're you looking for?'

'What d'you think? Didn't do your homework? Nodules, sensitivity, weight loss.'

'Don't you need scales to prove that?'

'Uh-uh.' Morgan waved his mouse-filled hand. 'Precision is the curse of small minds. Once I had a sign I should display here: "To enjoy the flavour of life, take big bites. Moderation is for monks!" '

Pauli nodded. Morgan's waving the mouse around like a furry frankfurter gave her the shivers. After it squealed once, she asked, 'Ever hear of stress as a cause for cancer?'

'This one's already got cancer. You're too late. All right, Miss Bleeding Heart, I'll put her back.' Morgan eased the animal, belly down, on to the shavings, where it scratched itself, checking all parts, then cowered into a foetal lump.

Pauli shuddered. Suppose a cancer virus floated in the very air here. The sophisticated filters that kept the world's air out also sealed this room upon itself.

For the remainder of the tour along the corridor Morgan pointed out the electron microscope and preparation rooms for samples. ('36 degrees in there and sterile. The cold room. Don't believe these laetrile types who tell you they can manufacture a pure sample in a slum room in Mexico with the temperature at 99 degrees and flies buzzing in).'

They ended up in his own lab and microscope room beside his office, where he slid out a grey-green drawer and steel shelf. 'My mouse surgery. I do my own, you know. Coral helps sometimes, but usually I need too much.'

Pauli nodded, recalling angry Coral, then tipsy Coral, plying Morgan with sandwiches at the party.

'That's funny.' Morgan was squatting now, groping on to the lower shelf of a trolley. 'I left a full box of disposable syringes here this morning. I suppose somebody put them away. Can't keep anything. Yesterday I lost a whole carton of fresh Petri dishes from the refrigerator. Just vanished. Maybe Arthur or Edward messing around.'

'I bet Arthur took them as a souvenir. He loves this place so.' Pauli lifted her briefcase. 'I better go now.' But Morgan was puttering again. The night shadows and images of mice in all stages, uterus onward, of their journeys towards death chilled her. Must be the air-conditioning. Morgan was pleasant enough, pleasanter and more verbal than Stevens most of the time.

'I better go,' she repeated. 'Will you let me out?'

13

The red, blue-and-white striped airmail envelope, thin almost to non-existence, stood vertically in her mailbox, propped against a drug ad and a medical magazine. As Pauli pulled the lot from her large box at the side of her brick apartment building, the scribbles – Lizann's new name and return address in Paris, all bunched as usual towards the ends of the lines – set Pauli's back crawling.

What could Lizann want after all these months? To cut the pain of her departure, Pauli had never written more than a Hi-how-are-you? holiday card.

Reclimbing the stairs, she opened the apartment door and carefully placed the pieces of mail on her kitchen table like parts of a time bomb she lacked courage to assemble.

A crisp, sunny Saturday, 10 a.m. She'd slept badly, tossed by nightmares ending in horror. At an elegant banquet table Sara from Pauli's magazine, swathed in black velvet and greasepaint, operated a hidden button that electrocuted all female guests, one by one. The death jolt hit Pauli while she attempted to revive the blonde woman beside her . . . Chilled and shaking, Pauli had awakened to her own cries.

Frank would be calling. Besides the mail, she also lacked courage as yet to phone her mother for the latest health bulletin, thus enmeshing herself in another Saturday of fetching and hauling. Take the initiative. Make something pleasant with somebody else for today.

Grabbing her Chinese red phone (when the repairman installed it, she'd joked about the Hotline to Nowhere) before she could change her mind, she dialled Rainette. 'Hi. It's Pauli. How about the beach today? It's a gorgeous day. You could sketch or finish your suntan.'

'Pauli, that's nice. It would be fun, but Tom invited some people over, and I'm fixing food. Want to join *us*? Like 4 o'clock?'

Pauli hesitated, having forgotten the futility of asking a married woman to do anything on a weekend – or a single one, except for herself, on a Saturday night. Everybody acted as whirlwinded as the jetset with sailboats or Cessnas.

'Look, with your fair skin you shouldn't be sitting in the sun, you know.'

If that was Rainette's idea of consolation – ' Oh, I just wanted us to get together a bit. I've been working hard, but I don't want people to feel I'm totally asocial. How's the Institute going?' Now that she was banished from its daytime existence, Pauli couldn't resist asking.

'Grotesque. Harry has a fit every other minute, mostly over trivia. Yesterday, if you can believe this, it was over who took a library book and that Siamese cat statue off his desk. The book turned up on a lab bench. Any robber would be off the wall to steal a 10-pound pathology textbook. The silver statue we're still looking for. It's all paranoia from what happened to Dr Stevens. Anyway, Harry locks his office if he only goes to the bathroom. Which means I can't file correspondence or get papers I need to answer the phone. The whole place is hell right –'

Pauli interrupted. 'What . . . what do people say about Stevens' death?' Still she couldn't use the word 'murder'. 'Do the police have any leads?'

'Only Coral – you know, the mouse-surgery lady, the one with the mosaic hair – talks about it openly at lunch. She's gossipy anyway.' Pauli remembered Coral of the white coat and red ruffle. How Coral had stared at Pauli and Stevens whenever she passed them in a corridor. Anger? Jealousy? Women's woes in science?

'The police finished taking all our statements days ago. And they came back to go through Stevens' desk and the labs. It's sort of business as usual, but *I* miss Dr Stevens. He was so calm and polite. Harry's a madman by comparison.'

If the police had seen Stevens' letter . . . Pauli shivered. 'Harry's under a lot of tension,' she finally answered, then wondered why this surge of charity towards Harry? She must be sick. Why not slash him behind his back as he'd done to her. *Nice girls finish nowhere.*

'I heard the government is withholding the grant until Stevens' murder gets cleared up,' Rainette continued. 'It'll help them keep their own noses clean by not funding anything that's got into trouble. To avoid publicity mostly.'

Ah so, one more reason for Harry's budget-cutting, firing frenzy. Stevens' death was toppling dominoes all around. Maybe Harry would lose his job; maybe he killed Stevens.

'Rainette, you work with all of them. Do you think Harry did it?' Loose lips lose lives.

'What? Slit Stevens' throat and castr –'

'Just answer the question.' The details still sickened her. She was glad the local newspapers had mostly avoided them. The police had released only one photo of Stevens alive and one photo of the death room. The papers had photographed the house, and reporters had written the usual rubbish, but Pauli knew the official story: an 'unknown intruder', lured by the open hall door to the front room containing artwork and Stevens' safe, had killed to avoid detection. Then he or she exited, perhaps mingling with the drunken, candle-lit guests on the way. If attempted robbery preceded accidental murder, then why hadn't the 'intruder' returned later to finish the heist? 'Intruders' may rape women; they rarely molest men.

Rainette was asking, 'Why would Harry kill somebody he invited to run the place, especially the research details he can't stand?'

Pauli laughed; it sounded hollow. 'Whoever heard of a research director who can't stand research?'

'But it's the truth,' Rainette protested. 'Look at the Arctic explorers who wind up paranoid about snowflakes . . . Pauli, I'm glad you can mention this again. After I called you that night, how you were the last to see him and all, I felt horrible.

I work there but I couldn't figure why *you* cared. It was just a part-time job.'

To the question in Rainette's voice Pauli remained speechless until the silence got awkward. 'Well, of course I care about the work I do. When I don't care any more, I'm a hack, right?' She changed the subject. 'Okay, I'll come this afternoon if I can make it.'

She hung up, grateful for the invitation but doubtful she could endure a chattering group of people, gossiping about their summer. Just like the last party – but without Stevens to anticipate. Without Stevens ever again. Both talking and concealing about Stevens exhausted her.

Lizann's three toned envelope stared from the pink enamel table. Not yet.

When the phone rang, it was Frank as expected. 'Hello. I didn't think you'd be in. It's that high-powered social life you've got . . .' Frank's banter seemed normal. Instead of recoiling, she loved him for it.

'What? Visiting Mom?' she asked. 'How are *you*? Frank, I can't take another Saturday with her tantrums. I'm going for a drive today. The humidity here has finally pushed out.' New plan: call Heather.

'Frank, what're we gonna do?' Pauli hoped the 'we' would rouse him to shared responsibility. 'The housekeeper I got from Social Services lasted a week before Mom wanted her fired. Just like the last one. Luckily the poor woman quit full of apologies for not pleasing Mom before it ever came to the big scene.'

'I know. You wrote,' Frank answered drily.

'Did I? I can't even remember.' Pauli sighed. 'Anyway, I phoned a Mrs Quinn and got Mom's name on to the lists at two nursing homes, but it'll be months, maybe years before –'

'She'll never enter a home. You know that,' Frank chided.

'Well, *help* me with this goddam situation!' Pauli exploded. 'If she'd just fall over and die, it'd solve the whole problem. Funerals I'm good at. It's *living* that's the problem.'

'If that's the way you feel, no wonder she won't cooperate.'

'I don't *say* it to her . . . That's right – criticise me because she's in a muddle. Look' – Pauli brightened – 'how about you take her out there? You've got a house and business. And she likes you better than she ever liked me.'

Silence. No familiar protest that what Pauli and her mother suffered amounted to jealousy of each other. Not even the rasp of Frank's breathing.

'But the house here has stairs and the mountainside. Who'd watch her in the daytime?'

'Frank, I don't care. She's driving me crazy. If it isn't a fall like last week, it's tantrums over food, clothes, dishes. Help me.'

Again no answer. Come on strong, you frighten people and don't get help; come on weak, they edge away with relief.

'Does she know about the nursing homes?'

'Whenever I mention the subject, she hobbles into her room and slams the door. Frank, please come? She'd love to see you. You're some god to her. You stay too far away to get on her conflict list. She never liked Daddy, but she loves you.'

'Maybe you're acting too strong about it?'

Pauli groaned. 'Well, if I'm weak with her, she does what she damn well pleases. Orders groceries, falls down trying to reach her purse, needs the landlady to peel her off the floor. I told her to let me do the shopping and get the Biasin boy downstairs to close her bedroom window before he leaves for school. It's a casement that's got no screen and –'

'Okay, okay. Don't relive it all. You'll drive me nuts too. Your problem is you care *too* much. I'll arrange things here.'

'What do you mean?'

'My business.'

'Oh.' Disappointment sagged in Pauli's voice.

'I'll try to arrive early next week. I'll phone Mom today. Can she reach the phone all right?'

'I may be away. There's a conference I need to attend.' Raw hunger for a change of scenery. How could Frank blame Mom's tantrums on Pauli's caring first too little, then too much? Goddamn double bind families get you into.

People make you crazy; people will make you sane. Maybe – if you're an optimist with leisure to do something about it.

With a green paper napkin Pauli wiped perspiration from her forehead and underarms. The bra between her breasts was soaked too. The essence of caring too much: your deodorant fails. If anybody could succeed with the nursing-home idea, it was Frank. Maybe if they just got her to tour the brighter, cheerier one in Eastdale. At $700 per week any place was extortion, but Mrs Quinn seemed sympathetic, certainly no monster who tied the senile to bedframes. Only two patients with broken hips had even been in bed. How to explain to Frank her aim wasn't to create a wall of guilt but to achieve some action in a situation that was gnawing everything it touched? Was Frank, the kid brother, still expecting her lead in every social situation? But this one had paralysed Pauli's will for months. Her mother's creeping paralysis merely underscored the misery.

If only she could use Stevens' storm of comments and questions in the research papers to deduce who'd killed him . . . But after poring over pages and figures until midnight she had to agree with Morgan Dianis. Stevens was an equal opportunity critic: *everybody* seemed to receive the lashings of his tongue or pen. She must have got the only tenderness he had left to give. *Stevens, tell me who killed you*.

To calm down, Pauli brewed a pot of de-caff and munched some sugarless cookies. She avoided two mini-Danish from yesterday's office party. No sense adding a hypoglycaemic high to the official list of Golden woes.

Her apartment lay clothes- and dishes-strewn from a week of rushing to work at 8 a.m. and returning at 9 p.m. As long as she hovered in the kitchen this morning, she could ignore it.

'Heather? It's Pauli Golden. How're you doing? How about a drive today? It's beautiful out. Maybe a picnic at Kent Falls?' Aim high. She layered the questions in a rush, fearing Heather would say no.

'H'lo.' Heather's voice arrived muffled. Pauli guessed the

call had awakened her. She envied people without insomnia or schedules who slept until 11 a.m.

'What?'

Patiently Pauli repeated her own name and added the string of invitations. 'Are you feeling all right?'

'I think so. I don't know. I just tried out this library job. They made a summer opening for me.' Heather was returning to normal consciousness. 'The system's computerised now. It's more complicated than it used to be. If you make a mistake, it gets recorded unto the sixth digit.'

'I know what you mean. You'll get used to it. The first time I used Medline, I figured a book or even last year's newspaper could have told me easier. Just inscribe your sign-on number in your soul and you'll do fine.'

'After this week that's just where it is. That what's exhausted me,' Heather admitted. 'By the way, sorry I was so morbid that last time. I was falling apart from the funeral and all. I'm better now.'

Heather's apology for what wasn't even her fault – something the murderer had stolen from both of them – touched Pauli. Lizann had never apologised for anything. Heather possessed such grace; why hadn't Stevens appreciated it?

Still nervous with this woman who had been his wife, Pauli retreated to the safe ground of planning details. 'Want to climb up the falls? It's an exquisite spot.' In another two minutes they'd settled on taking Pauli's car and a picnic lunch Heather would pack.

Was it masochistic to be lonely enough to spend the day with the wife of your dead lover? Was it the endless hours with her mother that had practised her at concealing guilt? In loving Stevens, she'd merely borrowed someone Heather no longer wanted.

After washing and dressing in sandals, sleeveless gold blouse, and wrap-around Indian skirt ('bleeding Madras,' according to the sales clerk), Pauli felt energised enough to slit open Lizann's letter.

My dear Pauli

So far, so good. If only 'I regret ending our life like I did. I'll be back. Will you have me?' had followed. It didn't. Pauli deciphered more of the jumbled writing.

Here life is quite different and so the pace, rhythm and energy are also different. People are still into the *agréments de la vie* – eating, walking in nature, conversation, wine, the arts, etc. I have calmed down and I am taking things more easily with less hysteria. I feel better in Paris.

Claude is a good companion. I'm not passionately in love with him –

Then how the hell are you running a marriage? Jealousy stifled Pauli's breathing. She forced her eyes back on to the page.

but he's devoted and affectionate. We get along fine. He has children from a previous marriage living in the south of France.

I will always love you, Pauli, I assure you, but our life together just wasn't working. You must see that by this time. If I hadn't made a scene, I never could have left. You must see that.

I'm working at –

Pauli dropped the letter on to the table, recalling that 'scene' from the 'life together that wasn't working', despite twelve years' acquaintance and ten living together. When budget cuts destroyed Lizann's final job teaching French, Pauli had painfully watched her lover's self-esteem plummet. Instead of rehitting the CV and phone trail, Lizann had crumpled into an ever smaller but irritable lump upon the suede sofa until they shared no more conversations. And the love-making, at first so exquisite, always tender, also ceased. No more spaghetti or veal dinners, with wine flowing throughout, the delightful prelude to Lizann's leg-between-her-legs, her tongue caressing Lizann's face on the way to their double bed.

And all the ten good years (well, nine and a half, until Lizann slumped) counting for nothing the night of the final fight. Lizann shouting, 'We never were alike, Pauli. You imagined it. Why didn't I stay in California? Even the weather was better there.'

'Because I invited you here . . . Send out your CVs again. Are you helpless?' *And chock full of self-pity.*

'Maybe I am . . . Pauli, I need a . . . normal life. I'm sick of living hidden the way we do.'

'We're not *hidden*. And you're the first one to say you don't like lesbian bars.'

'That's the problem. Cindy's Place is the only place we ever go as a couple.'

'So you're sick of *me*.' Then Pauli tried a final time. 'Look, if it's money, I'll earn for both of us till you get back on your feet.'

'Pauli, I've been seeing a . . . man. In the daytime. He's visiting here from France to study –'

'Why?' Pauli had shrieked.

Tears. And no answer except that yearning for the 'normal life'. And when Claude – pompous, pudgy man who looked like a chipmunk in plaid neckties – came courting Lizann, he made Pauli's flesh crawl. If she relived the scene a thousand times, she would never know what he offered Lizann that she hadn't already and gladly given her – a home, tenderness, love, money, faithful and good sex. Claude offered a new start in Europe, marriage, children. But Lizann hadn't pined for any of these, even a new job, before meeting him. Indeed, her final school assignment had included a teachers' strike, a bombing and getting mugged in her classroom.

'You don't even know *what* sex you are. He's normal, and you're – nothing.' Their final fight, even after nearly a year, still stung and shrivelled Pauli. Not believing herself worthy of love, Lizann couldn't love anybody. Was that it?

No wonder Stevens got you on the rebound. If Pauli really was bisexual, then equally what was Lizann? How even to discuss these phenomena on what seemed, for most people, the omega edge of reality?

Pauli recalled the geneticist who had maligned a woman who refused abortion although he had informed her she was carrying an oddly defective foetus. Pauli had asked, 'Well, what *is* wrong with being a genetic mosaic? The child will have some XO and some XY cells. Maybe it's not so bad being . . . bisexual.' Was that the correct term? Perspiring, she had loosened her collar.

The doctor's jaw had dropped. 'Well, of course, without gross abnormality he may survive childhood, but think of the problems at adolescence.' Pauli noted the automatic masculine pronoun, then remembered her own adolescent years trying to decide whether she loved men, women, both or neither, until she met Lizann during her 'junior year with a broad', as they later joked.

In the kitchen Pauli had dropped Lizann's letter on to the table. When she raised her head again, she discovered the thumb she was biting had intercepted the flow of tears down her own cheek. Must be her week for bombshell letters. Ironic: Stevens, who never said he loved her, really had, while Lizann, who had declared love and attraction, forgot both in her frenzied quest for 'normal life' – whatever *that* was. What still hurt was not that Lizann preferred a man but that after making Pauli swear oaths of undying fidelity, it was Lizann who opted for open marriage in the form of a one-way ticket to Paris.

Speaking of muddling through, she now hid Lizann's letter under the bread-box, boiled water for more coffee and began to read yesterday's paper. The garden club was revving up for late summer, and the Decibelles, a ladies' choral group, desired volunteers, particularly alto, for the autumn.

Amazing that suburban women still had leisure and money to subsidise this wash of volunteerism. They were keeping alive the only work world Mom thought appropriate for ladies – genteel dabbling, financed by indulgent husbands. Anything else supposedly threatened the fragile male ego. Stevens, Harry, Jacobs, Morgan, Arthur, even Sara – a frail ego? Hah!

On the kitchen pad Pauli wrote in black block script:

1. See Sara privately.
2. Follow Stevens' final advice about Mom: Do what you can, but don't let her load herself on you. And don't let her make you feel guilty. No magic solutions at her age.
3. Phone Frank to share it.
4. Jog before bed. To hell with the heat.
5. Stop reading the social page.

14

      By noon Pauli and Heather were winding along the river road north towards the falls in Pauli's ancient red VW. The passing greenery, bright under midsummer sun, calmed Pauli. After a few comments Heather rested her head back and closed her eyes. Pauli watched the white water rapids tumbling within feet of the road. Every mile and curve brought a different fisherman complete with pipe and waders, his baitbox and deckchair onshore wherever the rushing river relented enough to allow a shore. How about driving Frank here? Would probably bore him after all the Colorado gorges. But these New England hills that had sculpted the falls and smaller rapids appeared more human-sized. You could encompass them at near view without needing to stand 50 miles off.

      The panorama of evergreen foothills unrolled before Pauli. Watching roses and ivy along picket fences and stonewalls, she felt grateful. Stevens' death, cancer, strokes, accident – all faded into the mountain distance. Mile by mile her zest reflowed. How about driving herself and sleeping Heather all the way to Canada? It resembled having Lizann again, except . . .

      'I need a vacation,' Pauli announced to the steering wheel.

      'What?' Heather jerked awake. 'Oh-hh. My neck. I kinked it sideways. Why didn't you tell me I was falling asleep?' She massaged her shoulder and neck muscles.

      'And have you fall over when we get there?'

      'Nap for the little girl, huh? But I'm older than you are,

aren't I? Well, all this week I've had this terrific pain around my stomach muscles. It goes away when I eat.'

'And how much weight do you want to gain?' Pauli grinned.

'I think it's just anxiety. You know, what they call "anxiety attack"?'

'I don't believe in them. My specialty is nightmares and insomnia.'

'Being alone in the house at night is giving *me* the creeps,' Heather answered. 'And I was never afraid of the dark. Every time some old floorboard cracks, I leap and look all around. I wish they'd find Stevens' killer. I imagine him coming back. Creeping up the stairs to my room and then –'

'Stop it, Heather.' Pauli laid a hand on Heather's arm. 'If it was a burglar, why didn't he steal something? It was . . . some work problem Stevens had. I *know* it's something with the research but I can't prove anything yet.'

Heather rushed on as if she hadn't heard. 'Sure. A burglar who specialises in antiques. I call the police. They just say, we're working on it. They're doing nothing.'

'They can't accuse somebody till they get enough evidence.'

'What evidence now July's nearly over? I thought they just falsified it and accused somebody anyway to get the case solved.'

'They can hardly do that with all the Institute and a quarter of the Medical Center's doctors involved.'

Heather relapsed to brooding.

Something with the research. Arthur's, Burl's, Merrill's, Morgan's Xeroxed papers – and Coral's face, floating between Pauli and the road. What with the research? Heather was speaking again. 'What?' questioned Pauli. 'I didn't hear you.'

'You were daydreaming. I said, I wish I had somebody to live in the house with me. All those big rooms just glooming around.'

'You know my brother's coming in a few days. How about the three of us doing something fascinating?'

Heather stared. 'What d'you mean? I'm really not up to . . . socialising.'

'Okay. If you don't like him, you have my permission to be nasty.' Pauli tried to joke. Was everybody paranoid? *Stop menacing me with your friendliness.* Maybe Heather's loneliness was a pose, though she hardly seemed the type to play for sympathy. Stevens had trained her well.

Heather laughed. 'I should warn you. I'm not the last of the bigtime cooks. Steve was so fussy I finally gave up in despair.'

Pauli bit her own tongue to keep from replying, 'Well, he ate my quiche and salad.' Maybe Frank's presence would work a miracle, ward off mooning over both Stevens and Lizann.

'I wanted one of those gourmet men who relax from the office by cooking everything in sight.'

'And you didn't get one?' asked Pauli.

'*Steve?* He couldn't boil an egg if the hen laid it in water!'

Pauli began to laugh so hard a back tyre swerved off the road. She changed gear to keep the motor going.

Heather had swept her yard of blond hair into a sort of Victorian puff secured with a pearl clip on top of her head. A study in white from tennis shirt over white jeans down to sneakers, she looked the bride at a hippie wedding. So this was the Heather beyond the ruby silk suit, who had outraged Stevens' more sedate tastes in women's fashions.

'Steve and I weren't . . . doing very well,' Heather confided. She stared out the window as if addressing herself. 'If I didn't produce a child, I was, well, worthless. Most of the time I just . . . hated him. Dependent hate.'

Why tell me? Again Pauli bit her lip. If Heather blurted out such things to anyone who gained her confidence, it wouldn't do at all for her to discover about Pauli and Stevens. Pauli sighed, realising she wasn't much more talented at deception than Heather. Whatever poise she possessed was hard won from interviewing 3,000 people, some hysterical with fear of surgery, doctors, drugs.

'Hey, don't torture yourself, huh? It's over now.' Maybe her genuine sympathy could penetrate Heather's exhaustion or self-pity, whatever had created the mood.

'No. It's not over,' Heather protested.

An hour later they had zigzagged up the path of log and earth stairs to the pines and meadow above the falls. Crunchy, fragrant needles carpeted the brown forest floor. Pauli had climbed easily, the cumulative effect of nightly jogging. Beside her, Heather stood panting at the rickety single-rail fence, all that separated them from the verdant, moist emptiness that hung above the crashing falls. Sheets of water had carved four separate terraces as they plunged a quarter of a mile down from the earth beneath Pauli's feet to the valley and river below.

Pauli breathed the damp air. Pine bark on the railing chafed her fingers. She had stifled her first urge, to put an arm about Heather's waist or shoulders, six inches above her own.

For the first time in weeks Pauli felt her own nervous restlessness quelled. Heather's particular gentleness relaxed her. Such a quality must be what had both attracted and held Stevens through the years and how Heather had endured the whole business. Wasn't this 'shelter from the storm' just what she had provided Lizann, now magically regiven for a few minutes, anyway, while they both gazed into the tumbling waters? Maybe it – this surfeit of comfortable welcome that Heather exuded – had begun to bore Stevens, as it had Lizann. Yet to have anybody truly on your side who lasted more than four dates still seemed a miracle to Pauli.

Again she ached for Stevens' body, the few months when he'd given most of her irregular urges some outlet, more than four dates' worth and at least enough to forget Lizann for a few hours a week.

When would she learn to be self-contained? Must be what fascinated her about Stevens, that paradoxical talent for commitment with non-involvement that she'd hoped would rub off. Never had yet; looked as if it never would. She sighed.

'What's the matter?' Heather asked.

'It's not your fault. I don't know.' Pauli cursed her own indecision. Couldn't avoid Heather, couldn't drop her either. That would cut her next-to-final link with Stevens, who had been inside both their bodies. Pauli started from her reverie and stared around. Distinctly she felt someone or something watching them. Must be nervous. Who even knew she was here? The feeling persisted though, and she shivered.

A mass of youngsters, grandparents and leashed collies that had climbed the first stage of the path upwards now paused at level three below them. Pauli watched bobbing heads, the multihued T-shirts and sweaters.

Heather sensed the mood. Suddenly she spoke, 'Pauli, I know Stevens was seeing somebody. It's not that he was different towards me. I told you about the marriage. It was just the times he was gone that he used to be – anyway, can you help me find out who it was? Because it's tortured me, who she is, what she's like. It sealed how we were no good for each other. Maybe it's why they killed him, a love affair, somebody at the lab. Damn that place!' Heather clutched at Pauli's hand. 'Look, Pauli, was it you he saw sometimes? Tell me what you know.' At first it sounded like an order; then Pauli realised Heather was begging. 'You're so . . . quiet.'

In confusion Pauli stared at the roaring water. *Yes. No. I saw him last but I didn't kill, never would have . . . I'm a lesbian who just yearned to put her arm about you. No true lesbian runs an affair with a macho like your husband. Damn*! If she said she had, Heather would drop their friendship. If she said she hadn't because no lesbian would, Heather would drop her hand – as well as her acquaintance. In any case, they'd walk down and drive back in silence stony enough to rival these mountains. Until the recriminations began.

The clutch on Pauli's hand increased. Heather's eyes darted from side to side. Was her gentleness, like Stevens' quietness, a façade that broke?

'Heather, I know . . . who it was, it isn't what you think. She didn't plan . . . to marry him. She thought he didn't love her! I –'

'Hel-loo, girls. What have we here? I say.' At the mockery in the hearty British voice behind her ear, Pauli whirled to confront a green vision of a man – mint silk pocket handkerchief, an alpine hat, fern tie and shirt under a

Lincoln-green jacket, mossy suede shoes. Edward stood there, looking freshly escaped from a costume party in Oscar Wilde's conservatory, from a potted palm in a bad British play. Must be rehearsing a spaced-out leprechaun ad for the Irish Tourist Board.

'Edward! What're you doing here? You've been spying on us,' Pauli managed the first comment. 'You scared us,' she scolded. Heather stood, mouth open, one hand against her chest, with her back bent out over the rickety railing. Focused on Edward now, not on Pauli.

'It's the noise of the falls, my dears. You just didn't hear me.' Edward sidestepped the spy charge. 'I'm parked on the road over there. Will you ladies join me for some refreshment?' He gestured through the pines and across the meadow.

Once beyond the shocks of Heather's confrontation plus a semi-stranger a foot behind her Pauli forced her lips together to avoid ridiculing Edward's outfit. 'You're looking very . . . natty today,' she remarked, attempting some neutral comment.

'I went to a workshop this morning.'

'Oh.' Pauli feared to enquire as to the organisation, if it wasn't Leprechauns Anonymous. Edward must be gay; but that didn't explain it all. Pauli could intercept those signals – and usually relax when she met them. Edward's superheartiness, whether met in corridor or woods, just dismayed or embarrassed, however. Either it meant nothing or it was concealing something. Anything to forget Stevens and quiet Heather for a few minutes, though.

'Do you have any beer?' Pauli asked.

'Sorry, my dear. Chablis, five years old, chilled to perfection?'

If we stay here, there's no way to shake him. In Heather's view Pauli rolled her eyes skyward, hoping the silent message was received. Guilt surfaced next; all Edward's personality and antics were interrupting was useless mourning for Stevens, not even her husband but somebody else's, plus a conversation that could end in tears or argument.

Heather appeared exhausted now, but only the uninitiated

would confuse that with grief. That must be one reason Heather had agreed to come; with Pauli she could cease playing Grieving Widow. When Pauli shrugged a shoulder, Heather announced, 'I'll get our food.'

'Don't trouble,' Edward offered. 'I'll drive my car to the lower park and meet you.'

'The walk'll do me good. Give me the car keys,' Heather muttered above the water noise. She strode down the earthen steps. Pauli's unexpected agreement to Edward's presence must have miffed her. She might not return at all. Well, then Pauli could escape by pretending to search for her. Damn – all these green, quirky angles to what had been a no-stress country outing.

Fresh fears surfaced. How long had Edward been watching? How much did he hear? Worse, was he following them?

'Your chariot awaits, mademoiselle,' Edward said, smiling broadly and pointing across the meadow. They started downwards.

'Edward, do you always talk like that? I can't stand it.' She wanted to add, 'At the lab they think you're crazy.'

Hurt distorted his face. 'You American women. So literal, so prosaic.'

'Come off it. There aren't many places in Britain either where you can ham it up like that and get away with it.'

'The work I do is so boring, soulless really. In my private life –'

'You ham it up.'

'What a crude expression. I did join a Playmakers group two years ago. This autumn we're doing *Man of La Mancha* and *Paint Your Wagon*. If it weren't for that –'

'What's the matter, Edward? Is it really your work?' All of a sudden Pauli felt ridiculously maternal towards this man who was nearly her own age.

'Oh, it's Dr Stornell. He's on my back all the time, every sick animal, every Petri dish.'

Pauli smiled, appearing charitable while she laughed at this vision of Edward, Man of La Mancha, tilting at Petri dishes. 'I know,' she commented.

Edward looked so relieved he didn't even enquire how she knew. If Rainette with all her marital and secretarial experience of male tantrums could describe the lab under Harry as 'grotesque', no wonder Edward was cracking his pea-green seams. Poor guy, probably about to be sacked, as she had been.

'The Playmakers are doing an evening performance near here today. Summer stock. Would you and Heather grant me the honour of your company?'

Your poor sick mother at death's door. Reality, not stage fantasy. 'Edward, I should check with Heather. She probably needs to get back, and I should look in on my mother.'

'We could have dinner,' Edward urged. 'Rustic country inn, hot popovers, relishes, waterfall, ducks, termites, all that bucolic sort of thing.' He stared at Pauli, who met his yearning eyes. Next, as if gauging his chances behind the final pine before the meadow and crowded car park, Edward leaned forward from the waist. He kissed Pauli loudly on one cheek. Somewhere between a stage bow and a goldfish gulping air, it was the most non-sexual kiss Pauli remembered since somebody's seven-year-old slobbered her cheek in exchange for cocoa with marshmallows.

Stevens' black hair and probing tongue resurged. Ignore it; maybe it'll disappear. 'Where's your car?' Pauli asked.

Nervously Edward indicated a wreck of a beige station wagon – amazing antithesis to his dapper appearance. Like me, probably can't afford anything newer. From another car, rock 'n' roll music suddenly blared. Now Pauli felt onstage.

'I'll get the wine and quiche, my dear,' Edward announced. Well, this would shame Heather's tuna fish and beer.

Slowly Pauli followed him across the pebbly car park. Was it only a few weeks ago she'd pitied Edward's lot as veterinary assistant and general clean-up man to generations of waspish scientists and doomed mice – 'cute little buggers, aren't they?' Plus swabbing counters, answering phones, filing reports, washing and sterilising dishes, the dirty work that even Leon, the ageing janitor, escaped by confining himself to floors and sinks, gardening and heating problems.

But Edward had worshipped Stevens, hadn't he?

Pauli stared at him, wondering what else besides theatre churned under his pointed Alpine hat. As he raised the tail-gate door of his car, Pauli could see the strangest collection of miscellaneous metal and unrecognisable junk.

'Props,' Edward explained.

Hoisting the wicker basket of food, he disturbed a wad of plaid flannel blanket. Metal inside it glinted in the sunshine, and before Edward hastily reburied it, Pauli had recognised it. It was the silver cat statue, gold-trimmed, onyx-mounted, whose thin Siamese face and slit eyes had probed her once from Harry's desk. His research icon from a building squirming with mice – now borrowed, stolen, dumped into the back of Edward's car. As Pauli stood on tiptoe to see what else he'd stashed under the 'props', Edward slammed the tail-gate door shut.

26 July – On the Road

Scared at first in the half-light. Your hand shook. Stage fright. Stevens' front, then back, lit like some idol. Who else would spend our victory party criticising papers, crucifying staff?

Weapon grew warm in your pocket, inside where he couldn't see. Second by second you caressed it. His last on earth. Large rat sacrificed. Terminal tyranny. Just another experiment for me to clean up. No big performance.

'You little prick! Can't get it up for work other people need. And mistakes. Shape up. Or I report to the trustees. And you clear out, no recommendations.'

Crucifying us in his holy war for logic and truth.

His penis like a shrivelled worm. And I feared him those years. Under his belt buckle soft like a woman.

Who's the little prick now?

Tell it to the worms.

15

After a few hours' fitful sleep Pauli lay first chilled, then perspiring, longing for someone asleep or awake to curl into. No help in that direction now. Stuffing a pillow between her legs renewed the shivers. Must be exhaustion – or summer flu.

Birdsong, a bluejay's screech, and what sounded like a goose honk came from the dawn outside her window. Did they perch on the roof among the TV antennae forest where she used to sun? She touched the remaining lump in her left breast. Still there. She sighed.

And next, what to do about Heather?

Yet Heather seemed to have done something about herself, a truce that would hold at present. All Heather's strength had exhausted itself in the one near-question, just as Edward had arrived, and in eating mechanically during the picnic. She'd slept through the darkness of the ride home. At first this had miffed Pauli, who blamed Edward and then Heather for derailing their outing, but wasn't a sleeping Heather preferable to a questioning one?

Pauli rehearsed ten ways to handle the awkwardness when it arose again: yes, Stevens and I made love a few times, but he seemed too preoccupied to give what you or I would call 'love'.

Great flirt but lousy lover who rarely returned my phone calls and then only when Sara was eavesdropping. *True.*

Who, me? *I know who it was; she didn't plan to marry him.* True and false. Pauli's own words now haunted her.

113

What of the nearer truth? I loved him. He loved me, but I never could have married him. I look and act like other women, but when somebody concludes I'm 'different', the game is up.

Truly I loved Lizann, but when she left to live 'normal' last October after ten years, I went wacky for a taste of 'normality' myself. It didn't work. Sorry it was your husband.

And how to camouflage any of it into something Heather wouldn't blurt out during the next police grilling? Heather, I fell in love with your husband, but he was the same deadhead who discouraged you. Because I thought he didn't care, I was ready to break it off.

That at least covered one corner of the truth, because all of it sounded more ridiculous: I took up with your husband because he challenged me. I was on the rebound from Lizann; I was lonely. You can understand, can't you? No. Who understands anybody who loves both male and female? If it isn't freakish, then it's promiscuous. Heterosexuals have a ball with serial marriages but theoretically only one at a time – and only from the opposite sex. How dull . . .

Why owe Heather anything? If she's tactless enough to force the issue again, drop her. Ease your way out because her anger will wind up on a police form headed with your name. Again Pauli sighed.

And what to do about Edward? The cat statue had no part, even as prop, in either of Edward's productions. The picnic had consisted of his mimicking several characters' voices in each play while Pauli laughed despite herself and Heather dozed on the plaid blanket, opening an occasional eye. Edward needed to be seen as well as heard; he thrived on an audience. How sad his loneliness.

Harry's statue getting lifted by whomever served him right. Spite on Edward's part – to be expected from a disgruntled employee. Again Pauli wondered and cursed her off-hours involvement with what should be a routine job like any other freelance assignment. Except that Stevens had been no routine lover. Get the facts; transmute them into something readable, plausible and timely; get paid and leave.

Why did the Institute refuse to fit this stable pattern? Instead, whenever she touched one part or captured it on paper, another part ballooned like an aneurysm barely containing problems, questions, dangers. Part of the mess must involve the nature of cancer itself, the disease that has either one cause or six dozen, that can be prevented tomorrow or can't be prevented at all in a polluted society. Maddening to interview and write about. Reaching the moon merely exploited existing technology and theory, which united in a centralised wart at Cape Canaveral, while curing cancer involved quarrelsome people and confusing events dispersed like viruses over the globe. Researchers like Arthur, Merrill or Morgan obtained 'significant' results one year, then dropped into nowhere if they couldn't reproduce or explain those results. Or the 'promising' labour later proved less promising, and people went on dying anyway.

Morgan's and Arthur's results were both impressive. If cancer proved to be a virus, Arthur had the cure and the Nobel Prize already in his saggy pocket. And in paper after paper, Morgan not only grew malignant tumours, he regressed them at will and on schedule. Animals that should have died at six months persisted to a geriatric two years. And that was but one of his projects. The man must be a genius to coordinate so many additional ones. Hadn't she seen and touched the animals herself? Morgan displayed them like precious children. No doubt he also enjoyed wowing the less than impressed among visiting doctors and Congressmen, whose first and last question amounted to, 'Dr Dianis, what relevance has this for humans?' If besides research, the Swedes awarded the Nobel for charm, Morgan deserved a standing ticket to Stockholm.

Something with the research. Stevens' question marks and pencilled comments decorated the reports – Arthur's, Morgan's, everybody's. Apparently nobody escaped the perfectionist red and blue queries: 'Check this', 'Why assume this?', 'Needs reworking', 'Doesn't follow', 'Arithmetical error. Can't you add?' One of Arthur's papers even merited an insulting, 'Doctor, check your medical dictionary for the differences between a bacterium and a virus.'

115

Coral, the needlepointer/mouse surgeon, had raised Stevens' ire when she neglected chart-keeping on how many animals she anaesthetised, cancerised, sacrificed or sutured back together. When Coral remarked before Pauli that paperwork wasn't her specialty, Stevens had replied, 'I'm not interested in your preferences. I'm interested in what needs doing.'

But if Stevens meted out equal punishment to everyone, then that must mean he singled out no one for permanent or special opprobrium. Anyway, it didn't bother Morgan. He could angle around anybody. Pauli re-envied these guys' endless ability to sublimate, repress, suppress, forget. How did they do it? Lousy memory? Self-conceit? Maybe breastfed by doting mothers until they entered kindergarten in blue-lace diapers? My son the doctor.

The frustration gnawing everywhere at her life gave her insomnia and now the flu. She shivered. Better get up, take two aspirins and call somebody in twenty years.

At 7 a.m. the local radio news – singing bank and car ads interspersed with Saturday night car crashes, burglaries and bar-room fights – blared through the kitchen while Pauli collected and washed a week of dishes, steelware, casseroles. Lemon soapy water warmed and soothed her chilly arms. If housework proved such stunning therapy ('good for what ails you' – her mother's hallowed but unfollowed adage), maybe Pauli should try it more often. Sure beats brooding on the Institute, fantasies of saving Stevens' life had she stayed longer that night, won enough of his trust to advise him out of the problem for which he died, helped peacemake between him and Heather. Now *that* was a masochistic special, but such might-bes had lulled her to sleep for months. Just give me good sex and I'll follow you anywhere.

Intent on the slippery dishes and her wobbly knees, Pauli missed the first mention of Edward Mistal's name by the fresh-from-radio-school announcer. '. . . 1 o'clock this morning. Campus security guards arrested Mr Mistal as he was making delivery of medical supplies, equipment and silver sculpture to an undercover police agent. The ring is thought to be responsible for the disappearance of university equipment and microscopes from the science building and from the Medway Institute for Cancer Research in the last few months. The total dollar amount of the thefts is unknown pending further investigation. Mr Mistal has been charged with larceny, burglary in the third degree and possession of stolen property. In recent months university staff had reported a list of missing supplies and equipment, beginning the police investigation.'

Pauli jerked fully awake. Edward! Captured and arrested last night in his Lincoln-green jacket, holding Harry's hot statue in his hand. After the picnic and play he must have returned to the city for his Saturday night fencing party. Clever little bastard. So that's how *he* sublimated hatred of Harry and a demeaning job. But Stevens had lured him – or he'd followed Stevens – to the job. Suppose they'd fought, and Stevens had told him what a pea-green ass he truly appeared?

Was he in jail already? The cat statue nagged Pauli. Say nothing. Let the police work it out. If they caught him hauling table-top computers and electron microscopes, what difference that you saw him with silver and gold before the 1 a.m. bust? No difference except that Edward must be a liar as well as a thief. And had seen Stevens and Pauli together once when Edward bumped a trolley ('Awkward devils, these!') into Stevens' nearly closed office door. She'd just put a hand over Stevens' on the desk. *Dumb, Pauli.*

But she and Heather had met Edward only yesterday. Would anybody having an affair invite the wronged woman on a picnic?

Yes.

Would Edward, to save his own gnomish neck and reduce his sentence, reveal any irregularities seen during lawful and unlawful duties at the Institute?

Why not? Much more credible – and necessary – than inviting your dead lover's wife to a country outing. Pauli began to perspire.

In the bathroom she squinted at the mercury in her thermometer. 101.5 degrees – not bad for an amateur. No wonder she sweated one moment, shivered the next. Maybe

Edward had given her malaria besides this bad and present case of the shakes. The wise action, for organised types who plan, would be to desert the apartment 'on vacation' before the police arrived back. But today's Sunday. Surely even a diligent homicide squad wouldn't investigate on Sunday? If they've spent three weeks without a break, they'll investigate any time.

The dilemma of living alone: no roommate to drive you and your car to the airport. Anything you don't do yourself doesn't happen – except if you own and operate a self-sacrificing daughter.

Ringing roused Pauli from a routine nightmare in which some faceless person, gender unseen, was pushing her face into a black hole. The ringing relieved the choking agony until she recognised it as the doorbell chimes. Maybe if she curled there very still, they'd go away.

Rejecting the frightened-mouse technique, she flung her aqua satin robe about her shoulders. At the end of the double bed she steadied herself. When the dizziness and trembling stopped, she heard the chimes again.

'Miss Golden, we took a chance you'd be here today.'

'I'm not. I've got flu or something. That's why I'm not dressed.'

Pauli peered out the open door. Grey-haired Tight Lip stood there with a different police assistant, more his own age this time.

Pauli shuddered. Good guess. Having grilled Edward into the dawn, the police were now paying a friendly Sunday morning – afternoon? – visit. She imagined streaking past them down the stairs.

'Come in. I'm not going anywhere.' Maybe the combined aspirin and cold tablets would dull her reactions so they'd get no more this time than the last. Stevens' killer should pay, but how to do that without losing both her jobs in a scandal? Jacobs tolerated what she'd told him on her private life with Lizann, but an affair with a man that ended in medical crime? Sara would thrill to any dirt.

Pauli sought a comfortable spot on the sofa, but every

change of position brought fresh flashes of shooting pain. *Don't squirm.* Her mother's voice.

After watching her, Detective Jordan opened a folder and began quietly – to put her at ease or because he was bored, she couldn't tell. 'We have your signed statement here, Miss Golden, from the day after the homicide. Let's see. You arrived at the Stevens' party with Dr Morgan Dianis. You greeted Mrs St Steven and listened to an Institute employee recite poetry. At approximately 11.30 p.m. you said good-night to Dr St Steven in his study. He seemed "preoccupied", you said, with his various work problems. You saw no one else enter the room. Then you drove home. Do you have anything else to add, anything you've remembered since that night?'

Tell them about Arthur's or Coral's problems. About the cat statue. 'No. I would have called you. Well, it's Rainette who phoned me at about 1 a.m. and told me what happened.' What did they want now? Must be about Edward. As Pauli tried to recall the orange room, brown rug, and warm, live Stevens, already the details floated, then faded from her mind. Had Stevens worn a belt or tie? What colour blue was his shirt? Even his face now hovered, then faded. How the living protect themselves from –

'We have new evidence in this investigation. In the light of fresh facts we hope for your full cooperation.' Did he stress the word 'full' or had she imagined that? To keep her balance on the sofa and focus her eyes, she stared at the men's white shirts and navy ties. It banished the fog. 'I'll try, but I'm only half alive today. What d'you mean, new evidence?' Sound dumb.

This time the other policeman (had she heard the name Rose?) spoke. He had a face as blunt and jowly as Jordan's was thin and calculating. Must be high blood pressure. Both men had bloodshot eyes, like somebody Pauli had interviewed once who claimed he prospered on three hours' sleep a night.

'Miss Golden, it appears from our sources you spent considerably more time at the Institute than you said. And you spent most of it with Dr St Steven. Correct?'

'Well, I was paid by the piece not the hour. I don't know exactly how long I spent there, but I never neglected my regular job if that's what you mean.'

Detective Rose smiled. 'While you were there, did you hear anyone complain of unusual problems, missing equipment, anything like that?'

'Not before Dr St Steven's death. Since then, well, I've returned to get folders of material he left for me. I write on cancer all the time in my job and –'

'How about missing equipment?'

'Yes. Dr Dianis complained about a box of missing syringes and some scalpels, but he's not very organised. And I heard about a statue.' Pauli wiped her forehead. This ramble all over was confusing her. Why didn't they just mention Edward and finish it?

'Were you having an affair with Stevens St Steven?' Detective Jordan suddenly shouted, multiplying the ringing in Pauli's ears.

She jumped, then bit her tongue hard to stay mute. She tasted blood.

'We have evidence from several persons that you saw Dr St Steven much beyond a few articles.'

'What d'you mean?' Pauli demanded. 'Who's saying these things?'

Jordan flipped a few more pages. 'Sara Spaulding at your magazine told us you're over there "all the time whenever her mother calls here". Miss Spaulding's phrase. She seemed to feel you neglect your mother.'

Pauli burned. 'Sara's jealous. You can't get anywhere in business – be a reporter instead of a secretary – without making somebody jealous. She probably earns half of what I do,' Pauli retorted, 'but most of my money supports my mother. As for neglecting her, I spend nearly every Saturday helping her. She's been sick for years, and I was just on the phone to my brother yesterday to get him to lend a hand.' Shut up or they'll push you any way they want.

At first Tight Lip seemed to ignore the advantage of ambush he'd gained. Detective Rose sat silent. Why wasn't he playing the good guy second who supposedly rescued you from his boss's nasty aggression?

'Miss Spaulding also mentioned your close relationship with Lizann Gates.'

Pauli gasped. Goddamn Sara! Avoid all loverly phone conversations, and somehow the gossips intuit anyway. Might as well wear lesbian lavender sweater and earrings and tell the world.

Detective Jordan smiled, having, Pauli gathered, now scored his second point. 'It's not illegal. These relationships – between women, that is – shouldn't be condemned. I've never seen a lesbian booked on any charge more serious than getting drunk. Well, a few got busted at a demonstration a while ago. But we never get them on prostitution.' Again his dry smile.

Only after they get fired from jobs because of people like you and Sara!

'So,' he continued, 'you repeat that your relationship with Dr St Steven was for business reasons.'

Pauli sat stymied, awash in emotions and fever. If Jordan wants to hang gay men (Edward?), how real could his tolerance for women be? Encouraging her on this topic must be in exchange for what he hoped to extract about Stevens. 'Of course, he's – Stevens *was* a married man.' How to exonerate herself without involving Heather, who also suspected too much?

'Then why were you seen embracing in his office?'

Next they'd claim they had porno photos from the motel. Don't fall for that one!

'Who's telling you this? Dr St Steven was a flirt. A certain amount of flirting helps me conduct an interview, but I'm not in the habit of fooling around with my male business contacts. For the reason *you've* just mentioned.' If painting herself lesbian lavender would release her from the hook, then lavender it was. 'Who,' she repeated, 'is telling you these things?'

More paper shuffling. Couldn't these guys remember anything without a reference book? If she dared interview people when she was so half-assed uninformed, they'd kick her out. Police are civil servants. Like teachers, they needn't show result – only effort.

'Coral Deming. 9 July interrogation. Well?'

'I don't see how grilling me on Stevens' personal life will find his murderer. It was a *work* problem. That's *all* he ever thought about – work.' Give them something; they'll go away. 'Look I've got paper after paper with his question marks on everybody's arithmetic, their procedures and results. He saw something wrong with the work. That's all I know.'

'Have you got these papers? Anybody in particular he singled out?'

Pauli fumbled around her desk for the blue folder. God, the letters from both Lizann and Stevens lay inside a magazine in the top drawer! Don't leave the room this time. She answered, 'Not that I can tell. He was a perfectionist, drove hard on everybody.'

Both detectives rifled her batch of Xeroxes. 'Did he discuss these question marks and jottings with anybody you know?'

Pauli shook her head. 'Not with me. I expect with Dr Stornell. Isn't that the logical person?' Oh boy, sending them to him – dumb, Pauli.

'Perhaps.' When Jordan smiled, the cleft above his lip barely moved. 'It appears he did discuss certain matters relating to the animal care with someone.'

'Who?' Pauli demanded. 'Tell me what you want. This conversation is driving me nuts. I don't have anything you need.'

'Then why do you have these papers? Considering Dr Stornell recently terminated your relationship.'

Pauli flushed. Fever multiplied fever. Let that one go by. Probably Harry told them himself, or Coral shot her mouth again to look important. What else do they know? She shrugged. 'I told you. I use the papers in my work. My magazine does a story a month on cancer research.'

'I see . . . Did Dr St Steven ever discuss Edward Mistal with you?'

Ah, at last. 'He mentioned him when I met Edward. Edward worshipped Stevens. I think he was father figure to a lot of men there. Got them grants, high-class postgraduate stuff to work on, brand-new electron microscopes, things their universities couldn't afford. A lot of people miss Stevens.'

'Apparently.' Irony intended? Pauli couldn't tell. 'You're a perceptive person, Miss Golden. In your interviewing work you have to be. Sometimes a person like you who visits a place infrequently sees more of the whole situation than regular or specialised employees do.'

'It's possible.' Good dry reply. Beat them at their own game.

Jordan smiled and stood up, the other detective following. Cross over Jordan, doublecross Jordan. 'Remember we're still checking and rechecking Dr St Steven's activities on the days before his death. If you recall anything else, let us know. We may be back to look through these papers. We can use all leads.'

'Of course. Uh, is it all right to travel? I have a business conference this week, in San Francisco.'

Jordan stared at her. 'If it's lengthy, just call in a phone number. That's all.'

Pauli staggered after them and got the doorlocks open. Perspiration dribbled cold along her breasts and abdomen inside the nightgown.

The folder of Xeroxed question marks lay strewn across the sofa. Why hadn't the men impounded it? Did they want to observe her again? Maybe pursuing some other theory of Stevens' death – some elemental passion to which a bunch of edited ten-syllable words didn't apply.

Maybe she was wrong. Why, after all, imagine the key to Stevens' murder lay in the one assignment she happened to be given? If Stevens had hidden a whole previous wife from her, what other relationships – worship eroded into hate – had he also forgotten to mention? And remember people like Arthur who never liked Stevens at all. Tell them about Arthur's feud. Tell tales like Coral and Sara.

Pauli relocked the apartment door. She'd continue with the papers. If Stevens had found fraud in them, or elsewhere, so would she.

16

'Rainette? Hi. It's Pauli. I'm phoning from my magazine. You remember when we were talking about Institute finances? Can you get me some financial information? I expect it's already in Medway statements or the quarterly reports –'

'What do you need?'

'A list of companies and people whom the Institute has paid, say, for the last three months, with approximate amounts. Is that too difficult?'

'No. It's all in my computer – payroll, taxes, mouse chow. But I handle only the small accounts payable. Dr Stornell has to approve or write any cheque over $1,000, other than payroll, which I have a program for. Morgan got us the computer company from his previous work because it specialises in scientific and medical accounting.'

'Is there any way Dr Stornell could maybe keep a second set of books or another ledger for his private accounts?' Pauli stared at her own office wall, where Jacob's chart of impending magazine deadlines loomed redly at her. When she heard a clunk, she said, 'Rainette?'

'Sorry, I've got to escort a visitor who just showed up . . .' When Rainette lowered her voice, Pauli's heart sank. But then Rainette continued, 'Duplicate ledger? No. There's only the one. Harry and I both use it for whatever cheques the computer doesn't print.'

'Can anybody there write cheques for cash for, say, extraordinary expenses?'

'Yes, I can. For people's travel, conferences. But only Harry can sign those. Well, the accountant who does our financial statements also, but he's hardly ever here. And then Stevens.'

Silence. Pauli swallowed.

'Pauli, what's this for? Because the police –'

'Oh, an idea I'm checking about . . . what happened to Stevens.'

'Yes? Well, you know I can't hear into Stevens' office from here. Coral's the one with – Oh, I can't say more now. I'll get the list from our June statement.'

'Thanks, Rainette.'

'Pauli? I hope you meet your prince. Soon.'

'What? As I said last week, I'm not looking to get married. Besides, all *my* princes turn into frogs – or rats. They're not nice like your husband.'

Rainette laughed. 'I'll tell him.'

17

'Coral, this is Pauli Golden. Would you be able to meet me for lunch near the Institute? I need your opinion on some cancer research papers I have here. Story for my magazine. I'll buy your lunch.'

'But I heard you're not working here any more.'

'Well, that's possible . . . My magazine's also doing a new piece on women in science.' *Do two half-truths make –*

'Really? But I can't meet you now. I'm leaving for a conference. In St Louis.'

'Oh. And I'm due in San Francisco. How about –' Pauli checked her calendar. 'Next Monday?'

'I don't know. Phone me that morning. Usually I'm swamped with work when I get back here.'

'Look, is there any chance we can meet today?'

'No! Phone me Monday.' Coral slammed down the phone.

Coral sat rigid at her desk, staring at the yellow pad, scribbled with the protocol paper she was trying to compose. If she could standardise and circulate the exact steps in the commonest kinds of mouse surgery, then the lot of them would have less excuse for not doing their own. Blast that phone call. Did Pauline Golden really want her opinions on women in science? The police had asked more than enough questions for the rest of her life.

She stared at the air vent above the spare desk, stacked as usual with empty carrying cages and plastic boxes. That vent and the duct behind it must have been a test bore for the central air system, a mistake never repaired by the contractor who had renovated an old mansion, surrounding it with a modern research facility.

As she'd told the police, she could hear any loud argument in Dr St Stevens' office, just by standing on the spare desk, pretending to rearrange the cages. But she hadn't sat here most of 3 and 4 July, right before the party. She'd worked on mice in the quarantine area, where Stevens had yelled at Edward over a messy cage.

But everybody knew that, and it fit Edward's present predicament. So she'd told Detective Jordan about the late argument she'd heard between Stevens and Harry over something with computer accounts or budget. And the exchanges with various staff, including Edward, over what Stevens called 'sloppy work'.

But the police didn't know about the new insults she'd heard at the party, from the dark front-porch swing whenever the air conditioner in that library room shut off. The orange drape above it wasn't closed either, but she'd dared only one peek through there. That night Stevens had threatened the worst yet – in language foul enough to anger her too.

How could he have killed Stevens anyway, without scream or struggle? She'd heard no violence, just that stream of scathing insults over money and mistakes, plus the crude reference to his anatomy. Any others, like Pauli, might have entered that room either before or after him. Coral had driven herself home right afterwards. But he deserved protection because he worked so hard, along with them all, didn't deserve abuse, firing without recommendation, bad mouthing to the Board of Directors. So she'd continue protecting him.

Suppose she claimed she'd taped conversations in Stevens' office and maybe elsewhere? She kept the micro-cassette recorder locked in her top drawer for her own notes . . . *No. We're all tense enough.* Why not get him alone, show him she'd like some companionship? She'd wear the new dress instead of this ghastly lab coat. Last Friday to help Rainette, he'd even done his own forms. 'To save you some work,' he said, smiling at Coral too, and treating her to coffee. If only Dr St Stevens had cared that much for employees who were supposed to be colleagues . . .

And now what did Pauline Golden want? Good idea to put her off – unless she *really* cares about women in science? Coral stared at the computer-printed sign above her own desk:

I MAY BE FORGOTTEN, BUT I'M NOT GONE.

18

By taking a taxi from the airport, Pauli checked early into the chandeliered and rubber-planted hotel lobby. She planned to avoid conference claustrophobia by walking along the Embarcadero or maybe up to Chinatown. At least she could read the programme and bulletin boards, orient herself at leisure instead of jostling four deep, awaiting attention from harassed staff.

So far, from the hotel bar where she sipped a mug of coffee, she saw no one she knew. This San Francisco hotel was too far west for all but the most dedicated or expense-paid easterners to venture. Perhaps one orthodox cancer type – somebody who'd lost either his job or his grant – would attend. And here (she flipped the golden brochure) he was on the programme: Dr Basil Radison, Ph.D., a founder of the National Cancer Institute and former chief of a toxicology section. She'd heard him before. A balding man with a soft voice, he spoke against the cancer slaughter created by both camps – the orthodox types who cut, burned and poisoned people into the grave and the unorthodox zealots who believed pus draining from an untreated, ulcerated breast cancer betokened the body 'curing itself'.

And how was poor Francine from last year's conference? Alive, Pauli hoped. But how could anybody with such a walnut-sized tumour treat it to a year of prayer and vegetables? Despite Pauli's urging to get the lump removed ('it'll give the vegetables less work'), Francine had departed either cowardly or unconvinced. Pauli never knew which.

To dispel Francine's hazel, suffering eyes, Pauli drifted through the programme sheet. 'Nutritional Deficiencies Associated with Cancer'. Now that made sense. Other talks probably wouldn't: the hair analysis and biological ionisation people, the goats' milk and raw-egg contingent (that guy invited patients with active tuberculosis to these gatherings; before she learned, Pauli had unwittingly eaten lunch with one who kept coughing). Then there was the 'Health Secrets of India' woman in purple who had wasted twenty minutes of her time last year vituperating against fluoridation as the source of mongolism, cancer, heart disease and sexual dysfunction ('mucus membrane displacement'). While 300 people sat fascinated in the ballroom at a talk that never mentioned its topic, India, Pauli had walked out. How ironic to be here again while her own lump busily enlarged.

Everywhere the lobby now boasted red-and-gold placards:

ALTERNATIVE CANCER CONVENTION
Hear famous, informative medical doctors, researchers, nutritionists, authors speak on non-toxic cancer thera-pies, diagnosis, nutrition, laws, information withheld from the American people. Meet recovered cancer patients with encouraging reports. Attend a delicious banquet. Vegetarian cuisine available. Lectures, movies, exhibits. Meet Miss Norway of 1934. SAVE YOUR HEALTH FREEDOMS.

Pauli sighed. Having suffered herself the malignant arrogance rampant at Stevens' orthodox place, she hoped the alternative people were right: fight cancer as a whole-body disease instead of as a few psychotic cells. However, anything non-toxic was also and probably non-effective against any but the earliest tumours. To get this assignment, she'd even stuck her neck out to Jacobs. 'If the establishment is dying over finding a magic cure, how about giving these other people a chance?'

'Okay. 2,200 words. No photos. Speakers' heads are boring. But get me a couple books or bios to excerpt for boxes.'

'Will you sign my expense account?'

'Okay. Now go back to work.' Jacobs had even smiled.

'Is this seat taken?'

'What?' Pauli's upward gaze found a swarthy man with blue-tinted aviator glasses under three inches of black curls. He was beaming a smile at her. Pauli jumped. How could Stevens' dark waves have mated with Morgan's charm? 'No. You can sit here.' She shifted her legs away from the chair beside her. As he put his glass of screaming orange liquid on to the vinyl-topped table, she noticed a Morgan-like white gabardine suit covering Stevens' blue plaid shirt. Again her insides quivered.

'The way you're studying the programme, you must be a real devotee,' the man remarked. He could be thirty-five, maybe forty-five and very healthy.

'I'm a reporter. It amounts to the same. To write the stuff right, I have to figure out what's worth listening to . . . Why are you here?'

His lips curved downward, as if denying everything he was about to say. 'I'm the "scholarly prophetic genius with the cure for cancer" they mention on the last page.'

'Oh, is that all?' Pauli laughed.

'Nah. I run a health-food store in Manhattan. My customers are here. I need to see what food supplements get fashionable. Also I give nutrition classes.' That half explained his snappy delivery.

'What do you think of these conferences?'

'Is this for the record?' When Pauli didn't answer, he plunged on anyway. 'Combine one part fantasy with two parts paranoia. *Voilà* – this country's alternative-health establishment.'

Pauli smiled. 'I see you really believe in your work.'

'Of course I do. And now you can't quote me because I won't give you my name.'

'Oh, I'll read it off your name tag somewhere. I bet you even have an exhibit table, bamboozling the masses with carrot juice and tofu.'

'There's my buddy.' He looked away from his glass and waved into the lobby. 'Hey, will I see you later?'

'Maybe. I'll be busy,' Pauli evaded.

'All right.' As he rose, something in his jacket pocket thumped into his hip. Must be the hip flask of carrot juice.

By 7.30 Pauli had examined all the exhibit tables, including a chat with the natural facelift man ('$30 will save you $5,000'). And been forearm-clutched by a grief-stricken widow who made her promise to write that chemotherapy in the biggest West Coast medical centres kills people. 'My husband would be alive today if they hadn't shot all those poisons into him.' Pauli escaped by agreeing the East Coast situation was just as bad.

Deciding to skip the opening talk (last year's, full of self-congratulation, reached only the already converted), Pauli strolled to the twilit harbour. One pier bustled with refurbished shops, stained-glass galleries, restaurants, gaslamps, wood ramps – a tourist orgy of Victoriana. Did natives ever visit these places at all?

A juggler in multicoloured striped baggy pants and derby hat was attracting a crowd. To watch the last rosegold clouds behind a ship, Pauli sat on a red bench near a violinist whose sad gypsy melodies kept blowing away on the wind gusts. Hugging her suede coat closer around her, she turned to a woman already seated on the bench staring ahead. Noticing the name tag, she remarked, 'You're from the conference. I decided to skip the opening talk.' Pauli bit her tongue. Suppose this lady was a revered speaker? Pauli leaned across and read 'Dr Ann Barrett, Chairman, Biochemistry' from an eastern university. 'Hello, Dr Barrett. I was wondering what brings people across the whole country for this conference.'

'I've had uterine cancer,' the woman announced blankly. She stared at Pauli from behind emerald-framed goggles, which exactly matched the green silk blouse that flowed under her suit.

Ask a dumb question, get a hostile answer. Pauli sighed. So much for the amenities. Back to medical reporter. 'I've done some writing on uterine cancer.'

'Nobody cares about uterine cancer. Who reads?' Then

132

the woman relented enough to enquire, 'For medical journals?'

'No,' Pauli answered. 'Popular magazines, although the news magazine I work for is for doctors and other professionals. Well, I am co-authoring some journal articles on cancer research. They'll appear next year.'

The woman sniffed. Must be the 'popular' that riled her. Already got more information than she gave you. 'I've just come from San Diego. I delivered a talk there titled "How to Succeed in Science without a Y Chromosome." ' The woman's eyes, barricaded behind the thick glasses, stared at Pauli.

Was this humour? 'Sounds like an accurate title for problems women scientists have.'

Tell her about Coral Deming? Skip it. Pauli had expected a bristling what-do-*you*-know? rejoinder. Instead the woman leaned back and emitted a ten-second, closed-mouth smile. Female Calvin Coolidge, New England comic. With paranoia or irritability so perfected, what sort of teacher could she make?

Pauli shuddered. She heard the wind snap the rigging into the masts of a tourist schooner. How had these tight-ass types become the world's chosen people? Another strain of gypsy melody drifted by.

'I'm going back to catch the rest of the evening,' Pauli announced. As she walked away, two T-shirted women flashed by, a blur of bicycles and racing shorts. She just made out the lettering over their bobbing breasts: HAVE YOU HUGGED A GAY TODAY? She waved, but they'd already reached the next bench. And she hadn't automatically hungered for Lizann. *Must be healing. San Francisco is good.*

In the exhibit room she mingled again with the crowd. After Dr Barrett and the equally chilled harbour, the coloured lights, scarlet table-cloths and booths became a delight. At several she introduced herself, left her card and reprints of a couple of her articles. Might lead to another job.

As she repassed the table nearest the ballroom, she heard, 'Miss Golden! Somebody here to meet you.' The voice came from a rosy-cheeked woman with a 1940s upward twist of grey hair, now returned to fashion. Suddenly Pauli regretted leaving her card. Her view of this shindig was unlikely to be favourable, or even objective. Better to have remained anonymous.

Beside the caller, however, sat the most stunning woman Pauli had seen since, yes, Lizann lit out. Crisp black hair waved naturally about her china smooth face. Her large eyes appeared a deep gentian violet. At her throat inside the draped collar of a grey blouse winked oblong links, a hand-hammered gold chain. On her lap she held a black binder of pages. 'I'm' – it sounded like – 'Jessie Anaya. Mary tells me your'e a medical writer. I don't want to impose, but I'd appreciate if you'd look over these pages and give me an opinion. I'll pay for your time, of course. I'm speaking tomorrow noon. The diet therapy section. I'm recovered from breast cancer they said was terminal. Five years ago.' She spoke rapidly, as if expecting rejection.

Pauli blinked, eager to concentrate on this new lady instead of her own lump. Jessie looked about twenty-nine – not a wrinkle, grey hair or burst capillary visible. As if the most serious thing she ever suffered might be a cold. Whether true cure, spontaneous remission, quackery – anyhow, amazing.

Ease away? 'I'll read it. And you needn't pay me till you sell it for a million. Okay?'

Jessie laughed with delight.

Pauli continued. 'Come to my room in about an hour. I can concentrate better there. Room 405.' She flipped through what looked like 100 pages in the black binder. Just the right amount to escape the talks and provide some personalised, at least less depressing angle, to this event.

'It's not finished. I don't know –'

'Don't worry. Come anyway. It'll give me some background for your talk.'

'Thanks, Miss Golden.' She grasped Pauli's hand.

In the tiger-carpeted elevator Pauli regretted her generous gesture. A similar impulse at a college reunion had netted a year of Bible annotated letters of gossip, gratitude and more bad poetry signed 'Your loving sister in Christ, Ruth'. Beyond a Christmas card Pauli had tried to ignore all of them. If she ever laid one finger of a really loving hand on Ruth, guess who would have screamed Sodom and Gomorrah in shocked celibacy? If Christian sisterhood and 'love' for her, begun with a manuscript, meant exactly nothing she could lay a sexual hand on, why begin anew with Jessie?

Because you're lonely; it hurts.

Jessie's cool, dark eyes appeared again. *Tell me where is gayness bred – in the heart or in the head?* The familiar jingle calmed – although Pauli could never answer it.

In the orange/chocolate room, whose harvest theme recalled Stevens' study (damn!), she set to reading Jessie's pages. Surprisingly the writing was not only sensible and useful but interesting. Jessie had depended neither on God nor lemon juice to save her from terminal cancer at age – Pauli rifled pages. Jessie was forty-five, but looked twenty-nine, with laughter and enjoyment to spare in those violet eyes. What the hell kind of vegetables could accomplish this second and third round of miracles?

And her name was not Jessie but Chessie. Anyway, Chessie had sought the sensible: surgery for a 1-inch lump whose malignancy a pathologist confirmed. Her breasts were large; it had hidden until one day when she was swimming nude in a stream. When the cancer spread next to nodes in her underarm and a suspicious spot in one lung, the oncologist recommended the unholy trinity – more surgery, chemotherapy, radiation. Having fought to preserve her breast, Chessie declined all the Big Three, found a diet and cleansing therapy programme and now headed alternative cancer counselling for her state.

The greens, wheat grass, sprouts, cabbage and other items of her juice and vegetarian menus even made some biochemical sense – high in selenium, vitamins A and C; animal protein only in eggs; no processed junk food.

However, Chessie's evidence and existence remained merely 'anecdotal'; she was a self- or cancer-appointed sample of, yes, one. Without controlled studies, etc., blah, blah, blah. That she was bloomingly alive meant nil to people like Morgan, Stevens, Arthur. She could relapse at any time; then she'd be sorry. Further blah, for when conventional patients relapsed, conventional doctors had no answers to that either.

Chessie's story was no doubt over-personalised, needed fleshing out with other people's evidence, plus interviews with her various doctors, but there must be a self-help publisher who'd be glad to add it to their paperback list. Chessie's second doctor, who'd screamed, 'If you want to keep that breast, you're a whore!' especially deserved a wider audience. Did every major city come equipped with these male hysterics?

According to the pages, Chessie seemed to live alone in a mountainside house. She mentioned sports – Colorado flyfishing, jogging three miles a day with her regained energy.

After a knock on her door Pauli checked the peephole and fumbled the locks open. Chessie stood there. 'What's doing downstairs?' Pauli asked.

'The full-light-spectrum man is speaking, and Miss Norway is autographing.'

'Do you think this thing's a big rip-off?'

Chessie blinked in surprise. 'With a measly $10-a-day admission? You can't even get snake oil for that . . . I think, maybe you shouldn't read my book.'

'I'm sorry,' Pauli apologised. 'I just get nervous when they either sell things or ignore the topic they're supposed to speak on. Look, I already read the book. It's fine. If you still want a few suggestions . . .' Pauli grasped the black binder and detailed her mental list: no need to examine cancer deaths in so many family members, everybody knows that, tell more of your own story and other successes using this therapy.

Then she expected Chessie to retreat from the encounter with thanks, dismay, protests. Instead, Chessie laid the carefully typed pages on the table, curled up in the chair opposite Pauli. 'Um, Pauline, can I call you Pauline? Now you've read a bit, maybe you can advise me about something. There's some, well, personal aspect of this I need to discuss with somebody. I know we're nearly strangers, but I hope I can talk with you?'

Pauli nodded, feeling it was too late to say no. Sexual cancers always had 'personal aspects', but even Pauli's interviewing mind failed to predict what came next.

'When they told me what I had, I guess I felt it was something like punishment for my sins, for the strange person I am.'

'Oh-h.' Pauli's answer emerged as a groan. Was religious conversion, an anaesthesia-induced recovery-room vision, setting in? 'You're not strange. You're a beautiful woman,' Pauli reassured. Sounded like gushing, but what a relief – at last, somebody who didn't flirt, rant or go catatonic.

'You see, before I got the cancer, I had a sort of wild life with men and with –'

Pauli laughed. 'Didn't everybody! An even stranger thing happened to *me* on the way to senility –'

Chessie arched an eyebrow. 'No. You interrupted me.'

'Sorry.'

'I mean I've had . . . relationships with both men and women and what I want to know, what I need to know, what range of hormones in the body produces breast cancer and what link it has with the . . . kind of person I am.'

Pauli stared, stunned at Chessie's openness. Chessie, the undefinable, had asked the unanswerable. 'Well,' Pauli tried to stick some words together, 'all kinds of people, including men, get breast cancer. There are recognised risk factors I'm sure you know about.' Chessie nodded. 'Anyway, people with regular sex lives, and no sex lives, get breast cancer – and some people like you who don't.' *Perhaps people like me.* 'Hormones get produced in such minute quantities that change every day depending on your monthly cycle. So there's no way to measure, let alone prove –' Pauli stopped, then stumbled on, 'Look, I know what you're going through. I know what you –'

'You mean you've had breast cancer too?' Chessie held out her hands, on which two gold rings glinted.

'No, but I've got a lump that wouldn't aspirate, and my mother's sister, Marian –' The words stuck in Pauli's throat.

'No, I mean the other. I've spent my life loving both men and women. Sometimes simultaneously.' Her body tingled. Why did the truth always appear both impossible and improbable, compared with lying?

'But you seem so –'

'Straight?' Pauli finished the sentence. 'I'm straight enough for all straight purposes – and a few that are even more fun.'

Now Chessie looked incredulous. 'And you've never found anybody?'

'I did.' Pauli stopped. *But he got both married and murdered, and she* – 'It didn't work out,' Pauli concluded, hating to play for sympathy.

Confusion and pain crossed Chessie's face. 'And now?'

Pauli shook her head. 'I work more than full-time. I got over-extended from . . . his death, his research. Plus my mother's ill.'

'It was a man.'

'Oh, there was a woman too. She . . . left. She went kind of, well, crazy. I hope she's happy.' Pauli checked Chessie's face. It was calm. And no handwringing or edging doorward as so-called 'normal' women had done in the days when she still bothered to explain herself. Nor could exclusively gay ones locate a correct category for Pauli. 'What do you do? Work, I mean.' Back to facts!

'I'm a teacher – weaving and silkscreening at a college near my house. You know, I have a russet headband that just matches your hair. Tomorrow will you come to my talk?'

Pauli smiled and nodded.

'My mother is part Native American, something like one thirty-second Santee Sioux. She weaves rugs. That's how I got into the rag and fabric trade.' Chessie passed this on like a family joke. 'I know that American Indians, descended as we are from Asian people, do get less breast cancer than whites. But that didn't keep my mother from getting it.'

Pauli's shoulders dropped. Too much to expect of a medical conference not to discuss disease every thirty seconds. 'Well, there's your answer. Never mind your strange hormones. Is your mother well?'

'You mean, I inherited the family curse?'

'Not directly, but any daughter of a mother who had it is always at higher risk.'

'My mother's fine. After fifteen years. But she lost a breast and chest muscles and part of her shoulder. The works. I wanted never to do that.'

'I understand. Any woman would.'

'My mother didn't. She thought I should too, just to be safe . . . But you have surgery coming? You must be pretty nervous?'

Pauli nodded. 'Well, my female chauvinist surgeon wants to check again next month. I've had a series of cysts, but this lump is the first solid item.'

'And you're under a lot of stress?'

Again Pauli agreed.

'You know, at one point my doctor said to me, "Don't write the pathologist's report for him. That's what *he's* getting paid for." '

Pauli laughed. 'Like, why flunk your exam ahead of time?'

'Exactly . . . Well, I better go now. Getting exercise and sleep is part of my treatment. I'll be thinking of you.'

At the door Pauli pulled her close, hugging Chessie fully against herself. Chessie was warm and smelled of cinnamon.

'Tomorrow? Promise?' Chessie urged.

'I promise.' When Pauli closed the door, for the first time in months, Stevens, Morgan, Heather, Edward, her mother's tantrums, the lousy lady on the bench all floated upwards, 3,000 miles away.

19

'And then you know what the bastards did?' Dr Basil Radison's explosive gestures were monopolising not only the circular restaurant table but the airspace on all sides.

At first Pauli had congratulated herself for getting him alone. Now, toying at her breakfast oatmeal, she realised it wouldn't have been hard. The man was a revelation in pursuit of an audience. Like Chessie – but with the love, beauty, concern abraded away. He was no natural hysteric, Pauli knew, remembering the mild man, genial scientist from two years before, now frustrated to desperation.

His bald head and Ben Franklin glasses shone. 'This is part of my afternoon speech, but I've got pages of documentation, results of toxic chemical tests just languishing in file cabinets. Cancers from hair dyes, spray paint, cosmetics, shampoos. You name it – animals have already overdosed and died from it. Plus sloppy research, unlabelled animals, quarantine animals in the same room with control animals. I'd visit a lab, diagnose the problems, try to make *them* get on top of it. Then back in Washington I'd get on the bureaucrats to release results of some valid tests I found. Always needed *more* evidence, they claimed. Millions get wasted, millions –'

'Wait a minute,' Pauli interrupted, aware of the gathering crowd around her getting a preview sample of Radison's cancer scandals. '*Which* labs did you investigate exactly? I assume they all had federal grants, but anything for breast cancer, for instance?'

'Oh, women's lib, huh?'

'Cancer doesn't discriminate. Why should I?' answered Pauli crisply. *Cancer chooses both sexes. Why shouldn't I?* 'I agree there's waste, fraud, incompetence. I know about the project where, to destroy the evidence, they destroyed the mice by gassing them with disinfectant.'

'Cleaning solvent,' corrected Radison with a half-smile, but she'd finally caught his attention. 'And guess who discovered that chicanery going on in Memphis?'

Pauli needed only half a guess. 'Wait a minute. Did you ever visit a Medway Institute in Connecticut? Maybe you know – they're all MDs or Ph.D.s – Stevens St Steven, Morgan Dianis, Arthur Huggard –'

'That bastard!' Radison re-exploded.

'Which one?' Pauli begged.

'Huggard, of course. Never trust a man with a square jaw.' For emphasis, Dr Radison rubbed the beard on his own jaw which, on a face with straight-rimmed glasses set above dropped jowls, looked sawn off.

No wonder he and the Feds had parted company. Politics being the art of the possible, never the ideal, Washington had neither psychic nor financial space for moral crusaders, even against a disease guaranteed to kill a quarter of the Americans that Congress supposedly represented. Political or financial reformers received brief hearings; moral reformers like Radison preached to the already converted at these weekend conferences or from the ghetto of Sunday morning TV.

'Dr Radison, do you –?' Loud male voice behind Pauli.

Pauli turned. 'Excuse me. Wait a minute. I have just two more questions.' Pauli won her own right to continue before Radison got assassinated or some other interruption occurred. 'You were saying about Dr Huggard,' she prompted.

'Well, he didn't poison his animals in Chicago. That's where I checked into him. Had an even worse gimmick. Took money for a contract to test – I think it was red and yellow dyes in cosmetics on every drugstore shelf. He filled the lab with control animals. Then when I asked to see the test animals, he claimed they'd all been sacrificed. He never did the research at all for the year he was paid. Said the new animal shipment was so he could *start*. There he was, running a health spa for white mice at a quarter million bucks a year.'

'Did you report him?'

'Of course. The report is still buried in my boss's files marked "classified". Unless he shredded it the day after I left. Anyhow, it's buried for the next century.'

Did Stevens know about Arthur's history? But Stevens hadn't hired Arthur. Harry must have. *Get out of here, Pauline. Put the folders down.* Pauli dropped her voice to ask her final question. Despite July air conditioning in San Francisco, she was perspiring as if the flu had returned. 'Suppose I get you new evidence about Dr Huggard and some breast cancer research. Viruses, immunotherapy, new serums. What would you do with it?'

'Only what I'm doing now. Release it to people like you, speak at conferences.'

Pauli sighed, exhausted. And her momentary inattention lost Radison to the next questioner, a rail-thin man who pressed on about why more money wasn't funding nutritional research and hydrazine sulphate to attack cancers.

'It's a good approach,' Radison agreed, 'but my specialty is toxic-chemical research.'

Even with cancer's unpredictability, it wasn't hard to guess why the emaciated man with the string tie had asked his question. Pauli pushed through the crowd, who were already lusting as always for free medical advice applicable to their own disasters. Some had grabbed Radison's coat sleeves, as if touching his garment could cure them. If he didn't stand up, he'd get smothered. Did the quacks and the miracle seekers, like the sadists and the masochists, always deserve each other? At least Radison offered solid information, wasn't pushing lemon-juice or kiwi-fruit cures.

Outside the restaurant Pauli wiped perspiration from her face and neck. The cocktail napkin she was clutching read, 'We're glad you're here!' Her navy jacket felt moist under the arms. If she rushed upstairs to the ballroom, she'd make some of the first talk entrancingly titled 'The Great Cancer Rip-off'. How could she feel nauseous at 8.45 a.m. when she wasn't even pregnant? Fever? Tension? Hesitating by the stairs, she found the man with the white gabardine and hipflask of carrot juice staring again at her. 'Can I help? Every time I see you, you're thinking furiously. Must be something good.'

Pauli managed a smile. 'I hope so. What're you doing today?'

'At noon I take a group out to see a clinic here. I just finished the arrangements.' He waved at the wall phones. 'But I have a couple of hours. Want to join me?'

'Maybe,' Pauli answered, surprising herself. 'I don't know about the clinic but what do you want to do?'

'How about a swim? In honour of how we got the hotel management to knock off the chlorine while we're here. Fighting State Health Regulation 972 –'

'Okay, okay, I believe you.'

He winked, not in flirtation but rather like self-mockery. She breathed more easily. He seemed a healthy respite from cancer and frustration.

'You know you're a lovely, spirited woman. I saw you in action with old Toxic Chemicals there. Since you refuse to tell me your name, I'll lay mine on you. It's Alan Lebentritt.'

'Mine is Cinderella, and I turn into pumpkin juice at midnight. Was that *really* carrot juice you were drinking yesterday?' How had everything, including social questions, become an interview where she flirted automatically to gain information? Yet she hadn't even got Radison's address! *Slipping, Pauli.* How to send him whatever she could dig up against Arthur Huggard, to continue what Stevens had died trying to investigate? Rainette or Coral would have more –

'Hey, where did you go?' Alan was asking. 'Are you all right?'

Pauli found his hand on her arm, then his left arm behind her shoulders. 'Sorry. I've got a problem I wanted Radison to know about.'

Twenty minutes later they dove into the blue hydrangea-coloured liquid of the pool. With the pre-dawn swimmers long gone, they had the pool to themselves. Pauli kicked and bobbed, imagining the tension drain from her forehead out through her toes. Maybe the cure-through-visualisation people were right: the mind screwed the body every time. Imagine everything washing down the drain. Clean new life. If she bought tapes or transcripts of the talks, she could avoid all of them but Chessie's. She'd never played hooky at an assigned conference before. *Cancer freaking me out.*

'Hey, come here,' Alan called as Pauli trod water a few feet away. He began a splashy butterfly stroke towards her. Suddenly she found his arms about her in the azure water. She squirmed away.

'How would you like a body massage? You're so tense – for somebody so tiny. I mean that last as a compliment.' He gleamed a smile at her.

'I'm all of five feet one. But, thanks, I'll get back to the conference.'

Another stunning smile. Blast him for the curly black hair and the banter that recalled Stevens. Phoney? Better never fall in love than stay haunted like this. *Chessie*. The water was chilling now. Besides the chlorine, the pool people must have lowered the heat.

'Seriously, why did *you* come to this conference?' *Return him to reality.*

'Serious again, huh? Like I told you, I come to learn the latest fashions in vitamins. But there's also something about these people.'

'Good, bad, crazy?' Pauli probed.

'Well, most want the magic bullet that'll cure their disease without touching their lives, but it's their . . . single-mindedness I like.'

'Sure. Some of the exhibitors live, breathe and would die for their alternative treatments. You mean, their moral purity.'

'Yeah, something like that. They're not fractionated like I am, running a business that caters to all kinds, trying to make a buck, living in a filthy city.'

After his words followed the image of Chessie beside her mountain stream. 'I think you're idealising them, but I know what you mean. The clean sense of Us against *Them* – the bureaucrats, the medical-industrial complex, the chemotherapists –'

'But I'm caught in the middle trying to earn a living.'

Aren't we all? Pauli imagined the luxury of writing thoroughly on one topic instead of careering through sixty different subjects a year. 'Hmm. Selling $9 watermelons because you call them organic?' she asked.

Eyelash flicker and sharp glance from Alan. 'There's no such thing as an *un*organic watermelon.' He evaded Pauli's question.

'Right. That kind's only $4.'

'Well, have I passed or flunked all your tests?' His voice held a pleading that caught her.

Pauli was yanking the top and bottom of her coral-flowered swimsuit. The weight of her breasts had dragged on the wet, strapless top. Why couldn't they construct a bathing suit that stayed decent (including lumps) without choking you?

Alan held out his hand. 'Leave it where it is. I like the view.'

Instead of a sharp retort, a pang of envy overwhelmed her. How simple to be heterosexual and watch only what you're programmed to watch – for him, half-bared breasts on the opposite sex. For Pauli, there was no opposite sex, merely a community of need exploding everywhere. She could watch Alan as naturally as she watched the graceful curves of other women's breasts. Next she tried to dump such emotions into her carry-all category, long ago marked 'U' for Useless.

'Hey, why the pain? Your face!' Alan asked.

'You wouldn't believe it,' Pauli answered.

Then Alan reached out, gathered her to him, began stroking her soggy hair. Sitting beside him at the pool steps, she relaxed against his leg. Her father's face darted through her head. He'd comforted her when she'd pitched forward on roller skates, torn open a knee and lost a front tooth to the pavement. Although too ill to work more than six months a year, he'd been a kindly man. Why hadn't her mother ever seen that? When he died, it was merely his ultimate failure – daring to leave Mrs Golden a widow. A new category blossomed – 'PU' for Post-Useless.

'Come upstairs with me. The massage?' Alan murmured. He was kissing her hair and forehead.

'No ... Thanks. I'll get back now.' Using the pool ladder, she pulled herself upright. 'Uh, see you around.' Grabbing the fluffy hotel towel, she rushed towards the ladies' locker room before Alan could follow. As she hurried into her clothes, her fingers automatically checked the lump to see what cold water had achieved. Smaller . . . and harder. Damn!

On the way to the elevator Pauli noted a fresh graffiti scrawled across the artificial respiration instructions:

CIVILISATION IS THE DISEASE
CANCER IS THE CURE.

Anybody who'd write that must be sick, she decided.

20

'Miss Golden! Wait a minute.' Outside the ballroom Pauli heard a man's voice booming behind her. It was Basil Radison. 'You disappeared this morning. I wanted to give you my card and this report.' Having rushed towards her, he was out of breath. His bald head gleamed under the ceiling lights. 'If you can document anything going on at Medway, especially by Huggard, call me. Or send what you can. Now I'm out of government, I can't do anything short of suing them, but I have a few press contacts who always listen.'

After her swim and more thoughts of Chessie, Radison's insistence returned Pauli to reality. Ah yes, politics of Medway and cancer. 'Will you look at some reports I'll send? Give me an opinion on them?' Stevens' questionings inside all the baby-blue covers surged into her mind. 'I can't make a pattern yet, but I'll mark some things Dr St Steven questioned too'.

'Sure,' Radison answered, 'but remember reports and articles can be falsified, padded. They write what they want you to believe. To get the truth, you must see the animals. They can be destroyed but not faked. Either they have cancer or they don't. Either they die or recover in a few months.'

'Maybe you'd visit Medway with me, except they're paranoid there since the . . . well, one of the co-directors got killed a few days ago. Somebody murdered him.'

Radison's square jaw fell squarer. 'You mean Harry Stornell?'

Pauli shook her head. 'Dr St Steven.'

'Terrible . . . I met Steve once and sort of followed his career. Seemed like a nice fellow. Why –' He stopped. 'Seems like Harry who should have made the enemies. He was part of the grant committee that funded two of the places I investigated. Got his fingers in too many pies to do anything well.'

'What do you mean?'

'Besides the grants committees, he showed up at oncology and immunology conferences. Yet I doubt he's ever treated a live patient since he left med school. He's a wheeler-dealer bent on getting known.'

And a bastard. Pauli nodded. 'I'll send you something. Soon.' With Radison reading the reports and a final session with Coral, maybe she'd piece Stevens' apparently random questionings into something definite and then tell the police? Would Rainette have more financial info about Harry? 'Are you going to the next diet talk? It begins in a couple minutes,' she asked him.

'No. I've had it for today,' Radison answered. 'I'm sure this isn't your business, but who . . . what happened to Steve?'

'It was a big party and –' Shouldn't have mentioned it. Pauli's throat closed. 'They just arrested somebody for stealing lab equipment. They're grilling him about . . . the killing also.'

'And did he kill Stevens?'

Pauli shrugged. 'Is being a thief enough to make you a murderer? I don't know. Neither do the police. I wish they'd charge *somebody*. It's eerie – being there now.' *Skip how Harry already fired you.*

'You can quit. Don't you work somewhere else?'

Pauli winced. 'Yes, but I really got involved there for months. It's like the one solid piece of work I have now. The other stuff I write ticks off a new disease every week.' And I loved Stevens, for better or worse.

'General assignment work.'

Pauli nodded.

Radison smiled and took her hand. 'Let me hear from you. Promise?'

His concern touched her, brought tears she fought down. She'd go to her room to cry, but who was she crying for? Stevens? Her mother? Lizann? Tears that always got diverted into work because they hurt too much . . . Chessie's mountain stream.

Radison shook her hand and walked to the elevators. Reassembling her face, Pauli realised she was happy to enter the ballroom alone. If she sat with somebody, it would be awkward to meet Chessie afterwards.

In the back aisle Pauli passed Dr Ann Barrett – in red with red glasses today. The woman looked like a torch. Pauli stared the other way. Chessie was gathering a good crowd. Pauli smiled towards the speaker's table, wondering whether Chessie had seen her.

The introduction proved blessedly brief although the moderator somehow managed to flash and describe his own nutrition book in the middle of Chessie's bio. At least he refrained from calling her 'martyr' or maybe 'victim'. Since cancer already had too many victims, and martyrs were several centuries outdated, Pauli sat eager to hear a heroine who'd remained alive.

Except for a bit of black humour about modern medicine – 'Promise her anything but give her cancer' – Chessie's ten-minute talk was suprisingly sober, straight-on. Pauli realised she'd been expecting proselytising of some kind. *Relax!*

Chessie must have heeded Pauli's advice about including other people's experiences, for she described a group of fifteen she'd lived with at the California centre and detailed their progress. Only six had relapsed over the five years. All except one were still alive. 'This diet plan is one answer to cancer. I follow it now and intend to follow it for the rest of my life. It's rugged at first but worth the effort because I know that without it, I'd never be alive here today.'

Chessie concluded by describing a group boardgame called Shanti she played on a squared cloth she had silkscreened. 'It's a game of journey. Its goal is cooperation, not competition. Everybody must win in Shanti for the game to end. I hope my talk will encourage your interest in non-toxic therapies for cancer and other problems. Nobody wins with cancer. Everybody can lose unless we all do what we can to purify our lives, our diets, our workplaces, and the environment we all share.'

Pauli found it a sensible talk that, like Chessie's manuscript, gave concrete information without the paranoid sallies that other speakers used to bolster their own courage. Chessie smiled and sat down behind the table while the audience clapped. She'd exchanged her grey outfit for an aqua suit that contrasted brilliantly against the red-velvet stage curtain and dove-coloured walls.

When the moderator invited questions, Ann Barrett rose, twitching an attention-getting arm over her head. She began politely, 'Miss Anaya, I listened with great interest to your presentation, hoping to hear something useful to myself and others who suffer this disease. I hear you're writing a book. Maybe it's all in the book, but I find your talk dismayingly vague on details of just *how* this diet and cleansing are supposed to operate in the body. It doesn't seem reasonable that the same diet can affect, let alone cure, all forms of cancer when cancer isn't one disease. I believe your cure is a fortunate – and rare – case of spontaneous remission. Possibly you'd have this good outcome with no special diet at all once the major tumour was –'

Boos and hisses interrupted, insistent beyond the insistence in Ann Barrett's voice. She stared around the ballroom, her face screwed into disgust.

Let 1,000 flowers bloom, if 999 don't kill each other first. Pauli mumbled to herself. Chessie was a teacher, used to public exhibition, but Pauli noticed the papers in her hands trembling now. 'By objective measurements that exist – the pathologist's original report, decreasing numbers of cancer cells and bacteria in urine, disappearance of my enlarged lymph nodes – I not only had cancer but have cured myself of that cancer. I continue to see my doctor. I'm not against doctors as long as they promote health instead of just treat disease.'

Pauli began to squirm. Chessie wasn't answering the question, and Ann Barrett's hand twitched again.

'I don't claim that this nutrition plan cures everybody, only that it returned me to health. And it helps other cancer patients maintain physical energy and with it, psychological hope. It also – particularly the coffee enemas – reduced the pain I began to have daily. People should use whatever methods, including those of the cancer establishment, keep them alive. What I know is, faced with death, I found a way to live.'

As the applause continued, Pauli found tears crowding behind her eyes again. Newly aware of her own lump and probable surgery coming, Pauli wondered whether she could be as brave as Chessie and cut so soon away from the medical establishment.

A man from the audience reported that the diet plan had just received a small private funding to study its laboratory results on animals. Pauli winced; experimenting on humans *before*, instead of after, animals was unethical. She prayed they had other animal research tucked into the background. 'But how will it look,' the man continued, 'when an outsider with a budget of $150,000 finds a cure for cancer? Of course, it'll make the big guys with the million-dollar budgets look like shit –' At the four-letter word some in the audience shifted in their seats. 'So they'll downgrade it no matter what's found. But at least *we* can spread the word.'

Instead of clapping, Pauli watched the confusion on Chessie's face. Hadn't she known of the new grant? Maybe she'd like to hear the latest on Medway's messed up million-dollar budget. But not here or now.

Knitting her hands furiously, Ann Barrett had sat down in a scarlet swirl. The programme flowed on to the next speaker.

On her way out Pauli checked the audience again for Alan. She couldn't spot any head of black curls that didn't belong to a woman. Near the food booths outside, she caught up with Chessie. 'I wish that woman would *try* something just once. All she comes is to heckle.' Chessie was simmering and muttering.

'How about inviting her to one of the centres or something you know in Colorado? Her address must be on the registration list. You know, she's had uterine cancer. And depression.' Damn! Why defend a bitter bitch like Ann Barrett? Too much objective reporting, Pauli.

Chessie answered without even wondering how Pauli knew Ann Barrett. 'All right. I'll try before she leaves.'

'What're you doing now?' Pauli asked.

'Let's take a walk. I want to get out,' Chessie decided. 'I have to be back later, though. I'm presenting one of the Golden Fleece Awards. This year it's to the National Laboratory of Mental Health for their $200,000 project to measure the lengths of stewardesses' noses.'

Pauli giggled. 'Did you make that up?'

'I wish I had. Their research paper's in my suitcase. They've got a worse one about measuring human reaction to a photo of an octopus in a barnyard. Ah, they're all sick . . . Let's take a cab to Golden Gate Park and breathe some trees.'

'How about the palms in Union Square? They're closer, and we'd get exercise.'

'No. I want the tea garden. The real thing.'

A half-hour later they stood on a wooden crescent bridge gazing down at the goldfish circling the shallow pools. 'See?' Chessie remarked. 'Not as tourist trappy as you claimed. Anyway, they're closing it in a while.'

'Want some tea?' Pauli discovered she'd forgotten to eat lunch.

'Only mint or lemon grass. That's what I drink at home.'

'Have they busted you yet?'

'Not for lemon grass, but I'll probably get arrested for practising medicine without a licence any day now.'

Practical aspects of life with Chessie could prove problematical. Apparently she never ate at restaurants, only bought vegetables and fruit at organic grocery stores.

'They've got homemade tea cakes over there. Get yourself some,' Chessie urged.

'How'd you know I'm hungry? But all that sugar –'

'You *look* hungry, my dear. You're so tiny.'

Attempting to swallow that as a compliment, Pauli

walked down the bridge and wound up with two super-sweet white gelatinous masses – all the Japanese saleswoman in kimono had left. They resembled tiny living pillows, Japanese ravioli. Pauli made gumballs of them to chew. Chewing proved possible, but swallowing the raw dough gagged her. To share the joy, she threw bits at the carp, which snapped at such delicacies. Poor fish – ruining their livers on stuff the tourists couldn't stomach.

Pauli and Chessie strolled onward and sat down inside the emerald shadows and delicious odour of a eucalyptus tree. 'May I ask you a rude question?' Chessie began.

Pauli jumped. How to field what she guessed was coming next? She nodded.

'*Are* you one of us?'

Pauli stared wildly from side to side. Oh God, *which* us? Health dieters, cancer therapists, women craftspeople, Indians, lesbians? 'Um,' she began, 'if I had to label it, I'd call myself . . .' She stopped. This would surely blow it if anything did. 'I'd call myself . . . a bisexual. Like I described last night.'

Puzzlement covered Chessie's face. 'But you talk like, like all my lesbian friends. You said you lived with a woman so I thought – but I can hear the paranoia in your voice and see the pain in your eyes. It's, am I one *more* person who's going to kick you?'

Pauli nodded, unable to speak. Chessie took her hand. 'Chessie, I have to earn a living. So I have friendships with men, doctors, researchers, computer people. In order to get information, I have to be at least affable.'

'Well, many lesbians have been married. Most of them have children. Do you think of all people, I don't understand? But just friendship's not what you mean.'

What do I mean? Don't let me blow this! 'Well, look what I am. It's a category in between that nobody – straights, gays, neuters – wants to touch if they know. There was one man this year, a doctor, the one who got murdered . . . I get, well, lonely. Cancer is hellish to write about. I'm sorry –' Pauli halted. 'You've actually had it. I shouldn't talk.'

'Talk. Please. I'll listen. Don't you think I know what it's like to be . . . dumped by straight women and straight men?'

'But gay ones have dumped me too,' Pauli protested, recalling Lizann. Desperately she scrabbled to avoid the immediate topic. If you can't face it, laugh at it. 'Well, my father was a man and my mother was a woman. No wonder I swing six ways to Sunday.' She sobered. 'No. That isn't right either. I liked my father, but my mother belittled him and all the rest of her relatives. So I had a constant fight to reconcile all the conflicting claims. Take care of myself because nobody else would bother. I learned to be both man and woman. Does it make sense so far?'

Chessie nodded.

Uncomfortable, Pauli dragged a broken branch from under her thighs; it snagged her skirt. She'd been sitting on the twigs without even realising. Endorphins working overtime, narcotising my nervous system. 'My father was the family humanitarian. He believed part of being human is helping people, sharing, educating them to better lives. I guess he's why I'm a medical writer, why I keep at it, even when it frightens the hell out of me like with cancer and stroke. Where it hurts the most is where the help's needed. My mother, though, still believes everybody's self-serving, not to be trusted, that people monopolise your attention and never give much back. They build you up based on their own needs, then tear you down if you fail at *their* problems. The horror is that's exactly what she's become. A massive problem she expects me to solve. I suppose I love her, but I can't stand her. Know what I mean?'

'Is she ill?' Chessie enquired.

Pauli blinked. 'She's dying. Not cancer. Stroke, which is equally –' Pauli bit her tongue to avoid saying 'grotesque'. 'Painful. My brother – he's from Colorado, like you – will arrive in Connecticut Monday to help. I shouldn't be here this weekend at all, but I'm glad I came.' With her free hand she grabbed Chessie's other hand. 'Ah, I was horribly lonely when Lizann took off. She was my –'

'Lover.' Chessie finished the sentence.

Pauli nodded.

'This doctor who got murdered. You keep mentioning him. You really got fixated on him, huh?'

'He wasn't just murdered. He got mutilated too. Horrible. 'Course, the police think it must be a homosexual, maybe a junior-grade employee they've already caught for something else.' She tightened her grip on Chessie's hands. 'But those senior research guys are all so straight, it's laughable.'

'Are you sure? Then maybe it's a phoney job to fool the police?'

Pauli nodded. 'Based on what I saw of Stevens – that's his name – he seemed to be the one honest guy in a rotten situation that must be wasting millions in research money. But I can't *prove* it yet. He disagreed with somebody over something crucial in these blasted reports I've got. His question marks overrun them, like the pox. But no one paper or person. I offered the police some Xeroxes but if they've deciphered them, I haven't heard about it.'

Don't tell Chessie you're a suspect too.

'You sound very diligent and professional. Driven, I'd say.'

'Well, sure. I'll die trying . . . Oh, that's wrong again.'

Chessie smiled. 'I understand. How could I mind what you come from when I'm made the same way? It wasn't my childhood although being even part Indian in a white man's culture is its own death trip. It was . . . I had a relationship with an older woman when I was a teenager. Then with a man in college. I liked men, but somehow the woman had come first. Just because you start eating bananas doesn't mean you stop loving peaches and cream.'

Pauli burst out laughing. Then she continued, 'This doctor, Stevens, reminded me so much of somebody I knew in school. One of those marvellous things that never happen again because the energy they need goes into work. You know, study all day, make love half the night, stagger home for two hours' sleep, stick your head under the shower, get up and make class. Then do it all over again about five days a week.'

Chessie laughed. 'And I thought I was doing penance for being the original nut in Colorado.'

'Only if I can be the original nut in Connecticut. Did you ever see that cartoon about two winos lying in a dump near Manhattan's skyscrapers?'

Chessie shook her head.

'One says to the other, "It's really hard to be the town drunk in a city this size".'

'I wish I had *more* competition. All I meet is gays *or* straights. I suppose you can hang between them when you're twenty-one, but they figure not at my age. Actually I've looked for a really new sexual preference,' she joked, 'but I haven't found one yet.'

'You can make it with kangaroos,' Pauli suggested.

'Thanks. I haven't tried them yet.'

'Good.'

'Pauli, I have to leave tomorrow early.' Pauli's heart jumped against her ribs. 'I have things to do at home. Well, I can't exactly afford this hotel.'

'Stay with me. Room 405. Simple.'

Chessie took Pauli's hand and held it again. She sighed. 'Simple? What we are?'

'I only meant –' Reality again. Dammit!

'Look, how do *you* keep your job?' Chessie enquired. 'I'm a teacher at a public institution. It's harder.'

'They already know. I mean I told Jacobs, he's my boss, a few months after he came. He said as long as it wasn't anybody in the office or anybody I interviewed.' *How about Stevens?* 'But there's Sara –'

'Is she somebody you –'

'No-o!' Pauli shuddered. 'She wants my job so she digs any dirt she can.'

'Jacobs thinks it's just with women.'

'Well, yes, I had Lizann then. I mean, I don't fool with a whole stable if that's what you mean.'

'Pauli, I'll be in Hartford. Another conference in about two weeks. School is on then – they cram in a second summer session – but I'm hiring somebody to do my classes. Can I see you?'

'Of course. Stay with me before, afterwards? I have a nice apartment with a doorman who – he's like Jacobs.'

'Sounds better than where I live. I have to watch every wandering glance. I don't have tenure and in a public university they can get you on anything. Posture, dress. They told somebody in the art department she didn't *smile* enough and that's why she was losing students. So they cancelled her classes and contract. Like she didn't exist.'

'What happened to her?'

'I got a letter from her. She's job-hunting out here in California. I can't see her, but I'll probably phone from the airport . . . Pauli, you know something? You forgot to kiss me.' Chessie sat back against the tree's fragrant knots. The eucalyptus grove stood quiet without a breeze.

Pauli imagined the orange carp recircling their pool. She sat confused. She reached to touch Chessie's face. 'Give me time, Chessie. I can't believe this whole thing. I was so incredibly depressed when I left the east. How could I imagine a damn cancer conference would rejuvenate me?'

'You never can tell who you meet at cancer conferences.'

Pauli laughed. Maybe it would be easy to forget Stevens, Lizann, people like Alan, if she had Chessie, living and warm, not anaemic airletters or a stack of lab reports.

As Pauli nestled her face into Chessie's neck, she asked, 'What kind of perfume do you use? It's driving me –'

'It's not perfume. It's oils I blend myself. I add them to my own face cream too.'

'I bet it's chopped muskrat sex glands.'

'Shut up. You're too analytic,' Chessie murmured.

When Pauli closed her eyes, her lips met Chessie's.

21

With the hotel's liberal check-out time, Chessie vacated her own room and appeared in Pauli's. Or by 4 p.m., at least her possessions had – a handsome red-and-blue woven suitcase, a cosmetic bag and a pile of medical papers and conference literature. And – oh yes, Pauli laughed to see the hotel's liquor supply of miniature bottles supplanted in her refrigerator by plastic bags of carrots, sprouts, low-fat cheeses, plus apple juice and non-alcoholic beer. Two kinds of whole-rye crackers now nestled in the top dresser drawer.

Before attending Chessie's Golden Fleece Awards ceremony, Pauli mixed herself a Martini and stared out at the skyscrapers. With every sip it seemed she could soar out her window upon the sea breeze, alighting on the Golden Gate bridge in time for –

Admit it – scared to spend the night with Chessie. Afraid you'll ruin it, make the wrong move . . . But you haven't so far, and after ten years with Lizann you certainly know where the noses go, not to mention all the other things.

Pauli lay down and stuffed a pillow between her thighs. She must have fallen asleep because when awareness returned, the honeyed shadows in the room had moved across the chocolate walls, and a key was rattling in the doorlock.

Chessie strode in, dumping more papers upon the other bed. 'Hey, you missed my Golden Fleece ceremony. I looked for you everywhere.'

'I'm sorry. I didn't mean to. I just nodded off, I guess.'

'Do you always sleep with a pillow between your legs?'

'Only when I lack something more exciting.' When Pauli began to giggle and get up, Chessie sat down on her legs.

'No. Don't get up. I give marvellous massages. Just let me get my good suit off and my oils out.' Soon Pauli had removed all but slip and underwear while Chessie, clad in bathrobe, worked above her, beginning at Pauli's feet with soft taps and twists. As Chessie worked her way up the legs and spine, toward the heart, into the shoulder and neck muscles, a delicious cloud of mixed scents – lavender, cinnamon, and two more Pauli couldn't identify – rose with her in the cosy room.

By the time Chessie reached her scalp and face, Pauli had relaxed in total bliss. Eyes closed, she turned on to her back, feeling as if her limbs could dribble into the mattress.

'Come under the covers with me,' she murmured, beginning to massage at Chessie's hips and back as Chessie sat beside her.

When Chessie leaned over, their mouths met in a luxurious exploring kiss. Chessie tasted as good as they both now smelled – somewhere between mint and cinnamon. Suddenly the robe fell away, exposing Chessie's firm, high breasts and strong belly. Pauli pulled her down under the chocolate covers and clean white sheets, beginning to kiss at her neck and feeling her own nipples harden at the caress of her tongue against Chessie's breasts.

'Oh, that's marvellous. It's been . . . so long,' Chessie whispered. 'Come closer. Ummm.'

'For me too,' Pauli answered. 'Uh, on your massage, there's one place you missed, and it really needs it.'

'What?' Chessie's large violet eyes opened. 'But my massages are always thorough. I learned the whole Swedish method.'

'Well, this is the American method,' directed Pauli, guiding Chessie's hand, gold rings and all, between her own legs, where it explored deliciously, then found both outer and inner lips waiting and wet inside Pauli's underpants. Pauli's hips moved in rhythm with Chessie's fingers, back and forth, then in and out.

'Hey, slow down,' Chessie called. 'We've got all night, dear, and besides, I save my super massage for there.'

When Pauli opened an eye, Chessie's tongue flicked at Pauli's nose.

'You harlot. How did you know I love that?' Pauli grinned, then removed her own bra and the moist panties. Now Chessie's fingers explored Pauli's upper half. 'You know you have breasts like a teenager? You're lucky they're so small. Why, I can feel your ribs.' Beginning with the nipples now, she massaged in circles. Although her fingers hesitated around the lump, she continued until Pauli again felt ready to melt into the mattress. *The hell with the lump*.

Now Pauli began to explore Chessie's milky skin, inch by inch, with her tongue, beginning with her ears, while her hands rubbed at Chessie's back and buttocks. To tease, she slid a couple fingers between Chessie's legs, withdrawing them immediately.

'Again, again,' Chessie begged. 'I love it. I love *you*.'

'Of course,' said Pauli, 'it's my American method – with stops at Greece and a few other places.' *I love you*.

'Don't stop anywhere.' And then as Chessie was about to cry out with wanting, Pauli understood and covered her with kisses and tongue, filling her with gentle, then insistent fingers, one, two and three, stroking and pulling her nub of pleasure until Chessie moaned, and Pauli began rubbing herself in joy against Chessie's ecstasy until dusk, rising off the blue water, softly darkened the room about them . . .

'Pauli, are you awake?'

'Umm.' In the darkness Pauli spooned herself against Chessie's warm back and breathed into the soft curls about her ear.

'What happened?'

'What d'you mean?'

'I've never done . . . all that on a second date with anybody. We really got carried away.'

'I loved every minute of it!'

'I did too.' Now Chessie giggled.

160

'You know, before you arrived this afternoon, I was afraid I'd do something to, well, ruin things.'

'That's just what I was lying here worrying about. How did you know?'

'I love you, Chessie. Just enjoy what we have together now. Promise?'

'Promise.' Chessie wound her fingers through Pauli's.

22

Back in Connecticut, Pauli's stomach sank when Heather's morning voice came across the phone.

'I tried to get you last week. You've been away?'

Chessie, I need you.

When Pauli didn't answer, Heather continued, 'Pauli, I want to apologise for the other night, our trip. I really wanted a day in the country, but I was lousy company. And what's his name, Edward, frightened me. How he crept up on us like that.'

'I know,' Pauli agreed. 'I should have held him off, but sometimes he's amusing. I know him better than you. I could have angled him off. I sensed somebody watching us. Anyway, did you read the paper? They . . . got him. Must be grand larceny. Stealing so much stuff. Do you think they'll charge him with the . . . killing too?'

'I don't know. Steve – the Institute has enough problems without people getting rich at everybody else's expense. But the police did ask me again about Harry and what I know of Institute finances.'

'So Edward's pointing the finger at Harry?'

'Looks like it. Pauli?'

'What?'

'I apologise. I mean, I know if you had anything to do with Steve's death or you . . . saw anything, you would have told me. I feel you're an honest person.'

Heather's wrath Pauli had rehearsed, but Heather's praise? Pauli sighed. 'This thing has messed up all of us. I just flew in from San Francisco. My mother's very ill. I phoned my brother, Frank. He's coming tonight. Maybe we three of us, as I suggested, can go out and have fun. Get drunk some night?'

When Heather accepted readily, Pauli squirmed. The idea would provide Frank with somebody to talk to. But how could the apartment hold both him and Chessie if she actually showed up? Well, Frank never stayed very long. Once he realised a situation was hopeless, he got angry or otherwise eased his way out, leaving it to Older Sister. At least he could help visit and evaluate nursing homes.

'Heather, do you know any decent nursing homes around here?'

'You think it's time to enrol me?'

'No-o.' Pauli laughed. 'For my mother.'

'There's a place out in Branford my neighbour used. I'll get its address or phone or something.'

'Thanks, Heather. Oh, I have another request. If it's too much to consider now, let me know. I have somebody else besides Frank arriving soon. That person' – what a description of Chessie! – 'can stay with me. But would it inconvenience you for Frank to stay at your place? I expect he'll leave promptly. Illness never interested him one bit. He's a mining engineer, has lots of adventure stories to tell.' Say yes; say yes. Or try Rainette, but her husband vetoes these things. No point in calling either of the lesbian couples she knew, begging hospitality for a man. Silence. Had she said too much, too little? 'I'll get him at the airport, and he's used to cooking for himself,' Pauli cajoled.

'Tonight's not the greatest.' Doubt now oozed from Heather's voice.

'I know. I should have asked before I left, but I wasn't sure exactly when he'd arrive. *I hadn't met Chessie then*.

'Tell you what,' Heather rallied. 'I'll get a bed ready on the sun porch, and you can pick up a key from the neighbour in the white house.'

'What time?' How accommodating Heather was. Stevens must have been blind.

'Oh, after 8.'

'Fine. Thanks again. I won't forget it.' Pauli hung up,

realising it was insane to indebt herself in any way to Heather. But if Chessie actually arrived, to evict Frank from her living-room sofa, while she and Chessie shared her double bed, would look suspicious, tactless, impossible. If Chessie never showed, plenty of time then to take Frank off Heather's hands.

On her way out Pauli unlocked her outside mailbox. No letter from Chessie yet. *I'll call you from Hartford. . .* Promise? *Promise.*

At work Pauli phoned Coral, who hadn't returned yet.

23

The message arrived from the hospital at 10.15 the next morning. Somehow Sara, who wasn't the receptionist, got the information first anyway and left it as a powder-pink memo on Pauli's desk. Why hadn't she interrupted Pauli's and Jacobs' meeting on article emphasis and lead stories for coming issues?

With Sara, better not ask.

Two sentences: 'Mother ill. Come to Medical Center. Frank.' By the time Pauli discovered the note, Sara had already left for lunch. She must reason with her about the wisdom – not to mention courtesy – of relaying life and death messages more promptly, although there was more satisfaction in not seeing Sara than in seeing her . . . Who needed one more shrug and complaint about overwork, life was hectic, and didn't Pauli know Jacobs hated his meetings interrupted?

As Pauli rushed to her car, she informed Jacobs. His jowls nodded wisely. His only reply was, 'It's been going on a long time', from which Pauli intuited, I wish you well, you'll do fine. In one way Jacobs reminded her of Stevens – the same tired, quizzical but benevolent non-involvement. Perhaps Jacobs had missed his calling, should have auditioned as a gynaecologist.

Fifteen minutes later Pauli met Frank amid the rubber plants, potted palms, fountain and bustle of the hospital lobby. Her own surgery would probably occur upstairs somewhere here unless she could convince Dr Williams to do it under local anaesthetic at the surgeons' office. *It moves easily, Pauli. Good sign.* Chessie's lovely voice.

A 40- by 20-foot blow-up of red blood corpuscles (sickle cell anaemia?) adorned one whole wall of the lobby. If this study in shades of grey was somebody's idea of inspiring art . . . Must be op art, because individual black sickles danced as Pauli stared.

Frank kissed her hello. To his raised eyebrows she answered, 'Sorry I'm late. Somebody who's not the receptionist took your message. So I just got it . . . How is she?'

Frank sat down again on a squeaky beige-vinyl sofa. Staring away from the death-dancing corpuscles, Pauli took his hand. 'Well, she's conscious, but they don't have the brain scan results yet.'

'So they did another scan. You mean it's another stroke? You arrived just in time.'

Frank nodded.

Pauli felt every muscle tense. 'Is she in pain?'

'Yes. She moans a lot, but maybe she's just trying to communicate. I don't know.'

'I'm sorry. I know she's in pain. I just feel the whole thing's been a mess. For her and us.'

'You're torturing yourself again,' he chided. He wiped a swatch of hair from his forehead. He was parting it too low again on one side, continually losing to gravity.

'How's life with Heather?' Pauli enquired.

'My absentee landlady.' Frank twisted his lips. 'I met her when I arrived last night. That was it. She was gone this morning. I'm on one floor; she's on the next. If you had matchmaking in mind, you better pick a less elusive lady.'

'You know I didn't,' Pauli insisted. 'So it's working out? She complained she was lonely, and you needed a place to stay. How's the house? She's scared of being there, you know.'

Frank nodded. 'Well, I did hear her on the phone this morning fighting with the police about taking some kind of seals off that room by the front door. When they wouldn't agree, she ripped them off. So she doesn't see them every time she goes out, I guess. Cheery house you fixed me up at,' he went on. 'I'm on the back porch. Good thing I got used to fresh air and birds in Colorado.'

Pauli tried to change the subject. 'I just met an interesting teacher from Colorado at the San Francisco conference. She may stop over at my place while she attends an East Coast conference.'

'Oh?' Frank questioned.

Mistake. Drop it before he enquires whatever happened to Lizann. 'Well, I better visit Mom's room. You coming?'

'No. I been here all morning. I need some exercise.'

'Wait for me? Have lunch with me?' Pauli suddenly pleaded. Any session with her mother proceeded better if she had a reward to anticipate.

'All right. Uh,' Frank warned, 'she can't talk at all now.'

'I know. Just screaming. Frustration tolerance zero.'

'No,' he disagreed. 'It's worse now.'

What could be worse? A coma would be a blessing; only consciousness was worse. Reluctantly Pauli left the lobby hustle of people, announcements, normal life and movement.

In room 2316 with the blinds drawn she couldn't at first distinguish her mother's white hair and skin from the tangle of white sheets. As she switched on a wall light behind the bed, her eyes followed the transparent worm of an IV from its steel tree down into a thin wrist. 'Mom? Can you hear me?' Pauli took one limp hand, expecting to find it cold, but instead it was warm, as if fevered.

Pauli drew the plastic drape on its ceiling runner about the bed and sat down in an orange armchair, one of the back-sloping kind that made it impossible to touch the patient without perching forward on your own spine. Another inert body lay in the next bed beside the window.

Suddenly Mrs Golden awoke. When her eyes batted open, her jaw fell slack against the pillow. Just as Pauli leaned forward to kiss her forehead, the mouth began to moan, rapidly attaining a piercing wail. 'Mom, please stop! How can I talk with you? It's me, Pauli,' she begged. 'If you want to see me, please stop crying.'

The wails grew louder, longer. Mrs Golden had already learned to do them breathing in as well as out. This must be the moment when competent parents lift the fretful baby, but how do you console a woman who weighs more than you – with hoses sticking from both ends?

Familiar fires of impatience, then rage, then guilt flared in Pauli. 'Mom, please, shut up! I rushed from work to see you. With that bawling, all I can do is leave.'

The wails increased – horrid animal moans. Where could a dying body find the force to produce such banshee sounds? Summon the nurse? Forget it. They'd got enough to do for the living.

Minus teeth, glasses and hearing aid, her mother's face had become a red and black hole from which horrors issued. Impossible to know which side the new stroke had affected, since her whole body, except for the wail, lay limp.

With a final clasp at her mother's shoulder Pauli fled the room avoiding the nurses' station. Frank would have the latest doctor's report. God, how do nurses stand it? They don't care, they couldn't care. That's how. No wonder Stevens acted . . .

At the corridor's end as she hurried into the second-floor lounge, a wave of pain attacked and immobilised her midsection. She collapsed on the nearest chair, clutching its arms with damp fingers. Heather had complained of stomach-muscle cramps. Must be spreading. New disease. Rigor midriff. Prognosis: non-fatal, uncomplicated unless gastroenteritis ensues.

Pauli rubbed her stomach and abdomen, gasping for breath. From the time of meeting Frank, she'd stiffened her muscles, ribs through abdomen, and restiffened them to perch on her mother's chair. Now they sought revenge. *I can't stomach this*.

When she finally reopened her eyes, she jumped at the figure in the wall mirror – her own whitened face, hair awry, one eyelid trembling.

'Can I help you?' Somewhere behind her a soft voice enquired. She turned, instinctively looking upward. Instead her gaze met a woman in a gold robe very like her own dress, seated at her level in a wheelchair just one foot behind Pauli. The woman's right arm hung in a sling. 'Are you all right?'

'Yes. No. I don't know. My mother isn't doing very well.' Again Pauli rubbed her diaphragm, coaxing the tension to unknot. At this rate, Frank wouldn't need to take her to lunch; she'd never swallow another bite. Case of terminal tension.

'Where is your mother?' the woman was asking.

'Room 2316. She's had another stroke.'

The woman nodded. 'I've been here a month. I know everybody. I get around.' She smiled. 'Your mother must be new.'

'She's not new at all.' Pauli groaned. 'Well, she entered this morning, I guess. I was at work . . . How're you doing?' Anything to banish the image of her mother – and her own failure to comfort.

'I have pain sometimes, but the nurses are very good here. They sit with me. I got . . . cancer.' She stumbled over the word. Pauli stared. 'It was . . . breast cancer, but last month I was lifting my turkey pan from the oven and my shoulder just broke. But I didn't drop the turkey,' she added proudly. 'My husband grabbed it.'

Whatever Pauli wanted to discuss, it wasn't cancer. But, 'Do you have a lot of pain?' was all that her mouth put together.

The woman's long, straight nose crinkled as if smelling something noxious. 'Yes. But the nurses give me a cocktail. They're very good . . . What do you do?'

Pauli continued to stare at the woman until her eyes scrunched up. She was amazing – dying of cancer metastasised to the bone, needing morphine every few hours, and here she enquired how and what Pauli did. Pauli bit her lip to quell tears that threatened inside her eyes. 'I'm sorry. My mother's condition gives me a pain in the stomach.'

'I know,' the woman answered.

'How?'

'My daughter comes to see me every other day. I watch her eyes.'

'Why, your daughter must be just a little girl.'

The woman laughed. 'She's twenty-two and I'm older than I look.'

'Well, I'm a –' Pauli hesitated. Bellydancer? Would

explainthe spasmed stomach. As desperately as she attempted something light and funny, all that occurred was the truth. 'I'm a medical writer. Mostly cancer and surgery and hormone stories. Those are the hot news items. Unfortunately.'

'That's very useful. If I had . . . things to do over, I always wanted to be a writer. It's a gift. Is it hard to write about cancer?'

'It is. For every theory there's a counterattack theory. It's maddening. You wind up wading through pages of gobbledegook. Some paragraphs have a ten-syllable enzyme every other word.'

'You have to learn a lot then. I *know* they'll find a cure for cancer soon. I was reading the other day of a better test to detect breast cancer earlier. Maybe *you* wrote it.'

Pauli blushed. Just then a stocky nurse in flyaway cap peered around one doorway of the small lounge, calling out, 'How you doing today, Alice?'

'Fine. I got a nice lady to talk to here. I have such a busy life, you know.' She was mocking herself.

When the nurse continued the sentence, 'And you're gonna live it with style', Pauli realised it was a game between them. The nurse winked and disappeared.

Pauli sat stunned with admiration for this Alice, sitting crooked and broken but so alive in the wheelchair. In pain, days away from death, yet sure a cure for cancer would come 'soon'. Was she real?

Relaxing her own shoulders, Pauli discovered she now could coax the abdominal muscles in and out. Maybe up and down would follow if she was a good girl. No muscles, no sex. Damn. But with luck, she'd eat again. 'I'm sorry. I should go,' she announced, trying to rise. 'My brother's waiting downstairs.'

'Will you come back and see me?' While maintaining her dignity, the woman allowed a hint of pleading to infect her voice. 'I have . . . so many questions my doctor won't answer. And the nurses are so busy. I bet you could answer them. I'm so happy to meet you . . . Can I ask you something? Will you let me hold you?'

Pauli smiled before Alice continued. 'My husband used to hold me. Then they took my breast away and he said the scar was ugly. Once when I begged him, well, too much, you understand how I mean? He said I looked like . . . a freak.'

Alice in her gold robe and pink nightgown a freak? At the word Pauli's muscles contorted again. Tears swelling her eyes pressed behind her nose. 'Alice, maybe he was mostly scared of illness, not of you.' True? Who could know? 'Anyway, I'm a freak too.'

'You?' Alice giggled. 'You're a lovely young woman. You can make some man very happy.'

Except that I like women as well, so nobody trusts me. 'I had someone this year, but he isn't . . . around now.'

'I'm sorry. Will you do something for me?'

Pauli steeled herself.

'I'll hold you and maybe you'll hug me?'

Expecting to fall over, Pauli nevertheless reached out. Where do you hug a woman with a broken shoulder and devoured breast? Rubbing Alice's back, she drew the woman towards her chest. Alice felt soft and smelled somewhere between lilac and lily-of-the-valley. 'I would have hugged you anyway before I left. You didn't have to ask.'

'That feels good,' she whispered. 'You know something? I'm the only person I know who tries to masturbate with an aspirin bottle?'

Still hugging Alice, Pauli rocked with laughter. 'Does it work?' Tears overflowed her eyes, laughing and crying mixed.

'Well, my only other choices are a table knife and a thermometer.'

'Stick to the aspirin bottle,' Pauli advised. 'Will you do something for *me*?'

Alice nodded.

'Maybe if you get time, you could look in on my mother? Room 23–'

'16,' the woman finished. Morphine certainly wasn't dulling her. Which meant it no longer dulled the pain either.

'First bed,' Pauli added.

With a final grasp of Alice's hand, Pauli left the lounge.

What a gift Alice was. Despite Medicare stringency on reserving hospital beds for the acute not the chronic, patients like Alice didn't get transported to the end of the line – a nursing home among strangers. Doctors and nurses united to keep them going as long as possible. Who could resist such cheer and will and strength in the face of the unknown and the monstrous?

Pauli recalled her mother and shuddered again. If only Alice's character and courage were infectious like viruses or maybe even cancer itself.

24

Dinner with Morgan at Fitzsimmons' restaurant was proceeding swimmingly. One Martini was gradually renewing Pauli's San Francisco amnesia from her mother's dying, Stevens' death, Lizann's defection – in reverse order of recent chronological disasters. All blurred, tragedy transmuting into history, physical facts that might have turned out differently but hadn't and now never would. If one Martini changed passion into philosophy, what would two do?

For the first time Pauli was glad she'd buried herself in work during the weeks since the party. With ample time to consider any of that trio of hopeless problems, she might have popped an exclamation mark and wound up wandering Grand Central or Union Station unable to recall who or why she was.

Fitzsimmons Finn had been a rum-running sailor, and his namesake restaurant lay shimmering before her. Arched windows punctuated antique brick walls from floor to ceiling. Commas of potted Boston ferns drooped from high hooks. She and Morgan sat on varnished churchpew seats inside a nook made of scarlet-velvet curtains hung on brass rods. Pauli parodied her childhood prayer, 'Bless me, Doctor, for I have sinned.' Did this fascination with doctors stem from the fact they had replaced priests as the world's purported miracle workers?

Besides hinging to the stairs, the section of pews and tables where Pauli and Morgan sat swung by ceiling chains a yard away from the walls on the other side. Pauli felt adrift on a boat, almost dizzy as she leaned and gazed straight down upon the heads of diners below. Above the dish clatter and grill sizzle, pleasantly dissonant jazz played somewhere, loud enough to intrigue, soft enough to encourage conversation.

Fitzsimmons' must be a lovers' or businessmen's restaurant, and Pauli wondered why Morgan had brought her here. Must be a small reward for the nights watching mice, building tumour slides, scanning badly Xeroxed papers.

Morgan seemed as voluble tonight as Stevens had been taciturn. From the number of women's names, Pauli gathered he gave everybody a rush, then dropped both her and her name after three or four dates. 'Let's see, it was Norma I took to the theatre and disco. She's –'

'It's okay, Morgan. I don't really need to know your love life.' Pauli sat annoyed. Was he revealing all this stuff to attract – or repel – her?

'Morgan, you like women, but I think you don't trust them very much?' *Like you with men, Pauli*. She allowed the hint of a question both to give him room to manoeuvre and to rechannel the subject.

Ceasing the prattle, he blinked in surprise. The waves in his ash-blond hair caught light from the hanging Tiffany lamps. Instead of answering, he looked away and read the motto attributed to Fitzsimmons, who probably found rum-running more profitable than restaurateuring: 'If you are constantly watching fires, you may as well cook with them.'

'Wait a minute,' Pauli protested. 'That reduces women to some evil you tolerate, then use for all it's worth.'

'My marriage wasn't . . . much of a success. My wife left me for another man. Our beginning was all right, but then she got like a rattlesnake always striking out, bitchy when things didn't please her.' Again Morgan gazed away, unwilling to meet Pauli's eyes.

Was Morgan's impromptu confession true?

Pauli sat confused, head spinning. When in doubt, stick to the facts. 'When was this?'

'Years ago . . . I grew up everybody's model son. National

174

Merit finalist, Williams College, Harvard Med School, Mass. General residency.' He intoned all this in a single rush of breath. Did it now bore him? 'I . . . had a breakdown second year of medical school. I'd just got married; we had no money; my grades sank. I bought a motorcycle and began ballroom dancing half the night. I wanted to drop out of school and become a professional dancer.'

'What stopped you?'

'My father. He was a lawyer, very popular with clients. I thought I'd never measure up to him, either make it through school or make it with private practice. So I chose pathology at the last possible moment. The dismal specialty.' When he smiled, Pauli assumed this was a joke, the contrast with obstetrics, supposedly everybody's 'happy specialty'.

'No. What really stopped me was the dean, who also happened to be my faculty adviser. When he threatened to flunk me, I wanted to yell and scream and tell him off, but my throat froze. I made it outside his office to the street in the back when the rest of me just went dead. I couldn't move an arm or leg. I was suffocating. Somebody dragged me to one of those granite walls coming off the back steps. I was terrified. If I couldn't be a doctor, my father would wipe me out. And if I couldn't *move* at all, I'd never be a dancer either . . . Look, why am I telling you this?'

'Because I asked. Hysterical paralysis,' Pauli diagnosed. Morgan winced. 'Model son who finally rebels. What happened then?'

'I literally could not move or speak for the next hour. Somebody got the idea of putting a yellow pad and pen in front of me. They thought I'd had a stroke, but nobody called an ambulance. All these diagnose-it-yourself medical types. Anyway, everybody was in class till 4.30 so I didn't look like a total ass to more than about three people.' Morgan closed his eyes and seemed to relive the event against the music beat that had shifted from contemporary jazz into Big Band trumpets and clarinets.

'I knew if I could just force hand and eyes and brain to make one sentence on that yellow pad, I'd be all right. The pen kept falling out of my hand until they held it for me. Still I was suffocating.'

'What did you write?'

' "I" – the worst word was "I" – "am going to be . . . a doctor." When I reached "doctor" – it must have taken ten minutes – I dropped the pad. I can't remember what happened next. I felt somebody rubbing my arms and legs, and suddenly it was all over. I could stand again. They drove me home.'

Intriguing as Pauli found this confession, she squirmed. All focused on Morgan's apparently vanished dilemma, it touched nowhere on her problems. Like listening to Frank discuss the terrors of Colorado politics and mining engineering, as if medical writing held none of its own. And she envied Morgan the luxury of a disappeared problem that could be discussed with ease, if not clarity. To be randomly victimised by emotions you couldn't admit – Pauli lived that too. *Lizann*. And when would Chessie ever phone?

'Did you write any more?' Pauli finally asked.

'That night I stared at that one sentence. I knew it was a letter to my father I was trying to write, saying I was dropping out of med school. Instead it turned into the opposite.'

'But you were meant to be a doctor. Look, all your research, how good you are at getting grants, not only here but for Europe.'

'And that's the unfortunate essence of everybody's medical research – stalking grants and felling them with the blast of a pen.' If Morgan hated his work, she didn't want to sit through any more snideness about it. So his smooth, ironic self-assurance came from surviving med school and his father's orders, plus the sheer advantage of being male with blond hair in a white male world. Whenever life developed nodules, rip them out – no problem.

'Did you like your father?'

'He terrified me would be more like it. I remember even in grade school I took the long way home to avoid an older boy who *reminded* me of Father.'

176

Was Morgan possibly the only American she'd met who had a 'Father' instead of 'Dad' or 'Daddy'?

'What about your mother?'

'Oh, she was there, but she didn't matter. She had headaches a lot. She must have feared my father too.'

Change the subject. Nobody can solve, resolve, the nuclear family. 'What do you think of Edward getting arrested?'

'It was obvious our stuff was disappearing. I hope they find my scalpels, syringes and culture dishes in among his loot. Stevens liked Edward, but the rest of us found him a bit of a dandy. Know what I mean?'

'I know what you mean, but what're you saying? He's gay, and that's why he steals Bunsen burners?' What simple-minded asses straight people were – anybody weak enough to be gay automatically qualified for any other crime or vice. No doubt the police were still grilling him.

'I don't care what he does with his private life,' Morgan insisted. 'But that total dedication to Stevens did make him useless to the rest of us. He had a routine set by his hero Stevens. If Harry or I so much as asked him to clean a cage, he had to clear it first with the great white doctor St Steven. The other day I asked him to wipe a counter. He told me to check with the janitor. I told him to go to hell. But you know even Stevens dressed down Edward about something the day he died. I mentioned it to the police.'

Even Stevens. 'Do you know what about?'

Morgan shook his head. 'Since it was in Steve's office, I didn't bother to ask. Now I'm tipping Leon a bit to help me with the clean-up.'

'Do you think Stevens died, well . . . because of a homosexual thing? Because they found –' She halted the sentence.

Instead of the robust denial that Pauli expected, Morgan frowned and sighed. Then he shook his head.

'What I mean is maybe somebody . . . Edward liked him, but got furious when he didn't . . . respond.'

Now Morgan blinked and began a counterattack. 'Look,

you had a thing going with Stevens.' Pauli's back and neck prickled. 'I read his letter.'

Gulping down the last of her drink, Pauli jumped, sliding the green olive whole down her throat. With total effort, she choked back the saltiness and refrained from gagging. Nothing, however, escaped Morgan's diagnostic vision. 'Easy, girl.' His sudden concern reassured, but she feared those gimlet eyes.

'Don't ever try to lie, Pauli. Or bluff at poker. You won't make it.' Then he smiled.

With her throat nearly controlled, she seized her red napkin and wiped her nose and eyes. This conversation must be a trick: begin by granting her intimacies in exchange for – what? What did he want? Blackmail? Her silence on something yet undisclosed?

'Surely you don't believe I killed him. I mean, I came to the party with *you*.'

'Don't worry. I'm not using the letter. I didn't give it to the police but –'

'You Xeroxed it just in case?'

Morgan pursed his lips.

'Actually,' Pauli began, trying to sound convincing. 'I wanted to break off with Stevens. Either he called my office when I asked him not to, or he claimed he was never in when I called him. Besides, for a marriage that's breaking up, the other woman is just a ricochet thing. Instead of telling it to the bartender, *she* gets to listen to it all. So I was ... upset to find that letter. Yet he was so *silent*. Something very touching, like you feel he needs your comfort, but maddening too. I finally decided he's a frustrated perfectionist who broods all the time, even –'

'You know, Stevens stood me up once,' Morgan interrupted. 'Last spring. We were going sailing one Saturday afternoon. I paid $200 to borrow somebody's power boat and gas it up. 1 p.m. came; I sat there in the cabin. About 1.30 I phoned. No answer, with nobody on the switchboard. Finally I drove to Medway. There was Stevens writing up quarterly reports for some board of directors' meeting. I can see why he snapped up your writing talents. Well, he'd not only forgotten our sailing afternoon; he looked surprised when I walked in wearing a windbreaker.'

'What did you do?'

'At first he seemed so engrossed I thought he'd say, 'Morgan who?' Nothing like the man he was at our other university project. Research – just part-time then – was a fascinating alternative to his frustrations with office practice. Well, I started by being understanding. Then I told him to go to hell. By that time it was 3 o'clock. I went sailing alone.' Morgan gritted his teeth, then sighed.

'Hey, you should have called me. I love sailing. It's my one chance at really fresh air.'

Morgan laughed and laid his right hand over Pauli's left on the table. She jumped. 'Uh, Morgan, when I mentioned that Edward probably had a crush on Stevens, I expected you to deny the whole idea of, well, a gay murder. But you just looked sad. Why?'

'*All* of us had crushes on Stevens. That's how he got us here. You know that?'

Pauli nodded. 'But you're the first one who's been honest enough to talk about it.' Just as Pauli feared she'd over-stepped the invisible boundary between pleasurable and painful confidences, Morgan shocked her by plunging onward.

'I'm not telling you anything I haven't told the police,' he insisted. 'I *know* it wasn't a gay murder because of something that happened before the sailing episode. To make up, I guess, for ignoring me during my first months at Medway, Steve invited me out for dinner late one night because he said Heather never cooks. Anyway, I was tired and a bit nervous so I drank too much. Then we drove back to my apartment.'

'I can't believe he made the first pass?'

'He didn't. I wanted him . . . to notice my work, to notice me.'

'Well, what did you do?'

'What would *you* do?'

'Try to get close to him somehow. With Steve, that wasn't easy unless *he* decided –'

'Well, he belted me one and left in a huff.' Morgan rubbed

his jaw, remembering. 'At that point I was too drunk to care, but –'

'So the sailing offer was a way to . . . make up?'

'Yes. But Steve never mentioned it again, and of course I didn't either. But I know he's invited others out too, when they first came.'

Say it. Morgan, I understand. I'm a lesbian who's finally met the woman of her dreams. Next she ached to discuss Lizann with Morgan, to gain forgiveness somehow from somebody for that failure. Finally, despite the Martini, cold reason surfaced. With Stevens' letter and their clandestine work arrangement, Morgan could already blackmail her tidily if he chose. She bit her tongue.

Luckily their suppers of broiled chicken and lobster arrived. She ordered another Martini and gratefully escaped into eating. Again her desperation surfaced to discuss the weeks' events with somebody who knew most of the facts. Neither Heather nor Rainette could be such a confidant. *Concentrate on the chicken; skip the confession.*

She lost. 'Actually Stevens was . . . the first man I liked in a long time. Must be the black hair. Like a boyfriend named Ron I had in college.'

'Passionate?'

Pauli nodded. 'Of course. That's the point of these things. Why else would anybody do them? And it's the main reason that I was breaking it off.' Pauli struck a second blow for the version she was proposing. 'It was a rerun, and besides, Stevens was married.'

'I'm jealous,' replied Morgan so casually Pauli knew he didn't care. Morgan smoothed back his own blond waves. 'I thought blonds have more fun, and here's Stevens getting all the action.'

'You know, you're a lot like him . . . Stevens,' she accused.

Morgan looked startled; his smirk faded. 'But Stevens was a pusher – a flatterer, and then he'd yell to get what he wanted. I came expecting – well, he pushed me.'

'I mean, I tell either one of you something,' Pauli insisted, 'and you lose your temper like Harry Stornell. Or laugh it off as though it were nonsense. Wasn't I sympathetic when you talked about the paralysis problem?'

'Yes, but that happened years –'

'So I'd like some sympathy in return if it's not too much trouble! Well, one thing I liked about Stevens was that sometimes I could tell him *anything*. He just didn't care. He'd heard it all before.'

Morgan nodded. 'I heard a new definition of soap operas you'll like. Forty million women watch them because unlike fiction or life, the men listen when the women talk.'

'How do you know?' Pauli gulped at her second drink, which had somehow arrived while she was attacking the tough broiled bird with pistol-handled steelware. If they built these fowl any sturdier, they could *serve* dinner on them, instead of eating them. Perhaps the creatures represented a newly mutated stock of nude bird, a variant of the featherless chicken. Food at the nearby restaurant was no better. That one called itself the Recovery Spot to capture trade from Sinai Medical Center next door.

Still, this restaurant's cosy red haze must be relaxing or she couldn't have got this far with Morgan. *I did love Stevens and Lizann. I already love Chessie.* 'My mother's quite ill now. I better not come to the lab with you tonight. I should stop by the hospital before visiting hours end. But I do have one more question for you. Do you think Harry Stornell is fiddling Medway accounts somehow?'

Morgan's jaw dropped. 'How did you know that?'

'Used my head. Do you know any details? Is that what you meant by "dealing with" Harry?' *So Harry is a crook? And is Morgan blackmailing him*?

'No comment. You tell *me*. You brought it up.'

Pauli shook her head.

Morgan returned to mouse business. 'If you can come for a few minutes, I'll show you some tumours I've regressed in the past three weeks. Amazing results using another protein serum I've purified. You'll see.' He smiled.

'Okay, I'll come. For a few moments. I'll drive my own car.' Now Pauli relaxed into the red bench pads. Whatever he wanted, it didn't seem sexual, just some variant of business. Or was this the beginning of blackmail by a man with a former father problem who already knew too much about her and about Harry?

25

At 8 p.m. Sara put down the phone. She'd never met Pauli's brother, but he sounded smooth, careful. 'I'd like you to relay a message to Pauli, please. Is she there? There's a family illness. Turn for the worse. Have her call me at the Medical Center until 9 and after that at –' And he gave a number which Sara recognised immediately as Dr St Steven's home number. So Pauli's brother was seeing Heather? Some grieving widow, that.

'I'm *not* the receptionist here,' Sara snapped. 'I'm working late tonight. In fact, everybody but Pauli is. Deadline for the next issue. But I'll do my best with the message. Have you tried her apartment?'

'Sure. She's not there. Do you –'

'She may be at the Institute. I can try that number,' Sara answered.

When Frank had hung up, Sara dialled Medway Institute. Busy signal. Probably Pauli getting it on with somebody else there now. That woman was ambitious, would sleep with anything in pants, or skirts, to further her 'career'. Now Lizann was sweet, blonde, honeydewed that day Pauli brought her to the Christmas party.

'My roommate.' Some roommate. The pair of them showed an attention to each other's looks and words that Sara had never seen in casual roommates, certainly in nobody she'd ever roomed with.

Maybe a woman like Lizann or Pauli could be homosexual and look normal, even sound normal. Sara could almost understand that. But then to go with men as well. That went too far; wasn't fair to normal women who had that much less chance of getting a man. Selfish really. People like that were freaks, deserved whatever they got. Couldn't even climb out of the sack long enough to make their dying mother's hospital bed. No wonder Lizann had left Pauli.

Sara dialled Medway again. Still busy. And like the magazine, too cheap to install a through-call system that got beyond the central switchboard when nobody answered it. At least the magazine was happily in the black this year – the figures on Sara's quarterly reports were looking rosy instead of red. Not like the Institute, a beggar for any private or federal grant they could scrounge.

Back to the cheque ledger, payroll book and the last of the quarterly tax forms. Above the receptionist's desk where Sara sat some wit had hand-illuminated a sign, parody of a medieval scroll:

TO BE A SECRETARY, ALL YOU HAVE TO DO IS

TYPE EIGHTY WORDS A MINUTE WHILE ANSWERING THE PHONE

ACCEPT BLAME FOR LOSING PAPERS YOU NEVER SAW

PERFECT YOUR ACROBATIC SKILLS SO YOU CAN VISIT THE LADIES' ROOM WHILE COVERING THE OFFICE AND –

GET IT ALL DONE YESTERDAY.

Underneath it, somebody else had scrawled what Sara liked better:

DOING GOOD WORK HERE IS LIKE WETTING YOUR PANTS IN A DARK SUIT –

IT FEELS GOOD BUT NOBODY NOTICES.

Now *that* one was true. Jacobs had always played favourites. Hard as Sara worked, she wasn't one of them, try as she might at her age to get his attention.

26

It was simpler with Steve out of the picture – might as well admit it. Harry removed his gold-rimmed glasses and rubbed his eyes. Also admit – he was totalling the figures – without Steve's expensive salary and extensive squandering on all those 'special projects', expenses had visibly declined during July and the beginning of August.

Even the back-up power generator was finally paid off. Harry had signed the final payment cheque on 25 June. Edward, that ass, would never again squeak out, 'They're unthawing.' Medway's whole first year and a half of tissue samples ruined during a blackout, which the power company blamed on Niagara Falls and God. Idiots! Well, now Medway had not only its own functioning back-up to power the freezers but a dry-ice supplier who promised instant service despite disaster if anything equivalent happened again.

But the final instalments from two small private grants would arrive in a couple of weeks, and then what to live on? Charles Rivers autoclavable mouse chow? Harry pictured Edward eating the fibre pellets. 'A touch dry, I must say.' Goddamn.

Steve had been hopeless at personnel problems, including conserving money. And he might have got himself murdered a few months later, when the big federal bucks were already rolling in. Well, Rainette could juggle balances some more, send partial cheques to the most insistent creditors and ignore the least insistent. The linen supply and towel people never noticed when they got paid. Must have a lousy book-keeper. Hope they don't fire her and hire somebody who can add up.

That deal with the computer rep was proceeding just fine. Night rates for day computer time in exchange for the guy's 'small consideration' that was too large but was still saving about $1,000 a month that everybody (here Harry lumped the animals with the people) needed. It was only robbing a computer corporation of some cash in twenty and one-hundred-dollar bills so Harry could support fifty-seven different varieties of mice and people, supplying the laminar airflow and sterilised everything to which they were addicted. The SPCA would be proud. Like the mice, the pedigree researchers don't stay either if you skimp on their facilities.

Harry heard the switchboard phone ringing from the lobby. Place needs a nightwatchman again as soon as the bucks start rolling in. Leon leaves at 5; no point in wasting money paying him time and a half.

Harry debated about answering. Let whoever's expecting a call get it. Probably some desperate wife with a sick-kid problem. People never understand mouse doctors specialise in rodents, not humans.

Who's here tonight? Probably only Arthur. If ever was a man lacking sufficient charm to capture wife or girlfriends, it was Arthur. Guy doesn't even like mice, only cells in test tubes.

Ignore it.

Harry thumbed the newest sheaf of pink purchase orders from his various labs for equipment and supplies to replace what Edward had fenced into oblivion. How the hell had he (they) lifted most of an electron microscope out the door? Must have used a dolly. Two dollies. Let the police earn their salaries by retrieving the stuff before he'd waste time and money ordering new. Morgan seemed to be functioning with the old optical microscopes, for instance. Plus:

Petri dishes
2 new mini-refrigerators (the hell with that; use the large walk-in instead)

one set of scalpels (how could any surgeon leave *those* lying around?)

1 carton (2 dozen) water bottles

vials of antibiotics

1 rubber tree for the lobby

4 jumpsuits (Edward and his buddies must be staging *Star Trek* in drag; his ears and head were pointed enough for two Spocks.)

Harry read on, feeling nauseous.

Let's see what the police could recover. The great white hero Stevens had never serviced any of these financial gut details that make a place function. Harry groaned.

Again the phone rang. This time Harry arose. Better switch the call through to Arthur. Must be for him? Who *is* here tonight? Check the car park from Steve's office.

6 August – Near the Lab

Research is like whoring – same hustle to make a buck.

Some guys with small pricks get ten kids. Hustlers like him operate a big one – no results, no grants. Then dumped his problems on me. No wonder he had no kids, screwed us to death instead. The French say, 'If you lack the goods, don't open the shop.'

I'd do it again to watch him squirm.

Tell it to the worms.

27

Fitzsimmons' expensive coffee and driving her own VW had sobered Pauli sufficiently, but cancer cells on Morgan's newest set of glass slides still danced and blurred greenly in the microscope field. Pauli yawned and fidgeted on her stool before the lab bench. If she propped her elbows and head for another five minutes, maybe she'd see clearly enough to make cell drawings. Jacobs liked an original medical illustration now and then to supplement photos. 'Histological section of benign breast tumour biopsy specimen (Patient C.S.) Source of grafts for nude mouse Triad 10.' Now there was a spicy title. At least, it was a way to laugh, instead of cringe, at her own breast predicament.

She shared Morgan's fascination with learning all she could to help people visualise abstract concepts like 'health' and 'disease'. Unlike Harry and other bureaucrats, or even Stevens, who preferred human medicine, Morgan seemed also to enjoy these hands-on animal and slide sessions. Or was he just showing off, figuring without his labels she wouldn't know what she was viewing anyway?

Suddenly she sensed, then turned to see, Morgan behind her. He had opened the french windows of his lab that faced on to the corridor and was peering at her.

'What's the matter?' Pauli asked. The only sounds she heard were the breeze against the window and rodent scrabble from one of the plastic bread-box cages on the bench beside her.

Next Morgan leapt towards her. 'Come on,' he ordered.

191

She felt his grip pulling her arms hard through her blouse and tweed jacket. He was forcing her towards the wall near his office door. 'Quick. Get in here. Somebody coming.' In an instant Morgan had grabbed the slides from her hands and was shoving her shoulders, handbag and notebook into the supply cupboard.

'Who? What?' she protested.

'I'll deal with him,' Morgan sputtered. 'Just get *in* here!' As quickly as she shoved one of his hands off her, she felt the other clamp on, and one of his knees thrust into her back. From the radiant microscope field Pauli found herself flung at the floor into complete darkness. Bright after-image circles danced behind her eyelids.

She heard a clicking above her head. Damn! Morgan was locking the door from the outside! An intruder she would have flung a cage at, but how do you protect yourself from a man you've worked with for months?

Was it Arthur out there? Some other woman? So Morgan wasn't as fearless or heedless as he claimed. *What if somebody notices us? Forget it. I want the work done.*

Next she pictured him hiding the key, first in the hand behind his back, then easing it to one of his lab-coat pockets. He always wore the starched coats to protect his pinstriped F. Scott Fitzgerald specials.

Now she heard voices – somebody's gruffness, Morgan's steady but higher-pitched responses. So Morgan's visitor couldn't be a woman. Didn't sound like Arthur either. Kneeling, Pauli felt round the door edges where light crept under the smooth metal. How dreadful to be blind and comprehend the world only through echos and feels.

When she leaned back and tried to sit, something dug at her spine. Glass sounds tinkled. Sh-hh! Feels like a shelf. Must have jarred a shelf.

He *must* have some reason for this. Perfume odours assailed her through the black. Her nose tracked them to somewhere above the glass. Must be soap or detergent.

Make noise. Embarrass him for playing this jerky prank. Maybe Morgan was stealing his own equipment, and his fence just showed up. So was his dinner tirade against

Edward the senior pot calling the junior kettle black?

To avoid the shelf, she now squatted, leaning her head and right ear against the door. Still impossible to distinguish words. If not Arthur, then who owned the gruff voice? Another problem with freelance consulting: you never meet – or hear – more than the one or two people you work with, and if your man gets fired or assassinated, you've 'consulted' yourself right out of the place. Renewed rage at Harry and the lot of them made Pauli perspire into the closet's antiseptic stuffiness.

Was it Harry out there? He had a voice gruff enough to role-play twin male-chauvinist-pig bosses. Maybe Harry, contrary to rumour, did concern himself with research details, and Morgan didn't want to admit his work needed any supervision, especially at night with a woman Harry thought he'd fired. If Morgan gets the axe, I'll *never* get paid. Damn!

The effort of listening, plus racing her mind like a rat in a treadmill box deprived of oxygen, was making Pauli sleepy. How could Morgan *do* this to another human being with whom he just spent an hour spilling his guts? Free psychotherapy with bargain-rate articles tossed in – that's what these bastards want. Oh, and sex. Well, suffocating in Morgan's closet ought to be sufficient aversion therapy to cure her for ever of Stevens.

Chessie, Chessie, where are you?

Pauli's head dropped again into the door. Softer this time. Either she was blacking out or layers of cloth cushioned her head. The rough fabric smelled clean, somewhere between rubbing alcohol and aftershave lotion. Abrasive on one side, coolly silk-lined on the other. Like Morgan. Felt like one of his suitjackets.

Now the closet grew cramping, painful. Like when her father had shut her into the coal cellar, that cupboard, for sassing her mother. Only she'd sobbed and screamed then until he relented, released and hugged her.

Kneeling again, she began to finger Morgan's sleeves into the inner silk pockets, then outside to what seemed like slanted pockets without flaps. Must be some jacket he rarely wore. All his others featured classic flaps.

Pauli poked her right hand into what felt like the right pocket. Uhh – hh! Biting sting. Then she felt blood flow from the side of her hand. Quickly she withdrew, thrusting the wound into her mouth. How dumb to bleed over one of Morgan's tailored specials.

What the hell was in there?

Her intact left hand refelt along the outside of the pocket. Something hard and long. Pressing her nose against the jacket to steady it, she reached in – cautiously.

Like a butterknife. Was Morgan stealing from restaurants? But no butterknife had these razor edges ... A scalpel. Must be a scalpel. But Morgan had reported his favourite set stolen in the heist.

Now the cut palm of her hand stung hard. Coppery blood-taste filled her mouth and oozed down her throat. Edward had a bloody shirt. Some news bulletin said so, but he claimed he'd got it in a fight. The blood proved to be his own anyway. Morgan would love her for spotting his coat and snooping his pocket. If she could only see enough to blot it somehow.

She tried elevating the ooze, pressing it against the metal door. Beyond the shock of cold steel against inflamed flesh, she felt no ugly trickles down her wrist now into her own wool sleeve or his jacket. Maybe her blouse had sopped it up. By the time Morgan decided to open the door, maybe she could hide it behind her back instead of balancing on her knees, one arm aloft, like a frozen yoga devotee. But how to drive home with a car that needed shifting at every corner?

Light stabbed into Pauli; she fell forward. Morgan caught her shoulder. 'Sorry. He's gone now.'

'Who? What happened?' At the last second, as he helped her rise, she remembered to give him her good left hand. 'Come on. What the hell happened?' she insisted.

Morgan squinted, then decided to answer. 'Harry claimed there's a phone call for you. Something about your mother.

Of course, I told him you're not here. He told me your red VW's in the car park and –'

'What about my mother?' Pauli interrupted, sucking her breath deep towards her abdomen. 'Never mind Harry.'

'He didn't say.'

'I bet it's a coma now. It couldn't get worse – or better.'

Morgan nodded. 'I'm sorry,' he added.

In the fluorescent brightness again Pauli brushed past Morgan's jacket to grab her handbag and notebook from the closet. The jacket was a beige polyester that blended exquisitely with Morgan's summer tan. No blood on it, at least outside. She must have bled into the pocket lining, but withdrawing quickly had spared the outside. She remembered that jacket. Where?

The night she met Morgan outside Stevens' house for the party. Evening sun through the ancient maples had printed leaf patterns on it.

The night Stevens died.

'All right?' Morgan was enquiring.

'I don't know,' Pauli answered. Her hand was leaking again. With her right thumb she angled a Kleenex between the cut and her skirt back. She stared at Morgan. Get out of here before he notices.

28

It can't be Morgan!

Morgan traps people in closets, but he didn't murder Stevens. Lord, don't make it Morgan. Any of those bastards – Arthur, Harry, Edward, bitter Coral – but not Morgan.

The night before, Morgan had eased Pauli out the side door as usual. If Harry saw her drive away, well, let Morgan explain it. The newest hospital crisis proved not a coma but a fall. Like an uncoordinated infant, Mrs Golden had somehow rolled herself towards the edge of the bed, where an aide had forgotten to raise the steel guardrail for the night.

Frank, who found her on the floor, had screamed at the aide, who burst into tears. Then he'd phoned Pauli. When she arrived, glad of the darkness to hide the cut hand, he was mumbling about suing the hospital over the scarlet bruise, now enlarging to a purple bump, on Mrs Golden's forehead. 'Stop it, Frank,' Pauli reasoned uselessly. 'She's fallen before. Her bed at home has no rails at all. As long as nothing got broken –'

'But you bought carpets for her place. No supervision here at all.'

In the emotional blaze over disciplining the dying, Pauli forgot to ask Frank never to phone Medway again.

Awaiting Basil Radison's phone call now, Pauli sat fidgeting at her living-room desk, trying to drive the hospital scene from her mind. Like the rest of reality: everybody's fault, nobody's fault. Having taken the afternoon off, pleading her mother's crisis, she felt guilty that instead of rushing to the hospital, she was again leafing through Institute papers and the financial printouts supplied by Rainette. Better than dragging 10 pounds of the stuff to a hospital phone booth. Should call Frank at Heather's place to see how he's bearing up, but post-lunch sleepiness had descended, making her unsure she wanted to learn just yet. One crisis per hour seemed about her limit these days. Frank had come to do his duty; he was sticking right by the hospital, no longer threatening to return to Colorado. She should be grateful.

The scalpel in Morgan's pocket could be innocent. All surgeons walk around with lucky knives in their pockets, don't they? For impaling stray mice or patients.

Morgan's not a surgeon. Stevens was the surgeon.

Come off it, Pauli. Maybe Morgan's an ex-Boy Scout, always prepared, manly hunting knives, that sort of thing.

Morgan's not a Boy Scout. And what sort of quarry is a 3-inch nude mouse, already moribund from something tragic?

Maybe he locked the jacket and scalpel in the closet to keep Edward from ripping off his last favourite and decent tool. That *must* be it.

Besides, nobody had proved a scalpel killed Stevens. According to an ancient forensic medicine text she'd consulted at the magazine, all a medical examiner can estimate by studying the fatal wound is the length of the murdering blade, not its style, its substance, or even its sharpness. A nervous amateur can produce a hacksaw gash with even the sharpest blade. Two qualifying 'unlesses': unless the weapon leaves behind identifiable metal particles; unless identifiable blood appears on it. Oh sure! *Your* blood in Morgan's pocket.

And nobody, so far as she knew, had even seen Morgan enter the murder room. After you but before Harry discovered Stevens dead.

Damn, Pauli, got yourself in too deep. Like Stevens' question marks decorating the reports, everything could mean something – or nothing. His red pencil-itis could yet prove only the doodlings of a perfectionist bureaucrat.

The jangling phone startled her. Instead of announcing, 'Pauli Golden' when she lifted it, she remembered to say hello. Basil Radison's voice boomed. She jumped. The mild type she used to know had already vanished into the person of this . . . crusader/agitator. Whenever Pauli imagined herself in twenty years – little old lady in tennis shoes, T-shirt and hoop earrings haunting cardiac and cancer conferences – she shuddered. Cardiac arrest.

She realised she was holding the phone away from her head and hadn't heard much beyond Radison's 'Hello!' explosion. '– can't really tell because I'd need to see the animals, but you're definitely on to something. No one document is suspicious; they're all written in standard atrocious scientificese.'

'Wait a minute. I wrote two of them,' Pauli protested.

'Yes. I noticed your name under Dr St Steven's. Well, anyway, I'd question your Mr Morgan Dianis, since he seems to have done the most stuff. For instance, who has corroborated his results with either his cancer cure serum or his phenomenal success in transplanting human malignancies into the nude mice? Benign tumours, human melanomas and, of course, various mouse cancers will grow in mice, but I never heard of anybody's succeeding at his rate with the stuff he claims to be transplanting. Nude mice can die of infection before many cancers manifest, anyway. Besides –'

'Wait a minute. He says his results are preliminary. If he announces too soon, especially with the serum, people will misuse it in inappropriate doses for all kinds of work, then declare it worthless. And he'll be screwed for their errors.'

'He'll be screwed anyway if he continues to claim miracle results for something nobody else has tried.'

'But it's the virology man at Medway, Arthur Huggard, who proclaims he's God's gift to cancer. Well, Stevens did complain Morgan refuses to answer colleagues' mail and questions. I don't know the reason. But he's quite open with me.' *Skip the closet.* 'Invites me to the lab more than I have time for.'

'Sweetie,' Radison's voice condescended, 'you're a charming woman. The man *likes* you.'

Pauli gulped. 'Oh, I bet he just figures, she asks so many questions, what could she know? No threat to him. Typical doctor type. Questioning people – and ungarbaging their answers – are my job.'

'You're not one of his patients, are you?'

'I hope not! He's a pathologist. Well, I do have a breast lump scheduled for surgery next week. Benign, I hope.'

Radison sobered. 'I know it's hard to think when you're worried about that. Well, the man is working an incredible number of things simultaneously – six of his own projects plus some hospital staff position plus consulting on, what is it you wrote here?' Radison rustled papers. 'On "Twenty different projects elsewhere in the US, Canada and Europe". You know that means sending biological samples, test results, lab protocols, data sheets out at least monthly. Does he do all that? He'd need a staff of three minimum plus himself to keep all those balls in the air. How many people work for him.'

'Nobody – except maybe at the hospital. He says he can't even get the lab assistant to mop a floor for him. There's an Institute secretary, but she's Harry Stornell's property, book-keeper, woman Friday.'

"Then it's impossible. Unless he works twenty-two hours a day and naps in the mouse house. Do you know the penalty for falsifying slides, records, lab samples, tests or other materials pertinent to a government contract, grant or project extended without additional funding?' Radison seemed to recite a litany. Holy Mary, Mother of Mice.

'Not really.' Pauli's mind was clicking.

'Okay. It's a criminal offence, and the last guys who got caught and tried were five executive officers and the director of animal testing at a New Jersey company. The director got five years in the cage, the others got fined, and the company filed for bankruptcy.'

'How convenient.'

'Exactly. It's a waste of time to sue a bankrupt company. Unless it sells gold or fur coats. By the time most stuff is auctioned, it's nearly worthless. What am I bid for 10,000 geriatric mice and a five-year-old refrigerator? You see?'

'Only too well.'

'My dear, why're you involved in this? Take it to the police. It's *their* job.'

'I'm already involved. And I did. Show them Stevens' question marks. About what I showed you. And Harry must have supplied more because they weren't interested in my reports.'

'Call them anyway.'

Detectice Jordan's cardboard square hung in Pauli's head. Sure, and find out what they already know – some motel clerk or Sara or Coral has blabbed I'm a lesbian having an affair with a murdered man. She'd misplaced Radison's voice again.

' – in a word,' he was concluding, 'it smells.'

'I know. I already figured it or I wouldn't have involved you. Thanks.'

'Let me know what happens. I have an account to settle with Stornell and Huggard from way back. And I hope your surgery turns out all right.'

One more call. At the medical library Heather happened to be returned from lunch.

'Frank appreciates your hospitality,' Pauli began.

'Actually I hardly see him. He's out of the house. From the way he hovers about the hospital he's really a good son. We did have breakfast together this morning.' Heather giggled. 'And I pulled up the kitchen blinds. I hope the neighbours think we're living in sin. Once I thought I wanted that house, but I am so ready to unload it now.'

Had the neighbours already reported Heather's new housemate? Well, that was her problem. 'Have you put the house for sale?'

'Not yet. I can't bear to just yet. I keep saying, next week. I guess I'm scared nobody will want to buy it so soon after –' She stopped.

Change the subject. 'What I called about is a computer question. Since you're the Medline specialist there, you're the perfect person to ask.'

Heather groaned. 'That thing is the agony of my life.

Before it moved in as the latest piece of technological junk, researchers located and Xeroxed their own material. Now I spend half my day dialling Yale and Bethesda for them and the other half calling to check why their literature search printouts haven't arrived. And finally untangling wrong amounts on their bills. The system works, but our equipment isn't meshing right with it yet. It's hell.'

'I know it's frustrating,' Pauli sympathised. 'Look, my question is: suppose on printouts I keep finding something that says, "Charged at 50 per cent" or even "No charge" next to the computer time or log-out or whatever it's called. Isn't computer time – the compute part contrasted to the connect-time part – supposed to cost something like hundreds of dollars an hour?'

'Yes. More from a small time-sharing place. A large place can give the better rates.'

'Well, what about it if somebody's getting it for half-price or even nothing?'

'It could mean two things. If the customer's terminal set-up is brand new, it usually indicates some enticing deal the systems analyst negotiated to attract that customer. You know, three months introductory half-price special to assure customers they won't overspend while they muck around learning the equipment. It's possible somebody just continued the original arrangement, forgot to bill the customer online at the full rate after the honeymoon period.'

The Institute's been around for two and a half years! 'Negligence then,' Pauli replied aloud. How to tell Heather her husband was a crook? 'Who oversees this billing or whatever?'

'Not the programmer the central computer sends, or the users at the terminals. They're just poor slobs who want magic done on their data. Usually it's the chief financial officer at the facility who negotiates first with the systems analyst, then with the systems administrator at the central computer.'

Harry Stornell! He was there signing cheques before Stevens. Negotiating with whom? 'And if they still get a cut rate after a long time?'

'Then they may be ripping somebody off. But it's hard to prove. The bills arrive here, for example, screwed up about every other month. They've even billed part of our time to another account. Great for us, but I can tell you I got one hostile call about it from a head librarian near Boston. Some of our terminals also do various other data work, like internal book-keeping, payroll, monitoring number of requests for particular titles. I mean, they connect internally or to places besides other libraries. Look, what's all this about?'

'Oh, a story I'm working on for the magazine. Thanks, Heather. I'm leaving for the hospital now. To keep Frank company.'

Something with the research . . . and now the computer time . . . and the scalpel.

How to prove any of it? And whether to get the police to work on this new information? Short of going to the Institute, how to ambush Coral? Pauli held her head in her hands.

29

Pauli had already noted her visits to the hospital blurring into one unending visit of alcohol with bedpan odours, airless rooms with plastic snakes dangling from steel trees – the stuff of nightmares. Following the tumble from bed, Mrs Golden slid to and from consciousness. Meanwhile, Frank hovered to stroke her hand and utter encouragement whenever her eyelids fluttered. A total coma would be a relief; comatose patients at least didn't crawl anywhere. Mrs Golden's skin remained pasty grey, nearly laundry colour. The rose nightgown Pauli had given her mocked the face above it on the pillow.

Frank's tenderness amazed Pauli, then made her alternately jealous and ashamed. Her mother had long ago exhausted Pauli's patience supplies. Were older sisters always expected not only to fend for themselves but to spare something to buoy up younger brothers? Was that the start of the automatic sympathy she showed all the men she interviewed – childhood guilt because Frank always expected more than she could spare? While she rejoiced that he, new to bedside depression, had tenderness to spare, she ached for some to bathe herself in. His quick cliché, 'How are you?' whispered bedside, hit her more like a cold shower.

As she hurried into the lobby, some realist's definition of a nursing home loomed in her mind: a million-dollar project to benefit the nearly dead at the expense of the living. She'd planned to pass the afternoon bedside as an alternative to acting on Morgan or on Radison's and Heather's disclosures.

When Frank appeared however, Pauli found herself following him from the room after the five minutes of watching the IV bottle, rubbing Mrs Golden's hands, hearing her gasps.

Half-way down the khaki corridor Pauli overtook Frank. 'Hey, you gonna talk to me?' she enquired, hand on his shoulder. He wore a handsome silk shirt between tea rose and cantaloupe that pleased Pauli.

'What's to say?' Frank massaged his temples and eyes. In the last three months he'd grown a beard exactly the auburn of Pauli's own hair. Viewing herself transmuted to this male form still shocked and delighted her.

Pauli tried a compliment. 'Well, I mean you're here so many hours a day. Somebody should thank you for your devotion, since she can't.' Pauli's head motioned toward the room they'd just left.

'It's obvious *you* don't care about her!'

'Is that what I get for complimenting you? I do care about her. I just won't be blamed for her problems. Also I've done it now three years. You've visited maybe twice a year. What do you –' As a Filipino nurse walked by, Pauli strangled her own tirade. 'Come on down to the snackbar. Want some lunch? I got a question to ask you.'

When the menu's strongest items seemed to be lemonade and coffee, Pauli settled for decaffeinated coffee with an egg salad sandwich. Frank grabbed a carton of milk and a perspiring piece of lemon meringue pie.

'What's the question?' he asked between munches.

'Will you please apologise? Getting all twitchy at me won't solve her problems, but anyway, what're we going to do about a nursing home? The hospital won't want her here beyond a couple of weeks. Shall I call the better one I listed her at and tell them about the latest stroke and fall? Not that we can get an immediate bed but –'

'But this is a hospital!' Frank exploded. 'They're supposed to take care of dying people, not get rid of them.'

Pauli bit her lips. Try again. 'I know. But she could live two days or two years in and out of a coma. Once she's no longer acute, we need alternatives. I can't supervise a full team of nurses at her apartment, do my job and finish all that stuff for the Institute.' In the air conditioning Pauli shivered. 'And *you* shouldn't have to either.'

'Why are you still there?' he asked suddenly.

Pauli's face twisted with confusion. 'There? The Institute? I need the money. It's impossible there now, but I'll hack a way through it.' Don't admit you've done six months' hard labour at something for which two or three frauds, a murderer and a thief won't kill themselves paying you. Damn!

Much as she expended herself deciphering the wonderful world of mining engineering and petroleum exploration, Frank never returned the favour. Could he believe women don't work at anything serious, shouldn't complicate their fluffy little heads? 'Frank, why don't you ask something sensible about my work some time? I'd appreciate it.'

Frank looked blank. Next he toyed his fork into shards of sticky crust. 'I guess . . . I guess I've always had Mom's attitude. You pursue everything so intensely, I never want your fretting to affect me. It's like there's no room for me in it, anyway.'

'That's not true. Don't you care about your work? How do you run a company and meet a payroll, then? I believe you can't stand to see a woman – except for Mom – doing what you call "fret", because it reminds you of everything *you* never dealt with!' Pauli's anger surged into her throat.

'Hey! Fighting won't help her.'

Pauli felt a sudden hand grasping hers on the table. 'You're right.' She conceded the point, now that Frank had tendered the first olive twig. 'Let the nursing home slide. The hell with it. Let Doctor Breen force the issue when he gets tired of Mom wasting his Medicare days here.'

'So,' Frank continued, 'don't mention the nursing home until we have to?'

'All right. But if you're not here, that makes me deal with it alone.'

'I'll *be* here. I promise. Don't you think I know a visit every six months is not enough when somebody's dying?'

Pauli managed a weak smile.

'I can see you're all up tight. *Why*'re you alone now? Is

Lizann away?' At last, a shred of curiosity about Pauli's existence.

'Yes. She's gone. Got married in Paris.'

'And you're not dating anybody?'

'Not really.' My last lover got murdered, and my last date probably killed him – that's all. It can't be Morgan; it can't be!

'Sorry to hear that,' Frank was continuing. Pauli sighed. 'Well, look, those relationships have a lot of jealousy problems. You can't expect Lizann to pass up the chance to be, well, normal, can you? Anyway, guess it's hard to be a swinging single if you don't find anybody who swings the same –'

When the jauntiness entered his voice, Pauli spat out, 'Goddamn you! If you think that's a joke. If you're so certified normal, why the hell didn't you marry? Why don't you produce the 1.8 grandchildren Mom wanted?'

From the next table two swarthy orderlies turned and stared. Lucky that hospitals are used to scenes.

'I don't have to answer that.' Frank sat back, smugly stroking his beard.

As Pauli struggled to her feet, she knocked her chair backward. Metallic clatter resounded. 'All right. Mom's all yours. I've had it,' she announced. And ran for the doorway.

Maybe Frank's gay too? Not bloody likely, she decided as she shoved open the glass door to the car park. About as likely as Morgan or Stevens? Frank knows I date men as well.

As usual, the VW's engine, overheated in August humidity, flooded and balked. Lucky I escaped Harry and Company last night. Pauli imagined herself marooned there until January, when snowploughs discovered her – or rigor mortis had frozen every problem. Who will stage fights around my death bed? Thank God I lack kids to burden with that mess.

It isn't Frank's fault. Addicted to Mom, then you, solving all his minor trials on the home front from skinned knees to trigonometry answers and term-paper outlines. When women have or make problems instead of solving them, he can't cope. About time he grew up! Why forgive everybody (don't think about Morgan), which is interpreted as a cosy invitation to ignore you and your work (don't think about payment for it either)? Pauli laid first her arms, then her head on to the red steering wheel. The car sat in the same stuffy noon air as the hospital room. Pauli rolled down her window to breathe.

A man like Morgan (and unlike Frank) must have totally drowned the mother in himself, stopped identifying with her, even mentioning her. So his problem bloomed and loomed fully grown, projected onward from his father to any man a few years older and wiser who resembled his father – until that man, like his father, also rejected him.

At least Stevens had liked women. He eagerly accelerated whatever attractions would accomplish the work and minimise staff problems. Ulterior motive: anybody who's all or half in love with you is not likely to strike for a union and higher wages. Not if their emotional and/or sex life rides on it. Didn't you hesitate to present him even the one bill because it made you feel like – a whore?

Why had Morgan arrived at Medway? Had to be Stevens' scientific reputation, plus charm. Harry couldn't attract a honeybee to a flower show. *Stevens was a pusher; well, he pushed me*. Morgan's words from the restaurant. But Stevens and Morgan had also shared some project while Morgan was still full-time at the hospital and Stevens did private practice. Had Morgan arrived at Medway expecting to continue benign-father-acknowledging-prodigy-son relationship – and found instead an exhausted, angry boss who arranged assignations at motels or power boats, then forgot to call or appear? And pushed you unmercifully for results without a pay raise?

But if that were true, why was Morgan so genial compared to Arthur, Coral, Harry? He even *appeared* less hounded than Edward. Good acting, Morgan.

Did a human relationship ever exist where nobody got pushed by others' illnesses, rigidities, expectations, psychoses? Ah, paradise, paradise. Ah, Chessie's mountain stream.

But little boys like Frank – and Morgan – finally mature, take their place as carers as well as being cared for.
Or murder to avoid it.

30

Phone Morgan once more. Sound strong, reduce involvement with the mess to a minimum, let the police sweat out who killed Stevens. Rewrite Morgan's four articles, put the newest data into a fifth one – or just outline it. Pull together the rest of what he ordered, submit your final bill and be done with it. Plead your mother, plead tension, avoid more uncreative encounters with both Morgan and Harry. Rotten of Morgan to expect you to show up again.

Morgan's continued expectations of her now made no sense at all. If you murder somebody (Morgan a murderer?), you don't invite reporters in to stumble over weapons and evidence. Unless you're harassed by Stevens or burgled nightly by Edward. Unless you're cocksure or blasé. *Blonds have more fun.*

What's another corpse to a pathologist, anyway, after vats of used body-parts grey and floating in phenol? Pauli shuddered. Every med school stereotype about pathologists reassaulted her: swine who root among rotting garbage, corporeal exotica, fanatically assembling specimens of the abnormal and horrid. Calcified foetuses; dermoid cysts that never attained foetushood but ended as sci-fi-like bits of teeth, bone and hair; one-eyed cyclops born full-term dead, preserved in jars; 4-inch gallstones; 20-foot tapeworms, long as the intestine they sucked from.

Did formaldehyde fumes become slow toxins to patho-logists' brains, inducing chemical madness, chronic toxic psychosis, until their hungers, like cancer cells, metastasised? Who else would describe tumours dug from the sleeping and the dead as lush fruits? 'Big as an apple.' Or an orange. And if they hit the jackpot with an ovarian cyst, perhaps a pumpkin or watermelon? 'Cheesy' pus, 'currant jelly' stools. Sick.

The original vulture of them all was the sixteenth-century anatomist Andreas Vesalius, who began the whole business of scientifically dissecting the dead. Pauli had seen his portrait with scalpel poised over the naked, unlucky corpse, one of Vesalius' eyes gazing towards a crucifix (a bow to the Church?) from his lean, fanatical, possessed face.

Enlarged lab rats they all were, inhabiting the basement of every hospital, med school and nursing home in the world, stabbing, weighing, bottling.

To divert such horrors, Pauli paced her living room, staring again at the red phone. Just your mother eating your brain. Stop it! You'll get over it. Her condition, like everything, will and must pass away. No one inhabits even a coma indefinitely. They must pull the plug to accommodate the less ill, the still living.

Despite her air conditioner's breeze, Pauli was sweating again. Altogether the summer's weather had been wretched. Solid rainsheets during May and June. Simmering July heat, the night of the party. Now early August, like a rainforest special imported to the city, alternated showers with humid sun every morning and afternoon. At least San Francisco had a cool and dependable, although damp, ocean breeze. Five times since returning, Pauli had stopped her hand from dialling 303, the Colorado area code, followed by Chessie's number. Pauli had written it two places in case it proved unlisted or one of her addressbooks strayed.

Don't run after her. She knows you're interested. Let *her* contact *you* about the Hartford conference. Maybe she can't come, has to teach, couldn't arrange a replacement. Maybe it's too expensive. Denver–San Francisco plane fare is one thing; 4,000 miles roundtrip the other direction is something else. Fiercely Pauli reinforced her original decision: let her contact you. If you don't hear from her, phone in a couple days just before her conference. Chessie's dusky-rose skin and perfume reassailed Pauli . . . Offer to finance her plane fare if she still cares. Otherwise drop it. Who needs one more frustrating transglobal relationship? As with Lizann, remain dependent on letters whose lines you reread until they tatter and smudge? Who the hell wants a pen pal when you need a lover?

Stevens no longer counted. Even New England Telephone's wizardry had not achieved an area code to the afterlife – or the grave. *The grave's a fine and private place, But none I think do there embrace.*

Oh, pack up the morbidity. The penalty is tears and nightmares, tossing and fretting in the small hours. No wonder everybody sought business life to escape the horrors of personal existence.

Morgan again. Call him. Be strong. You'll do his stuff when you get around to it, considering how popular you are at the lab these days. He believes women are all blithering twits like his mother, images eradicated from any healthy man's head. He expects you to knuckle under and do what he wants – or buckle under and fear to do it. Surprise him. Half a year already. Finish it, publish it, get out of there.

Suppose his work *is* a fraud? Suppose he really killed Stevens?

As Pauli dialled, she found her right hand shaking. 'Dr Morgan Dianis, please. Pauli Golden calling. Morgan? Hi. This is Pauli. I'm working at home today. My mother's no better. It was a fall last night. She's barely conscious, and they don't expect . . . not too long now. Anyway, about our work there, the articles and photos –' Pauli gulped for breath and plunged onward. Hard as hell to think, talk and breathe simultaneously. Don't ever try out for Yale Rep Theater. 'I'll finish the articles as fast as possible and send my bill, but right now I need to put it off a bit until I can think better. My brother's here to help with my mother's problems, but even so, it's not simple.' Like he and I just had a fight. Morgan, help me. Don't mention Harry.

At first Morgan's voice arrived strained, then with an undertone Pauli hadn't heard before. 'You can't *do* this,

Pauli. I've taken care of Harry. Forget him.' Before Pauli could ask a double how, Morgan rushed onward. 'People like your mother remain in comas for months, years. Somebody at your magazine wrote about long-term coma. You can't drop everything like this. If you drop it, lady, you're fired – for the second time. No payment at all, no bylines. Clear?'

'I'm *not* dropping it,' Pauli protested. 'I can't afford to.' Dumdum, Pauli chided herself. Shouldn't have revealed the truth.

'Right. And don't worry about Harry.'

'Why not?'

Morgan ignored her. 'I can't help your personal problems, but the French have already rejected my application for January. So I'm counting now on either the Swedish Medical Research Council or the Swiss Science Foundation. I *guess* you didn't know that.' Morgan's sarcasm bit across the wire. '*I need those articles*' – he spat out the words – 'finished by the middle of this month to airmail to Europe. After that, I don't care what the hell you do with them here. Publish them, shove them.'

Up yours. 'Morgan,' Pauli interrupted, 'how can we settle this? I don't need one more problem either. Can you finish them? What about Arthur? Can he write anything?'

'You bloody little fool! You don't understand me. I hired *you* to do it. What's the matter with you? Don't you realise you've got the only copy of some of my print-outs, anyway?'

'I'll Xerox them –' Pauli began.

'You get over here by tonight. I'm here till 9 as usual. Bring everything with you. You got the afternoon to retype . . . whatever –'

'But Stevens never minded if I couldn't get –' Not true, but anyway.

'The hell with Stevens!' Morgan exploded, then hesitated a few seconds. 'I don't believe you. He pushed all of us, spun us round our tails for his results. Grabbed me out of a perfectly good grant in Boston. Promising miracles, including promising *me* all over the place to everybody's goddamn projects and post-Ph.D. stuff from here to Albuquerque.

Then when I got here, bastard wouldn't even give me personnel, let alone help me. All spring he crippled my work. Now I have to wind up everything in ten days flat. And I came here *because* of him!'

So did I. Just as Pauli hoped Morgan's wrath was ebbing into self-recrimination, he recommenced. 'Get over here tonight, Pauli. If you don't, I'll call your boss and report . . . your various activities. And I'll inform Harry.'

'I can do the same – before you. Right now,' Pauli countered. 'My boss already knows, and you just said not to worry about Harry.'

'About *all* your activities? I believe screwing people you interview is still considered somewhat, well, unethical? Not to mention what Harry thinks of people with Edward's so-called "orientation".' A nasty mimicry had entered Morgan's voice.

Instead of shouting, 'And what about killing the boss you made a pass at and fudging your data?' Pauli bit her tongue and flung down the phone.

Think, think! Get lost is more like it. Get lost.

31

So the dilemma appeared checkmate with Morgan. But was it truly, given Pauli's renewed luck lately? If Morgan dared call Jacobs to squeal on her sex life and the shadiness of continuing work after Harry fired her, she'd reveal who was paying her to do same, plus the scientific fraud of imagining data and faking slides.

Don't let him make you guilty as a woman for a sex life any man would envy – lovers who truly loved you. Even if one left and the other dripped to death on the chocolate carpet. Oh, Morgan's just furious that Steve loved you instead of him. At least, don't allow the bastard a gilt-edged tour of your guilts.

Just as Pauli grabbed the phone to call Jacobs herself and devise something more plausible than Morgan's slander, the red plastic thing rang. Startled, Pauli jumped backwards.

She paced the living room, determined to ignore the jangle. More garbage from Mogan. Then guilt, born of office years lived phone in one hand, scribbling pen in the other, tore her. Hadn't she told three Manhattan people – one researcher, one microsurgeon and somebody whose hand got sewed back on – to call her at home? Could also be the Medical Center or Frank regretting the noontime blather. Damn. Shouldn't miss any apologies that might be due me.

Gingerly Pauli lifted the receiver and listened without speaking.

'Hello? Hello?' A woman's voice. Pauli relaxed enough to sag on to the desk. A pile of Morgan's green striped computer junk tipped on to the carpet. 'It's Chessie. Pauli, are you there? Do I have the right number?'

'Yes, yes, Chessie. Of course you have the right number. I'm out of it this afternoon.'

'Are you sick?' The genuine concern flowing lively in Chessie's voice made Pauli want to cry. 'Your voice sounds so funny, low. What's the matter?'

'Well, it's alto anyway. A castrato I am not.' Pauli attempted to joke her usual way off the current crop of festering wounds.

'Pauli, I can come! Next week. I just arranged it with the school and finished bribing somebody to do my classes. I wanted you to know.'

'That's lovely, Chessie.' When Pauli's torso tried to dialogue with her legs, they buckled until she gave up, sat cross-legged on the floor and wedged her knees against the desk panels. *Don't let your problems kill her joy.* 'Look, can I, uh, help you with your plane fare? I know it's a long way.'

'That's sweet. I appreciate it, Pauli, but if I can stay with you after I give my talk and maybe just commute to the rest of the programme, I'll do fine. I can stay with you, can't I? You haven't,' Chessie stopped, 'changed your mind?'

'Of course not, dear. I can't manage to attend the conference this time, but call me and I'll pick you up. Oh-h,' Pauli groaned.

'What's the matter?'

'My mother. I told you. She's very sick. Let me give you the Medical Center number. If it's daytime, try my magazine first, then here, then the hospital at the Center. If it's nighttime, try here, then the hospital.' And the Institute? Fuck the Institute. Pauli mumbled numbers.

'Okay. How about a definite day? They usually make these things on weekends, but this one they didn't. If you can't manage, I can get a bus. The hotel's in Constitution Plaza. That should be right near everything.'

'Yuh, but Hartford's funny. It's like Stamford. They keep tearing it down or building it up or something.'

'I believe it's called urban renewal,' Chessie joked.

'No, don't worry. I'll be happy to come get you. God, can I use a break from here.' Kent Falls, anywhere.

'So. Wait till I call next Wednesday evening. A week from today. Ages! Pauli?'

'What?'

'I'm really looking forward to seeing you. I've thought a lot about everything in San Francisco. I hope we can –'

'Don't say it, Chessie,' Pauli begged. 'Not yet. Wait until we see how –'

'I love you, Pauli.'

'I – I know that,' Pauli stammered. 'Wait, huh?' A week from today. With Morgan and her mother's mess to wade through before then.

'I'll wait,' Chessie promised.

'I'll make you a nice dinner. Veal in cream with wine or something. We'll have a good time. I'm sorry, Chessie.' Pauli's voice caught. 'I'm gonna cry. I'm so happy you're coming, but life here's really messy now.'

'I understand.'

'Till Wednesday, then. Bye, dear.'

'Goodbye, Pauli.'

Pauli replaced the phone and stretched out face down on the carpet. Chessie's a vegetarian, dumdum. Doesn't eat veal. Well, let her concoct some sprouty spinach delight. Now Pauli felt as limp as a day-old body about to be tripped over. How many hours does rigor mortis last? She couldn't remember.

An image of Morgan hunched over his tumours, plus the impossibility of finishing five articles in as many hours, hit her like twin boulders.

216

32

Pauli would walk boldly to the front door, dump Morgan's stuff with the guard at the desk and be done with it.

Fuelled by fury and coffee, she'd left the phone off the hook and patched herself together enough to speedtype the written and edited articles into readable copy. For points still under research or not yet discussed with Morgan, Coral or Arthur, she faked some plausible wording, leaving room for alternate versions Morgan would have to worry about.

Next she prepared her bill based on the four finished pieces, including five artwork pages of computer data she'd built into graphs, plus a 'consultation fee' for the fifth outlined, but unfinished, article. She added a list of summary paragraphs from the four, destined to be the booklet Morgan had wanted. A page of stunning quotations she'd gathered on Medway researchers' use of computers followed. She couldn't type that without laughing.

At first she threw in for free her diagrammed layouts for the new lobby photo display on immunology research, for which she hastily composed captions in the milestone/isn't-science-marvellous? genre. On second thoughts, she added $50 to her bill for two earlier hours of *that* particular problem shoved by Harry on to Morgan. Morgan didn't even perform immunotherapy experiments involving viruses, but his charm, coupled with Medway's name, had attracted a useful and proliferating photo file from virus researchers round the world. That must be why he, rather than Arthur, had got the task.

Finally at 6 p.m. she grabbed a dented apple and some cheese from the kitchen, discovering the afternoon's discipline had wrought its usual magic: she felt both calm and exhausted.

To avoid uncreative encounters, she hoped for Medway empty but with the dwarf guard or Leon or somebody still at the open front door. Otherwise; she'd be forced, like some mendicant suitor, to bang as before on Morgan's ground-floor windows.

The streets lay blackened from a rain she'd never noticed during her afternoon typing frenzy. A tarry mildew exuded into the evening air.

With Morgan's payment she had planned to purchase first and at least an air conditioner and an FM radio channel for the VW – or perhaps a shiny new car (her first ever) if the VW proved too decrepit for electronic or cooling marvels. However, would she even get paid? When twitchy people decided to play cheap, they chopped your agreed fee in half, pleading budget cuts and indicating you're-damn-lucky-to-get-that-it's-all-you-deserve-I-could-have-written-the-stuff-myself-but-I'm-too-busy. Offensive frill added to basic fraud. No wonder some labour unions wind up bombing factories that underpay them. Pauli clutched the steering wheel to contain her anger, restore the calm of a few moments before.

She lost.

Why go at all? Bastard deserves nothing, and here you just worked your ass off for him like a schoolgirl. If only Stevens had lasted just six more weeks. But had he lived, she wouldn't have concluded the assignment till January, because Arthur's and others' experiments were still progressing. Freelancing like this with now thoroughly uncongenial, not to mention dangerous, people was the dregs – fringe existence without fringe benefits. Remind me, never again.

Thank God for Jacobs and the magazine to lick her wounds. The man was proving truly fine about her mother's illness. 'You've been working pretty hard. Take the time you

218

need.' Despite August vacations already leaving him short-staffed. Call him tomorrow and thank him. Pauli's absence usually induced a spasm of creativity in Sara, who would rewrite a few medical school press releases. Sometimes Jacobs used one – without byline – in the magazine's news item column. Did he pay Sara extra for the unsolicited effort? Probably not.

When her mother's illness finally ended, maybe she'd spend a lovely cool week with Chessie in Colorado. Chessie's mountain stream. Now that should rate at least one vindictive press release.

Back to reality. The Institute car park with – no! – Harry's Cadillac was not only still there but he was talking at the top of the front stairs with – Arthur? Burl? Who else could be so tall? She'd used one of Burl's virus papers for some immunotherapy captions. Would Harry recognise her car again? Plenty of people drive red VWs. She parked on the far side of the car park.

Don't panic, don't pain. Wait. Drive away. To hell with Morgan. Mail his stuff. It weighs 20 pounds. Dump it over Kent Falls. I want my money. Call the police about the curious scalpel in Morgan's pocket. So they're all crooks. I need my money. I worked like hell for it. No grandiose reason for exposing them. Passion for truth or justice? All I want is to eat, write – and make love. Are we all crooks with some habit that needs feeding and hiding from the world? With some people, it's called medical research.

Oh, c'mon. You want the bastards burned. They waste millions while people like Alice suffer and die – and poor Stevens got murdered.

Pressure on Pauli's stomach, beginning as indigestion from the half-chewed apple, escalated into the nauseous, weighted-rock feeling her body remembered from early pregnancy. Waves of stone. Either lie down or drive out of this heat. Since she was one of the few petite enough to recline in a VW front seat, she managed the feat with a few sickening abdominal wrenches as she angled around the gearstick area. When she twiddled the radio knobs, some vapid cocktail music annoyed rather than soothed her.

Dammit, you're afraid. If Harry's still perfecting his fiery-dragon routine at the entrance, go dump the stuff at Morgan's window. The ground is wet. Decide!

Elevating herself on one sticky elbow and peering over the car door proved Harry still there, hands thrust into pockets now. Must be narrating his memoirs – how to defraud the government and retire to Bimini or Pago Pago.

Suddenly Pauli sat up and leapt from the car. Flinging the keys into her purse, she grabbed the two shopping bags from the back seat. One of the handles ground into her wounded right palm until she adjusted a handkerchief over the sticking plasters. Meandering like a bag lady (dizziness helped), she started towards the hillside where the rear stairs climbed to the back of the white building. The front stairs were easier, closer, but who needed Harry? Who needed Morgan either? A rear entrance existed, but she needed the side door directly into Morgan's lab.

Safe now on the grass strip between the building and the pines, she recognised Morgan's window. He was the only one in the mid-section who 'forgot' to draw his white shade at night. It stayed either flung to the ceiling for the janitor to unwind or yanked unevenly until the edges tattered.

There he sat before the window, beside his microscope.

Guts together, girl.

Carefully neutralising her face, Pauli held up one shopping bag, then the other. Damn! He was nodding and smiling. What now? She'd geared herself for battle – $4,500 was worth it – but *cordiality*? Maybe testosterone, chemically similar to oestrogen, variegated these guys' moods; only they'd never admit it.

Morgan clicked open the side door that led into the larger of his two lab rooms. 'Glad to see you. Got everything there?'

Pauli blinked and stared at him. Play it sane. 'Yuh, all the printouts. The finished articles, the photo layout, and summaries are on top in the large envelope, plus my bill on my letterhead is underneath. You can retype the bill minus my name and just say "editing" or "consultation fee". Maybe Harry won't notice. It's a large amount.'

'Nonsense. *I'm* paying you. I told you that.' Instead of flipping open the envelope and folder to reach the bill, he stood smiling like some talkshow host. Not quite an apology for the telephone apoplexy but verging into his familiar charisma. God, the man must be an actor. Vincent Price of the test tubes.

'I'll go now. I'd due at the hospital,' Pauli announced. She turned, but Morgan had already reattached the door's antiburglar circuitry.

'Stay a while,' he begged, removing her shoulder bag, which he carefully laid on to the lab bench. 'I apologise for the phone . . . thing. Upset about deadlines, I guess. I've just made some new slides. Want to see them?' Why was he wheedling? Surely he wasn't morbid enough to have checked his pocket lining for her blood. Had he pressed the charm button because he knew the power of a disgruntled, unpaid underling to spread rumours and retard progress? Why did he care?

'This is the last. I promise,' he cajoled. 'And I won't even charge you extra for the pleasure of my company.'

At first Pauli felt her nostrils flare with anger, but when he winked, she found her lips smiling automatically. She cursed wherever women had learned to cuddle towards humiliators, begging forgiveness for somebody else's problems. It's not women. It's *you*, dumdum. Have to look normal; flirting's part of normal. Accept a pass in order to pass.

'Here, I left the optical microscope and slide viewer burning just for you.'

Pauli bit her tongue to avoid the customary 'I'm honoured' response.

'I'll even go into the other room and let you be,' Morgan promised. 'Everything's labelled. Just enjoy yourself. By the way, what happened to your hand?' He motioned towards the plaster display.

'Oh, problem in my kitchen,' Pauli lied.

He nodded and walked away.

Giving up, Pauli inserted the coloured slides one by one into the lighted viewer. Morgan had done it again: mouse after mouse began with tumours ulcerating across three quarters of its belly, progressed to half-size sores, finally to blackened scabs that would flake off in a few days. Cancer flaking off? Pauli reached her left hand towards her own entrenched lump. Morgan must be using his own variant of Arthur's wonder-cure serum, certainly not the antiserum that gave more animals breast cancer faster.

How did Morgan do it?

Maybe it wasn't the *same* mouse that hopped from near death to miracle remission in three easy slides. The lab and animal strain numbers read identically from slide to slide, but anybody with a ballpoint pen and some extra mice up his lab coat could arrange that. To quote Edward, little buggers all *look* alike anyway. And with Coral's refusal to play surgeon to Morgan's animals, which he birthed and pedigreed on his own, whoever even checked? Except maybe Stevens. Suppose –

'Morgan, I've got a question. Are these all mouse tumours here? Or is this human cancer you've transplanted?'

Morgan peered out from his office doorway on her right. 'Half and half actually. Look where it says either "murine" or "human". I wrote it on the back. You don't think I'd forget a detail like that.'

'Where's your control group?'

'Out in the animal wing. My own room, divided from the animals in the slides.'

'And has anybody corroborated this work? I mean, tested this serum yet?'

'Of course. I've sent serum samples to a dozen places here and in Europe. They're doing it as their own grants allow new testing and –' He stalled.

'Yes,' Pauli persisted, 'but has anybody really corroborated your results on mice or on humans?'

'On humans! You know I can't get permission for –'

'So they haven't,' Pauli concluded. Morgan, however, had vanished from the office doorway before she could launch her next two questions. What happens if your mice don't get cancer? Are the animals the same mouse from slide to slide?

She frowned. Get out of here. No. Stay; get some answers. No good. If his stuff stinks and this whole place is tarred by association with him, then what is the fate of *your* articles? Six months of work down the paper shredder. What editor, scientific or popular, will print any of them once this news hits the media fan?

Pushing aside the viewer, Pauli dropped her head on to her arms, which were flung already on to the black Formica top of the lab bench. Her shoulders ached. Exhaustion. Sleep for ever; wake up dead. Simpler than living. Her mother's faded face and gasping chest aroused Pauli.

Morgan is . . . a liar . . . a fraud . . . a cheat.

And a murderer. But can you prove it?

Who incidentally owes you over $4,000 for reading, editing and writing his science fiction. Ye gods and dancing idiocies. Serves you right for letting Stevens pull you between his legs in the first place. April to August. From for ever to nowhere.

So preface Morgan's stuff with a warning that his methods and results may be dangerous to your health, have been corroborated exactly nowhere, are *not* ready for human trials. If he won't accept some such statement, take your own name off his crap. Your crap. He never needed your name. It was your work, six months' work he could avoid doing himself.

To make more room on the lab bench, she tried shoving the microscope aside. Bolted down. Her shoulder muscles froze. Since Edward's multiple heists, they must have screwed down everything that walked, lived or smiled. The screwing directions blazed in red from all bulletin boards:

WARNING

Each employee is personally responsible for equipment and supplies. At the end of every business day:

Relock supplies and solutions into proper cabinets.

Place new or movable equipment (calculators, minicomputers, slide cases, titration apparatus, tools, etc.) into secured storage areas.

Secure locks or bolts on large items.

Return all keys to your supervisor.

FAILURE WILL RESULT IN YOUR DISMISSAL.

Harry Stornell, MD
Director, Medway Research Institute

How could people post such threats and expect employees not to gossip and scheme? Like Victorian schoolmasters, they don't ask to be liked, couldn't care less what underlings, like the mice, feel. No wonder somebody extra-desperate pulls a knife behind their backs.

Should get out of all this security. Pull yourself together. Get Morgan to unscrew the side door. Walk out for ever.

Suddenly a corridor door behind Pauli burst open. When she jumped, tilting her stool, she avoided falling at the last second by grabbing the microscope with an arm and a half. Must be Morgan playing a joke. Two places at once – office and corridor. As she righted herself and stared round, Harry stood there.

Face fuming red, pink note in hand.

'They were right,' he was shouting. 'You *are* here. Goddamn! I fired you last month. Who let you in here?'

Cool, cool. One at a time. 'What're you talking about?' Pauli answered. 'I came to return all the material to Dr Dianis.'

'Oh. Took your time, didn't you?'

No placating Harry tonight. The bastard glared over his half-glasses. All bark, well the hell with his bite. 'I'm leaving. Don't worry.' She stood up, switching off viewer and microscope.

'Uh, what they called about.' Harry's tone unfroze a few degrees. 'There's bad personal news. Your mother. I'm sorry,' he added indifferently.

Did guys like him have a mother? My son the monster and computer cheat. For an instant Pauli's head whirled crazily to avoid comprehending his words. All a nightmare. Doesn't exist. 'Is she . . . dead?' An edge of the whirl advanced, receded.

'I don't know, but I don't want any more calls for you here. Understand? You better leave now.'

Turning to grab her shoulder bag, she saw Morgan standing in his office doorway. 'What's going on?'

'My mother,' Pauli mumbled.

'What? Speak up.'

No chance Morgan would or could pay her now with

Harry aware. The hell with him. Both of them. 'Look, Dr Stornell, you want me out, but there's something you need to know.' Onward she rushed before he could cut her off. 'Morgan's work, these mouse slides. According to an opinion I got from a researcher and my own brainwork, some of this is, well, not accurate. Things claimed aren't true, slides fudged, doctored data that –'

'Shut up, Pauli!' Morgan's voice was harsh and froze in her throat the words 'that Stevens found'.

First Harry blinked. Then he leaped within a foot of her face. 'Listen, you bitch, the past or present work of Dr Dianis or any of my researchers is *none* of your goddamn business. Hear that? I fired you once. If I catch you here again, I call the police and get you removed. Clear?' As he paused for breath, she heard him mutter, 'Stevens and his whores!'

Rage. For a gun to blast both of them. 'You don't insult me without every newspaper and TV station in Hartford, Boston and New York getting into it. They'll *love* this coming on top of murder.'

At Harry's smack across her head Pauli reeled backwards. The single eye of the bolted microscope gashed her spine. Her breath exploded in a groan. Harry, purple-faced bear, claw outstretched, still loomed above her.

'Harry! Stop it! She weighs 90 pounds.' Somebody yelling. Why should it be Morgan?

Gasping for breath, she felt the pain coalesce to a brilliantly throbbing ball at the right of her spine. A similar shove from Frank on a country road had rammed her same back ribs into a fencepost.

Throwing herself towards Harry, she yanked his necktie with her left hand and slapped away at his fuchsia face with her right. She threw three good slaps at him, regretting she lacked a knife to slit his apoplectic throat. Her hand throbbed, stung. His glasses smashed to the floor.

As he recovered balance, his arms rose to grab her shoulders and throat. Sensing his hands, Pauli shoved her leather bag into his stomach, following it with her knee. Then she bolted from him out of the open door.

Along the shadowy corridor, past the empty guard

station. The car, the car. Down the front stairs, across the car park.

Her hands with the keys trembled so much she had to steady her right index finger between her teeth before she could coax the key near the ignition. The motor started; the car edged away. She got a mile down the highway and pulled off into a shopping centre. As cars whizzed around her, she sat limp, not daring to drive further.

Were they following her?

Three times she checked the rearview mirror and through the windscreen. Neither Harry's Cadillac nor Morgan's sports car appeared. No drivers approached the station wagon or the van parked on either side of her in this aisle near the road.

She began to breathe again, her underwear glued to her body like a damp bathing suit. Dumb to threaten as she had. They'd surely follow her with scalpels or worse. Even if they hated each other, needing to shut her up would unite them. Morgan's apparent chivalry – 'She weighs 90 pounds' – was faked. Like everything he did, nothing to trust. Nothing to trust.

Continue the scenario: Harry and Morgan would reach an overdue 'understanding', would both slander her as a conspiracy-seeking paranoid of a female reporter who imagined anything and everything but the truth of how hard-working male scientists cooperate to achieve break-throughs in the War on Cancer – if questioning arose.

What questioning? Nobody who mattered knew she was here. Even Frank, who must have placed the call that stampeded Harry.

Did Morgan know of Harry's little fraud game?

What did it matter?

As her shaking body quieted, Pauli pulled the VW out again into streaming traffic. When she failed to shift at a green light, horns shrieked behind her. Reach the Medical Center. Then stay with Heather. If Morgan and Harry arrived at her apartment, they'd get four empty rooms.

Phone the Medway Board of Directors, the trustees and every medical reporter you know on the East Coast.

And see the police about the scalpel in Morgan's pocket.

226

33

According to the Medical Center nurse, 'Mrs Golden expired at 7.05 p.m. I'm sorry.' So her mother was dead. Dead. The word raced in Pauli's mind as she flung nightgown, toothbrush and notebook into a suitcase at her apartment.

Out gallivanting with your other problems, Pauli, while your mother died. 'Gallivanting' – guess whose word that was?

She phoned Heather. Heather wasn't in. For ten minutes Pauli paced. Then Heather was in. It was Frank who was out. He was at the hospital already, signing and arranging. How had she missed him? Heather had told him the nearest funeral directors. 'When we couldn't get you, he had to go ahead.' She paused, then kept repeating, 'I'm sorry, Pauli. I know how close you've been to her.'

'No. It wasn't that way. I did what –' Pauli stopped. Let it go. Quit explaining yourself to half the world. 'Heather, can I stay with you a while? Frank and I can talk when he gets back.' Say yes, say yes, Pauli's head screamed.

'Of course, dear. Shall I come get you?'

'No, no,' Pauli bridled. Her face was sweating; her cut hand on the desk stung again. 'I'm not breaking down. I'm just a little upset.' Cracking up. Morgan and Harry wanted to kill me tonight. I'm out $4,500 for a job I've got fired from twice. 'Work pressures, I guess.' Damn. Why couldn't she ever tell the truth? Hide everything. Just like your mother. 'I'll drive over myself. How's half an hour? Heather?'

'What?' Heather's voice was soft.

'Thanks. I really mean it.'

Heather's house would be safer than alone in this apartment. But a house where somebody got murdered and mutilated just days ago? Pauli glanced at the bank calendar. Early July to 6 August. One month ago. Well, nobody commits two murders in the same house, unless inspired by the delights of the nuclear family, and that situation wasn't hers or Heather's any longer.

Admit it, Pauli: you're scared to live alone now.

34

'Heather, can I use the phone in your bedroom this morning? Some stuff I should take care of.'

Heather, dressed in a powder-blue angora sweater whose texture and tone made Pauli's mouth water, was buttering and pottering in the kitchen. 'Toast?' she asked.

'No, thanks. I can't eat this morning.'

'I'll save something for you. You know where the phone is.'

Get the little green book. Phone first, face Frank again later when he gets up. She glanced towards the screens around his bed on the sun porch. The organised life is not worth living. Lie down until your voice stops shaking. But you just got up. Phone and get it over with. Since when is the pursuit of justice like going to the dentist?

On Heather's puffy satin spread (how often Stevens must have sat or made love here), Pauli tried to read the swirling numbers on her address pages. Eeeny meeny – catch a trustee by – Try one trustee type from the general Medway board and one doctor type from the Board of Scientific Directors. If the trustee type didn't give a damn because he's basically a businessman, not a scientist, surely the science type should care. How to sound accusatory, but sane and competent?

In her apartment she'd left her black looseleaf book with the names and affiliations of all the trustees and the scientific directors. Too late now.

'Dr Ivors, please,' she said to the hospital switchboard operator.

'I'll page him. Are you a patient?'

'Yes,' Pauli lied. What the hell was Ivors? Urologist? She'd met him once at some function. Was he still even a trustee or scientific director? Damn. Why couldn't reality match those speedy TV dramas, where the reporter, minus even a phone book in the booth, always knows whom to phone? Somebody who answers instantly and listens enthralled. Must write the phone numbers on his shirt cuffs.

'Yes?' An irritated masculine voice.

'Dr Ivors? I'm calling about a matter related to Medway Institute. This is Pauli Golden. I work for *Contemporary Medicine Magazine*.'

'You're a reporter? Look, can I call you back? I'm just about to go into surgery.'

'Will you listen for one minute?' Pauli controlled the rage in her voice. The accumulated impotence from her whole year avalanched on her stomach, but she continued biting out the words. 'For months I've done various writing and editorial assignments for Medway, where you're on the board of directors.'

'That's correct.' Good. he was listening now.

'Certain, well, irregularities have come to my attention. I have evidence that various frauds are going on, both financial in computer services the place uses and scientific in the research of at least one doctor there. I believe the trustees should act on this as soon as possible.' She'd rehearsed this speech a hundred times. 'You know me. We've met at a Health Systems Agency hearing.'

'No. I don't remember,' Ivors was disclaiming, 'but anyway, do you know what you're saying?'

Pauli heard the background bustle of the hospital. 'I know very well what I'm saying. I've gone over hundreds of pages of reports. I was hired to make articles of some of them. Dr St Steven hired me. After he was murdered, I – '

'Yes, yes. Look, I have to go into surgery now. Call me afterward. I will present this to the trustees and directors at our next meeting and –'

'When's that?'

'Next week.'

'That's too late, Dr Ivors. The people who did this and are doing it know that I know.'

'Who's that?'

Pauli bit her lip. 'If you can't handle this, give me the name of another director who you know is available.'

'Is this connected with Dr St Steven's death? If you have murder evidence, you should call the police. Why involve all the trustees?'

'You're already involved. As a scientific director, you both approve Medway's budget and oversee its research, don't you?'

'Yes, but –'

'Give me the name of another director or trustee,' Pauli demanded.

Ivors backed down. 'All right. Try Paul Santorini. He's president of Citizen Savings here.'

'And may I have the name of another scientific director like yourself?' Pauli persisted.

'Oh, I'd have to get my index file. Look, don't call the police. Call my office this afternoon about 4.' Although he sounded a few degrees more sincere now, he was stalling until he could check either her or the situation with a buddy.

Pauli hung up.

Paul Santorini was – predictably – out. Bank presidents don't return phone calls anyway unless you leave a corporation name and they can smell money over the wire. They delegate some secretary to do it. Scratch Santorini.

From her little green book Pauli lifted the cardboard square with Detective Jordan's special number and the page of her radio, TV and press contacts. Try Jed in Boston. He owed her a dinner for the night he forgot his wallet at a conference and she'd charged it on one of her credit cards.

'Jed? You're there? Good. This is Pauli Golden. I have a red-hot story for you. You're still interested in the murder at Medway Institute? Now it's double fraud and theft too. I'm calling the police, but I wanted to give you first chance at it.'

'You mean you know who did the murder? What about the police?' But Jed's voice was always sceptical.

'I told you. I'm calling them next.'

'Okay. What have you got?'

'Evidence that Dr Harry Stornell has defrauded a computer company of terminal time for research. Morgan Dianis' work is fudged, plus he . . .' Pauli hesitated. If only she needn't continue. Was it sick to incriminate Morgan further, the last semi-decent guy in the place? If you don't, they'll kill *you*. Hating herself, she plunged on. 'Morgan, he . . . killed Stevens St Steven.'

There. It was done. She felt miserable.

'Wow. Why?'

'Didn't want all his games revealed, the twenty projects he took credit for when he did nothing. It's not just one thing wrong with his own work. Stevens attracted him there and then either overpushed or dumped him. Anyway, had no more time for him. Also massive father problem that Stevens ignored.'

'How much of this can you prove?'

'Jed, enough of it. Would I be calling you if I couldn't?' Pauli shivered. 'I have Morgan's papers with Stevens' question marks, plus testimony from a computer expert.' Heather would love *that* description of herself. 'Also evidence from an ex-government scientist who knows Medway. And Harry and Morgan threatened me last night. I had dinner with Morgan. He carries scalpels in his pocket. A jacket he wore the night of the murder, although he must have taken it off –'

'Okay. I'll discuss it right now with the powers here. Where can I get hold of you? Pauli? Take care of yourself.'

'Uh, my mother just died so I'll be in and out of –' And she'd given him half her apartment number before she changed it to Heather's. 'Detective Jordan of the police here is handling the case, but I wanted you to know first.'

Still came on not as grateful as she'd expected (maybe handling six other stories) but he did add, 'I'm sorry about your mother. I met her with you at some dinner, wasn't it?' Jed's voice had hushed.

'Yes. Medical writers' awards thing. Last year.'

'Take care of yourself.'

Four more calls: Hartford, New Haven, Manhattan, Providence. And screw Harry Stornell and Morgan from their wing-tip shoes and H. Freeman suits up to their lying brains. Snakes in the woodpile. Her grandfather's phrase. As Pauli dialled the final number – Jordan's – rage clotted her throat and shook her fingers again. The plaster from the scalpel cut was hanging. She tore it off and flung it on to the shaggy carpet. Detective Jordan promptly answered his own phone.

'This is Pauli Golden. I got some news for you. Sorry it took so long.'

'And I got some news for *you*.' Jordan's voice animated slightly. 'Yesterday a motel employee called. Says he remembers a woman with Dr St Steven at his place a few times last spring. His description could fit a lot of attractive women, but it fits you. He says the lady always registered alone in the middle of the afternoon. Some of the papers have run more of the doctor's photos.'

Damn. More snakes in the woodpile. Don't let him back you down. At least he was direct, not toying about where-were-you-last-spring-you-tell-us-first. 'When I'm on a story, I sleep when and where I can.' At such immorality, admitted or implied, Pauli sensed her mother turning in the coffin she didn't have yet. Frank would choose it this morning.

'But I've got some news for *you*,' Pauli repeated. 'Last night I went to Medway to return a bunch of Dr Morgan Dianis' stuff. I can prove by questioning about his slides and piecing together Stevens' queries on his papers that Morgan's stuff's a fraud. I believe he killed Stevens, probably with a scalpel I found in his closet. A jacket he wore on the murder night. Last night he and Harry Stornell both threatened me; Harry tried to strangle me.'

She rushed to finish before the detective stopped her. This time it proved easier. Talking to Jed must have toughened her. But you liked Morgan! Bad as those kidnapped hostages who end up loving their terrorist abductors.

'Where are you now?'

'At Heather St Steven's house. My mother just died, and I . . . couldn't stay alone any longer in my apartment. I'm scared.' If not chivalry, then perhaps a note of panic would rouse him. Did he believe her? Jordan would never reveal how much the police knew. Tight Lip. How much did he already know? Maybe that explained his lack of reaction.

'Also Harry Stornell's been stealing expensive computer time, according to Heather. She's a medical librarian.'

'Yes.'

'Yes, what? About Morgan? Harry Stornell? What have your people concluded about this? Did anybody *see* Morgan enter the murder room?' she pleaded. Her heart thumped.

At first he ignored her question, his answer disappointingly generalised. 'If we get a warrant and charge somebody, that would come out then. Will you sign a new statement for us? I'll send a man around to you and also check at Medway soon as I can.'

'Of course, I'll sign. I've worked hard enough on those papers. And add how the bastards cheated me of $4,500.'

'What do you mean?'

'Stevens – I mean Morgan owes me for doing his articles and layouts.'

'Pauli?'

'What?'

'Thanks.' And he hung up.

Pauli jumped at a wood thud behind her. Heather stood in the open bedroom door. Had she been listening? Better inform her she's about to become 'a computer expert'.

'It's Harry Stornell,' Heather began. 'He's downstairs to see you.'

'How –' Pauli grimaced.

'You mean *why*, don't you? Did the funeral home give you a hard time?' Heather gestured towards the phone. 'You look green. You've been in here so long. Frank's awake now. Come on down.'

35

Pauli found Harry – surprisingly – in the baby's room/library. Where Stevens had died. By daylight the cocoa carpet still showed bits of irregular stain. Pauli stared into the paisley print of Harry's necktie, then at the grotesque drummer boy, still on the mantel. Why hadn't the police tagged and taken it? How could she have envied Heather for owning this place with Stevens? Or passing his days with Harry drumming the funds to feed the mice?

After Harry had shut the door and walked towards Stevens' desk at the window, Pauli refused to sit down in either chair he indicated. Standing should eject him faster from the house. She balanced before the doorknob, one knee wedged into a bookcase. If Harry wanted privacy for intense conversation, that was precisely how Stevens got killed. An old-fashioned iron key still stood in the lock. She wondered about palming it. Had Morgan used it?

'Pauli,' he began without introduction, 'I believe we should work this out. You're an intelligent woman with a considerable . . . position. Morgan tells me you've gone off with misinformation, half-truths. You don't want to harm a valuable federal project like Medway, do you? I'm sure with Stevens' death, you agree there's been enough upset. Now it's yesterday's ugly gossip, anyway,' he oozed on.

'Since you're such a good writer, Dr Dianis and I both want to see you get all the payment coming to you. For the work,' he added.

Threat or promise? When he actually smiled, Pauli's knees

shook. Stevens' murder now dismissed as yesterday's gossip? No matter who the killer, nobody should downgrade murder. Confusion roiled her. Call his bluff. Demand your $4,500 cheque right now. How could these bastards live so crooked and still smile straight? Edward should be here to declaim his hunk of *Hamlet*:

> O villain, villain, smiling, damned villain! . . .
> My tables, – meet it is I set it down,
>
> That one may smile, and smile, and be a villain.

'I know how upsetting last night was to you,' Harry was somehow continuing, 'but the best thing to do is just forget. I expect you've, well, *overestimated* much of what you've seen at Medway. Naturally to someone not trained in –'

Before he could oil it further into 'My dear, there's a good girl', Pauli interrupted. 'I'm a journalist, Dr Stornell. I'm paid to remember and get things right, not to forget.' If first her information had been dangerous, now it had degenerated into ignorant snooping. Her brain struggled to cope with what her ears seemed to hear.

'Yes, but surely you see the wisdom of not inflaming an already tense situation.' Harry frowned, crunching his forehead straight up to the thinning grey strands he'd slicked down with some pomade that smelled like apricots around the small room. A new laetrile hairspray for people running scared on cancer? Or maybe almonds. Cyanide pomade to murder while you make love? Her mind was wandering.

He was continuing. 'I've had two phone calls this morning. One from Dr Ivors and one from a reporter. The reporter claims he's got what he called "fresh evidence" on Steve's death, but he refused to tell me his source. Is this some new story you've made up? To get attention?' His eyes narrowed. No smile this time.

What a motive: anybody who fussed over murder, mutilation and fraud just needed attention! Like her mother, who'd equated everything wrong in Pauli with needing either a feeding or a spanking. Or dismissed it as 'just another stage' she was going through. Simple-minded asses, the lot of them. Your mother's dead. You're supposed to be phoning about her funeral.

Surfacing again, Pauli detected something else in Harry's varying tones: he was running scared. His eyes glinted, renarrowed at her; above his belly, the shoulders slumped.

Carefully saying nothing, Pauli moved two feet to the right and leaned against a shelf of Stevens' walnut and medical bookcase. If Harry wanted to curse or strangle her into oblivion, even he realised the situation – minus a raucous, candle-lit party to camouflage falling bodies – required tact. The struggle to control one of his customary tantrums was tearing him. Perhaps people who staged tantrums were fortunate; they never repressed anything long enough to kill themselves or anybody else over it.

When Pauli remained silent, Harry continued, 'You're a talented young woman, but you know you got too much imagination in these highly technical research matters. We professionals have many years of medical schooling. We don't just hop in and write half-truths on a new topic every week.'

'I'm as specialised in my field as you are in yours, Dr Stornell,' Pauli retorted. 'I've had the same anatomy, physiology and biochemistry.' Leading nowhere. Trading charges. Get him out of here. 'But before you or Morgan plot to slit *my* throat, I want to help the people you forget while you little boys play ego and publicity games. How about the people who get cancer? Do they matter at all?'

Remembering Alice, Pauli's voice and courage hit top gear. Kiss your money goodbye. 'A few days ago I met a woman at the Medical Center. Her name's Alice; she's dying of metastasised breast cancer. Through all the pain, surgery, chemotherapy, you know she *really believes*' – Pauli spat out the words – 'you people are finding a cure for her cancer.'

Harry stared, then answered, 'Of course. You people in the press write junk. Then patients demand death-bed miracles. Besides, one patient's experience is anecdotal evidence. Don't you know better than to conclude anything from it unless she's part of some research protocol?'

'But she represents another half-million deaths every year and that doesn't even include Aids!' Pauli exploded.

'So?'

'So! People at your place hire reporters to write "break-throughs" that need ten years more testing. I don't invent the stuff I write. *You* whitewash surgery, diagnosis, chemotherapy. Then bury your mistakes in a cemetery and vacation on the proceeds. I bet you don't even send a sympathy card. That would indicate personal concern, and, of course, we can't have –'

Suddenly Harry was shouting, 'You're the sick one! Like cancer cells that've lost your right function. Morgan says besides chasing men, you're queer! No wonder the stuff you write's trash. Makes normal people throw up. Mind your own business –'

'I'm not paid to mind my own business,' Pauli screamed back. "Get out of here!' When she flung the door back into the orange wall, Heather and Frank both stood whitefaced in the hall outside.

Shoving Pauli into the woodwork, Harry stormed past, a flurry of navy serge and empurpled rage. As he reached the front door, Pauli yelled after him, 'Look for the police in Morgan's office. They want to know why he hated Stevens. Also about computer time at your place.'

If Harry heard the computer addendum, she couldn't tell. He wrenched open Heather's antique oak door, smashing it into the iron coat rack behind it. Heather's stained-glass door panels exploded, then shattered to the carpet.

36

Inside the hotel phone booth Pauli stood reading the graffiti. WHEN MY SHIP COMES IN, I'LL PROBABLY BE AT THE AIRPORT. Beneath it in red felt-tip on a bank poster, somebody else had scrawled, REMEMBER, WE'RE ALL IN THIS ALONE. Somehow those two slogans were more reassuring than the final effort, which seemed a joint production by two different hands: GOD LOVES YOU – WHETHER YOU LIKE IT OR NOT. With one finger she traced the angles of 'Remember . . .', then dialled before she could change her mind.

'Chessie? It's Pauli. I'm downstairs in the hotel. I'm really here.'

Chessie's voice bubbled back. 'Come up, come up! I gave my talk. I'm finished for the day. Let's have a drink or dinner or something. Uh, Pauli, I read the Hartford paper during somebody else's talk. What's going on at your place? Are you okay?'

Avoiding the second question, Pauli tried the first. She sighed. 'It's not my place. Not any longer. It was a freelance thing.'

'But your name's all over the paper.'

'Oh, I'll tell you about it someday when I have around five years. I signed a police statement about everything. The trials are coming. Oh, you can read something from the Boston paper I got here that makes more sense. Chessie, I can't wait to see you.'

'Well, come up. Room 916.'

The elevator dial crept; Pauli paced the lobby's ferny rug. When my ship comes in. Frank was flying back to Denver right now. Heather had driven him to the airport this afternoon. On Heather's front porch Pauli had kissed him goodbye, making no excuses for why she couldn't drive him.

The funeral and cemetery efforts had turned out decently. Even Alice, with a hospital aide pushing her wheelchair up the ramp and over the carpeting, made it to the funeral parlour. The mourners merely assumed she was Mrs Golden's sister. Although thirty years younger, the final grip of cancer had aged her so badly, etching crevices in her face. Jacobs sent long-stemmed creamy roses with pink centres.

Frank was now executor, and Pauli would purchase the gravestone. 'Phone me when you need me,' Frank had called as he and Heather took off. Maybe she'd surprise him, phone from Denver and introduce him to Chessie – if something good happened. If . . .

Was it Stevens who'd remarked in bed once, 'Pauli, you've got plenty of faith and love, but where's your hope?' She'd hidden her hurt – her too automatic assumption that Stevens didn't care enough to end even a failing marriage for her – behind the reporterly question, 'What do you mean?' Stevens had only smiled enigmatically. Like being in the sack with Buddha. Or was it the Mona Lisa? His lengthy love letter now reposed with Lizann's old ones in a gold-trimmed box that had belonged to her mother.

Room 916 seemed located down a ruby and lavender corridor whose wallpaper and floor crawled with garlands of some persistent but indeterminate flower. How could a new hotel look so gloomy? Must be the scarlet lampshades, faked to appear Victorian. Like the funeral parlour. The wave of the future is the past.

When Chessie opened the door, she and Pauli hugged each other tightly. Chessie's face felt smooth and warm under Pauli's hands.

37

'Chessie's chilled white wine in the crystal glass tickled Pauli's throat deliciously. Near the circle table she'd flung off her shoes and sat in the air conditioner's hum. 'I know what I wanted to show you – before we crushed it at the door.'

Chessie laughed. 'The better to see you. How can I love you if I can't touch you? If people weren't meant to love, they'd have hearts of stone.'

'Maybe they do anyway. Did you make that up? It's beautiful' Pauli confessed, blushing. Must be the wine. 'I have something to show you.' She retrieved the crumpled Boston newspaper from where it had fallen to the carpet. 'Read this. Then I'll stay the night or we'll leave and I can wow you with the fabulous apartment I have. And the health-food store we can visit in Manhattan. I know the owner.' Since the San Francisco conference she'd scarcely remembered Alan, but she gauged it was something Chessie would enjoy.

'When?' Chessie asked.

'When you come live with me.'

Chessie pursed her mouth. 'I thought *you* were coming to Colorado first. Then we can decide.'

Pauli grinned. 'I have three weeks' vacation. So read the paper while I sip my wine. Did you bring these decorated glasses all the way from Colorado?'

'Sure did. Wait'll you see the other lovely things I have. First, let me show you what the Hartford paper says.'

Chessie grabbed the paper from her open handbag on the floor. 'Is all this stuff true?' Her eyes opened wide.

'Probably not,' Pauli commented. 'Most things are even weirder than ever appears in print. I'll read this before you read mine.'

TWO MEDWAY STAFF INDICTED
FOR MANSLAUGHTER, CONSPIRACY
New Evidence in Mutilation Slaying of Cancer Researcher

12 Aug. – Detective Samuel Jordan of the Police Department today filed triple charges in the ongoing investigation following the murder of Dr Stevens St Steven at a 4 July party celebrating a million-dollar federal grant to Medway Institute for Cancer Research.

Charged with manslaughter in the first degree is Dr Morgan Dianis, a senior researcher at Medway. He has pleaded innocent to charges that he murdered and mutilated his employer. Dr St Steven, director of research, was also a Medway co-director.

Dr Dianis' trial will begin 5 September in -- Superior Court.

Also arrested and charged today was Dr Harry Stornell, financial head and the other co-director of the Institute. Dr Stornell has pleaded innocent to conspiracy to commit larceny in the first degree. He cited 'extenuating circumstances' involving computer use at Medway. Also charged in the alleged conspiracy is Paul Radcliffe, Systems Administrator, American Computer Systems Corporation.

These events follow the arrest of Edward Mistal last month on grand larceny, burglary and possession of property stolen from Medway and the University.

Pauli's spine tingled as she found the next paragraph.

Detective Jordan cited persistent efforts by his men, particularly Detective John Rose, in pursuing the investigation and securing the indictments. Also cited was a medical reporter, Pauline Golden, who provided evidence from Medway, where she was employed on freelance assignments.

'Police work long hours, but we can't do it alone,' Detective Jordan said. 'We need people like Miss Golden in neighbourhoods, businesses and on the street to follow whatever looks shady.'

Despite the praise, these terse sentences fluttered Pauli's insides. Months of work, love, hate, terror stuffed into a short report.

'Well?' Chessie asked. 'Did they really do what it says?'

'Harry certainly did. Bastard of the first order. Stevens and he never agreed on priorities – expensive research versus personnel problems and paying for everything. Stevens probably suspected Harry's creative accounting methods, but Harry had no immediate reason to murder Stevens. I mean, his whole career wasn't at stake, whereas Morgan –' Pauli hesitated.

'Why do you care?' Chessie asked, watching sharply. Rainette's question.

'I . . . got involved. Assuming Morgan killed Stevens, I hope they hang him high very soon – using my evidence and testimony. Or salt him away. It's just . . . until even last week he seemed the only genial human in the whole set of nasties. At least the dozen I interviewed, all bitter over something or other.' Pauli shivered. 'Stevens was easy to hate. Oh, there's a woman too. Coral Deming. She's mentioned in the piece I'll show you. Stevens was about to fire her for insubordination.'

'What's that mean?'

'Wouldn't follow his orders as the new research director, and the thing blew up as discrimination against women in science.'

'Of which there's plenty.'

'Sure, but Coral's a poor one to push it. She's not even medically educated. I mean an MA but no Ph.D or MD. But somebody has to push these things, or those guys would talk only to themselves. Without degrees, her second-class status infuriated her.'

'Will she be at the trials?'

'You bet. I thought I was the last to see Stevens alive. It turns out Coral got fed up with the party – sat alone on the front porch. She actually saw Morgan in Stevens' study and heard them quarrel. The police just found out. Before now, she protected Morgan, hoping he'd care about her. Coral burns to inform the world how women suffer from Medway's internal politics. The papers'll get some good quotes out of her. "Male Chauvinist Mouse Megalomaniacs". She'll accuse them of everything but sodomy.'

Chessie laughed. 'You mean, with the mice?'

'Yes, though I expect the prosecution, based on Edward – he had a frustrated crush on Stevens – will also tar Morgan as a suspected homosexual.'

'Because of the mutilation it mentions.'

Pauli nodded. 'Must have been rampaging fury that did that. Thirty-five years hating his own father. Plus Stevens' threat to ruin Morgan's whole life and career. To attract talent, Stevens encouraged people like Edward and Morgan to fall for him, then decided he had no time for them.'

'Is Morgan really gay?'

'Is there life on Jupiter? Who knows? All those guys who idolise themselves and their work have so little left over that it's a miracle when they love *anybody*.' *Yet Stevens loved you.* 'Well, if Coral is shy – she wouldn't meet me last week – I'll give them some more stuff. Harry not only fired me twice, he smacked my head and tried to choke me.' Pauli waved her own newspaper. 'It's your turn now.'

Chessie angled her chair into the lamplight and read the two-column editorial Pauli had circled.

ON CHEATING IN SCIENCE

A spate of irregularities concerning Medway Institute for Cancer Research made headlines this week. The mutilation-murder of one co-director, Dr Stevens St Steven, last month was followed by multiple indictments against the other co-director, a senior researcher and a junior employee. The murder of Dr St Steven occurred at the party that celebrated a million-dollar public gift to support next year's work at Medway.

Combined efforts of the police, aided by an alert reporter, Pauline Golden of *Contemporary Medicine Magazine*, who conducted her own investigation, have revealed these tragic doings.

Such events raise serious doubts about both direction and credibility in US biomedical research. Despite present budgetary austerity, federal financing of science, research and education has increased to over $56 billion. US Nobel laureates regularly criticise the red-tape paperwork involved in accounting for cash flow in science. They simultaneously decry reduced budgets to buy brainpower while maintaining that scientific creativity cannot be purchased like test tubes or Bunsen burners. However, Big Science still means Big Money.

In the words of one Nobel winner, 'This country is now falling behind in its commitment to science.' But even he admitted the old informal system of awarding unsupervised grants accountable to hardly anyone – certainly not the American people – 'will no longer wash. The more you start indiscriminately awarding money, the more scandals abound.'

'This is heavy stuff.' Chessie looked up. 'But you wade through it every day.'

'Like other things, it takes patience and concentration. Read on.'

Which returns us to the 'War on Cancer' and the multiple Medway tragedies. The 'War', begun by President Nixon in 1971, now costs over $1½ billion a year by itself. In the 1970s the easily deluded compared the 'answer to cancer' to reaching the moon. Yet the moon has proved easier than investigating the recesses of human cells. One official commented, 'In terms of hitting the moon, at least we knew where the moon was. In cancer we still don't know how many moons there are.'

Part of Dr Morgan Dianis' initial plea is that he

massaged his data in self-defence against his directors' persistent demands for quick results and completed, publishable research after a blackout destroyed much of the Institute's bank of frozen tissue samples. If these motives prove true, they are as tragic as cancer itself.

According to Coral Deming, the Institute's mouse surgeon, Dr St Steven found personal fault with his senior researcher and younger colleague, warning Dr Dianis repeatedly to organise his work, attend staff meetings, answer queries on procedures, and allow the veterinarian to oversee his private mouse colony. The day of the murder saw an argument during which Dr St Steven allegedly termed Dr Dianis a 'total flop' at continuing the significant work for which he was hired and at conducting himself ethically as a scientist.

Chessie pointed to the final paragraph and asked, 'What's that mean exactly?'

'It means first, Coral snoops outside people's offices, as well as on the porch.' Sara's squat body and ruby lips loomed before Pauli. 'Next, a stilted way to say Stevens thought Morgan had produced zilch since he arrived, hadn't contributed enough data or papers to land his own grant. And fudged what he did do. Should get on the needle, do some honest protocols. And Morgan needn't think their manly friendship would get him off the hook.'

'Isn't this trial by newspaper? Is Morgan vicious? Or was he just scared?'

'Both. Oh, Stevens wouldn't have publicised this junk and tarred Medway in the scandal. He was just trying to terrorise Morgan, shape him up.'

'Stevens doesn't sound . . . very bright about managing people,' Chessie decided.

'Oh, he was bright. Also rigidly honest – about work, anyway. But you're right. Remember those awful teachers who believe insulting students must improve their work because humiliation's so good for your soul?'

'You mean he was a sadist. I'm glad I teach at college level.'

'Sort of. He could be lovable – if you didn't expect too much,' Pauli commented. *Let it go. Let him go.*

Chessie looked puzzled. 'He was the man you were seeing?'

Pauli groaned inwardly. Now you've done it. Shut up. Tell her all the truth. No, shut up. 'He . . . fascinated me for a while. I told you in San Francisco. Finish reading. Please?'

Chessie's dark eyes found the printed lines again.

Science, like other human endeavours, must proceed on trust and self-discipline. Furthermore, compared to Ph.D scientists who do not treat patients, medical doctors who combine research with clinical care of humans should have additional impetus to work ethically.

Despite the Aids crisis, the 'answer to cancer' evidently won't occur tomorrow. But it will never occur without more 'avenging angels of accounting' from the media, the alternative cancer therapy movement, the Justice Department, and DHHS itself auditing frequently and remaining vigilant always.

'Well?' Pauli enquired as Chessie finished reading.

'Wow! I have a celebrity in my room. Can I have your autograph? Everybody raves about corrupt medical care, but half a person in 100 does anything useful about it. Seriously, I had no idea this is what you were into.'

'I didn't either. I get paid to do something else. This was supposed to be a pleasant part-time job, but I nearly got murdered.' Pauli clenched her teeth.

From across the table Chessie grasped her hand, then tapped the newspaper. 'They're bad stuff, those people. If I'd waited for some of them to cure me by killing me with poisonous drugs, I'd have been in the grave four years ago. At least the paper also mentions alternative cancer therapy.'

Pauli nodded. 'Oh, some good news about my lump. During all those trips to the hospital I had mammography and forced Dr Williams to look again. When she removed the lump under local anaesthetic it looked benign. We're still awaiting the report, but I can breathe again without that horror hanging over me.'

'That's great! But didn't I tell you so? When we compared –'

'I know, I know. Yours are bigger than mine.' Pauli burst into laughter. As Chessie stood up and pushed out her chest, Pauli grabbed her around the waist, inhaling the familiar cinnamon fragrance. As Pauli, still seated, nuzzled at her mint-silk blouse, she mumbled, 'Spend the evening in bed?'

Chessie looked down, rubbing Pauli's curls. 'You bet. But I still have one question about the Medway thing. Weren't you in a lot of danger? I mean, how much did the police know? And how much did you give them?'

With effort Pauli reconcentrated. 'I guess I'll learn that at the trial. They did catch Edward. Then through getting a warrant to audit Medway's accounts and bank records, they got evidence about the computer thing. Because of Coral, they were tailing Morgan, Harry and a couple others, but I gave them both the weapon and exact motive. If they tailed me, I've been too exhausted to notice. Actually I could have used them a few times. There's a problem with the weapon, though. In order to prove the scalpel I found in Morgan's pocket did it, they need steel particles left in Steven's throat that match the scalpel.'

'Have they got them? Whose blood is on the scalpel?'

Pauli gulped. 'Well, it's *mine*. The latest anyway. I cut myself on it after Morgan must have used it. If there's blood on his coat, I didn't see it. With the heat that night he must have removed it while Stevens and he were arguing. So he could put it back in his closet, where it usually hangs. About the particles, I guess we'll find that out at the trial too.'

Chessie stared. 'You mean he could go free?'

'Not if the prosecutor and Coral and I get our way! Even if Morgan gets off, he's tarnished. They'll wipe out his medical licence. There's the deceptive research too, remember.'

'Good.' Chessie clapped her hands and nodded. 'Pauli, come away to Colorado. At least for a vacation. Come back with me?'

'What? "Famous Murder-Larceny-Fraud Witness Disappears Before Trial"? Suppose they get me for contempt of court while they're formaldehyding Harry and Morgan into the next century! Of course, I'll come visit.' Still seated, she looked up at Chessie and hugged her hips. 'Then we can figure out how to stay together. I love you. I know I can help you get a college job here in the east.'

Now Chessie stared into the plum-velvet draperies behind Pauli's head. 'Considering I've got no tenure in Colorado, it sounds good. And you must see my house. But what about all your fraudulent friends at the trial?' Her nose crinkled.

'We'll send them a postcard from the Rockies.'